COUNT

*Not all romance books need to be serious.
Sometimes, you just want a little bit of fun, and
a whole lot of spice.*

"TEN BUCKS SAYS I can pretend-murder you in the next round."

Tristan just quirks a disbelieving eyebrow at me. "You're delusional. But you're on."

I immediately crouch low, circling my coach and friend on the mat as I get ready to shoot for a takedown. He's older and more skilled, but he's a few days away from his UFC debut and Coach has been working him into the ground, so he's sore and more banged up than usual. And I'll use any advantage I can get.

He feints a shot at a takedown, but I see it coming so I drop my hips back in a sprawl, already planning a counter-move that might get me on top of him instead.

Except, I over-exert on the sprawl and end up giving Tristan an opportunity to come down on top of me.

He wraps an arm around my head and under my chin, and before I even realize what's happening, he's used that grip to spin around to my side and take my back. It takes him next to no time to sink his forearm under my chin from behind, and even less time to squeeze hard enough to make me tap out in surrender.

"I'll take that in cash, thanks," Tristan says with a cocky grin as he rolls away from me.

"Shut up, you set me up," I mumble, coughing awkwardly to try to clear my throat after the chokehold.

"Bullshit," he responds cheerfully. "I'm running at like 60% right now. This was the perfect time to take me out. It's not my fault you're more preoccupied with school and girls than training."

I aim a glare at him. "That's not fair, and you know it."

He lets out a sigh as he lies down on the mat. "Chill out, man, I'm just kidding. Everyone knows you're a hard worker. You just need to work on your takedown defense."

I let out a sigh of my own and flop back onto the mat. "Yeah, I know. I should head over to the college again for some wrestling sessions."

"Take Tristan with you. He could use some lessons of his own," says a voice from the other end of the room.

I turn to face Remy, Tristan's girlfriend and one of my hardest training partners. If it weren't for the constant after-training eye-fucking, you'd never know these two were dating. Their love language seems to be bickering and hate sex.

"Why don't you come over here and I'll show you just how good I am at wrestling," he growls at her.

"You're on, asshole." She stands from her stretch and immediately launches herself at her boyfriend. Within seconds, the two are a rolling mass of limbs, each one trying to finish the other with a submission.

"Good to see nothing has changed between those two,"

Jax says dryly from behind the check-in desk. I smirk, knowing he's secretly giddy about the fact that his two best friends finally acknowledged their feelings and got together.

"I can't say I don't miss the days they were at each other's throats, but this is close enough that it doesn't matter," I admit with a wave of my hand.

"Except now it's considered foreplay instead of just sexual frustration in the form of training," someone says with a chuckle on my other side.

I aim a glare at *my* best friend, debating for a moment if I want to simulate murder on him before I end my training for the day. But then I realize I'm too tired, and he's not wrong.

"There's no need to point it out," I tell Max with a wince. "Dating or not, Remy still feels like a sister to all of us, so we don't exactly need to analyze their sex life."

"Here here," Jax echoes with a wince of his own.

"I had no idea our sex life was such a big topic of conversation," Tristan drawls from where he just submitted Remy with the same chokehold he got me with. "Would you all like to come watch next time? I'm happy to share the knowledge. Maybe you could even pick up a few pointers."

We all shudder at the thought, at the same time that Remy smacks her boyfriend's shoulder for the suggestion.

"You're an ass," she grumbles.

"You knew that when you said yes to me," Tristan says cheerfully, driving his body into her stomach and lifting her over his shoulder. He smacks her once on the ass as he carries her into the heavy bag room on the other side of the gym, her shriek echoing through the room.

Hearing Jax's heavy sigh, I turn to see my teammate's eyes following his best friends, looking almost... forlorn. Or conflicted? Which is odd, because I've never seen him be anything but cheerful.

"What's going on, big guy?" I ask. "Why the long face?"

He seems to shake himself from his reverie, his cheeks warming slightly when he realizes I just caught him staring.

Coughing awkwardly into his fist, he swivels back toward the computer in front of him, stammering through his answer of, "Uh, nothing. Doesn't matter."

My brow furrows as I glance toward Tristan and Remy again, then back to Jax. "Trouble in paradise? Or just jealous of the couple in paradise?"

Jax turns to glare at me. "Drop it, Aiden."

I raise my hands in surrender, confused about what could possibly be making Jax grouchy. Couples don't usually bother him, especially since he hasn't exactly shown an interest in dating anyone in months.

"Alright, whatever, I'll leave you to your sulking," I say, standing and stretching out my cooling muscles. "I have to get to class anyway, and I want to grab some food first." Jax just gives me an impatient wave before going back to whatever admin work he was doing.

It only takes me ten minutes to shower and get dressed, then another minute to smooth my hair into some semblance of order before I walk back into the main room—where Jax is still frowning.

When he sees me, though, he's bumped out of his bad mood. He quirks an eyebrow at my appearance.

"You know, when I was in college, I could barely bring myself to wear jeans and a t-shirt to class," he says dryly. "How is it that you have the energy to put actual thought into an outfit? Especially after a workout?"

I shrug and adjust my button-up as I answer simply, "Because appearances are important."

I do one final outfit check in the mirrored wall along the side of the gym: black button-up, grey slacks, nice shoes, and the glasses that I wear in class are safely stowed away in my backpack. When I'm content with my professional appearance, I grab my backpack and sling it over my shoulder. "Plus, the professor for my class tonight is the one that got me the interview for that paid internship I want. So it helps to not look like a slob."

"I never said I looked like a *slob*," Jax mutters in an annoyed tone.

I let a grin slide across my face. "Compared to me, I'll bet you did."

Jax just points a finger at the front door. "Out."

Chuckling, I turn to Max and ask him, "Fight night at my house tomorrow? I really want to watch the co-main event, and it's a free card."

He nods and goes back to doing his sit-ups. "Sounds good. I'll come by around eight."

I walk over to give him a fist bump before making my way out of the gym. I also force Jax to give me a fist bump, despite the fact that he looks like he wants to drag me into the cage for another round.

Twenty minutes later, I'm walking onto Temple's college

campus. I beeline to my favorite gyro food truck, starved from this afternoon's training session, and place my usual order. Then I stand aside and pull my phone out while I wait. When I hear my name called, I grab the bag of food and make my way over to Beury Beach.

It's not really a beach, especially in the middle of a college campus in November, but it's where every student comes when the weather's nice enough to be outside. I take a seat on the concrete border that divides the courtyard and the grassy area. I pull my water bottle from my bag and set it down in front of me before tearing into my food.

I'm barely two bites in when I see her.

She's across the courtyard from me, kneeling in the grass as she aims a fancy-looking camera at the resident Jesus-worshipper on campus. You know the one: the scraggly looking older woman who comes with a massive sign and yells about how everyone on campus is going to hell. Today, she also happens to be handing out condoms and pamphlets on being pro-life.

I sigh and shake my head at Mrs. Jesus before bringing my attention back to the photographer who caught my attention in the first place.

She's gorgeous. She's got perfect olive skin and dark, wild hair, and she has green eyes so bright, I can make out the color from all the way over here. Not to mention, she looks cool as shit in shredded black jeans and an oversized flannel. But that's not why she caught my eye, although all of those things make her really fucking hot.

She's gorgeous because she's hyper-focused on her art—

on whatever shot she's taking. She's uncaring of the dirt she's getting on her knees from where she's kneeling in the grass, and she doesn't even seem to notice the way her hair keeps getting blown across her face and catching in the camera. She's so focused on getting the perfect shot that she's contorting her body into a low position that has her practically lying on the ground. She barely notices the drunk college student that trips and almost falls on top of her. And based on the badass vibes this girl is giving out, something tells me that would not have ended well for the kid. Especially if the camera was a casualty.

I continue to watch her for a minute, my food now cold and completely forgotten next to me. I'm just staring in awe at what is clearly a master at work.

Sure enough, when she finally straightens and lowers the camera, there's a huge grin on her face.

The sight of it, of her bright smile and giddy expression, is enough to get me moving. I stand up and start walking toward her, tossing my forgotten gyro into the trash on my way across the courtyard.

She's still immersed in flipping through her pictures when I finally reach her.

"Did you get the shot?" I ask.

She looks up at me, grin still bright on her face. She nods and stands up, moving so close to me so quickly that I suck in a breath at the sudden proximity.

Fuck, she smells good. Like some kind of spicy flower.

"Look," she says simply, extending her camera so I can see. She's standing in front of me and slightly to the side, and I'm realizing now she's way taller than I thought she was. I'm six feet tall, and she's only a few inches shorter than me.

For a moment, I'm distracted by her closeness. Not only is her hair blowing in my face, but her flannel button-up has slipped off one shoulder, which means her smooth skin and the line of her neck are directly in front of me.

I feel my dick twitch in my pants.

When she looks over her shoulder at me to see what I think of the shot, I realize she's showing me a picture. I hurriedly snap my attention to the camera.

And then suck in a breath of surprise.

"Holy shit," I breathe, reaching for the camera so I can pull it closer. "That's the shot you just took?"

The look of pure satisfaction on her face couldn't be more obvious.

The picture is… breath-taking. It looks like a picture you'd see in a National Geographic magazine, or like something that might win a photography competition.

It's a picture of Mrs. Jesus, yeah, but it's so much more than that. It's not just that the camera settings are so spot-on that the colors and focus of the picture are better than anything the human eye can see—it's that the angle of the picture makes the woman the focal point, surrounded by the college students. And this girl has somehow made it look like they're worshipping the old kook.

The figures of the students are slightly blurred, which means their mocking expressions in real life aren't visible. Instead, all you can see is their hyper-focus on the woman in the center. And through the quality of the camera and the talent of the photographer, you get a clear vision of who she really is. You can see the fire in her eyes and the spittle flying from her lips, and the clenching of her hands on the sign she's holding. You can *feel* the bat-shit passion of the old woman.

"I was trying to get the angle right so it would feel like she's looking down at them," the girl explains, the proud smile never leaving her face. "I had to wait for the moment when the students parted enough to let me get the shot."

I'm still speechless, standing there with my mouth open and my attention stuck on the camera. "This is… incredible. Are you a photographer?"

My attention finally snaps back to the sexy brunette when I hear her chuckle. She steps away slightly and turns so she's facing me, although her focus is back on her machine.

"And here I was, hoping you'd be smarter than you are pretty," she muses. "Although, in your defense, you probably would've had to be a genius by that ratio."

I can only blink at her. "I can't tell if you just called me hot or stupid."

She glances up at me with a grin. "It's whatever you want it to mean, pretty boy."

Sign me the fuck up. I've met my dream girl.

"I just meant, are you a professional photographer?" I clarify. "Or are you just doing this for fun? Because if this is just a hobby, you might be in the wrong profession."

She finally gives me her full attention, lowering her camera to hang from the lanyard around her neck. She gives me a blatant once-over, before reaching into the bag that's slung over her shoulder and pulling out a weed pen. She slips it between her lips and pulls, then says on a light puff of smoke, "Don't worry, I don't like to do things I'm good at for free."

Before I can react to *that*, she turns and walks toward a nearby bench. I'm left staring after her in shock, until she peeks over her shoulder and gives me a subtle nod to follow her.

I'm not even a little bit ashamed to admit that I rush to catch up.

"You're not a student here, are you?" I ask as she takes a seat. I sit down next to her, willing some of my usual cockiness back into my stance as I stretch an arm across the back of the bench.

She starts to adjust some of the settings on her camera. "What gave me away? The lack of a backpack or lack of Temple gear?"

Both are true, but instead I answer, "More like the lack of fucks you give. Most college students are either unsure of themselves or going through an identity crisis. You're neither."

That catches her attention enough that she peeks at me again, a little longer this time. "You're not either of those yourself. Yet you scream college boy."

"Yeah, but that's because I'm not your typical college boy," I quip.

Now it's her turn to snort, this time turning back to her camera. "The arrogance is definitely college boy-level. You're probably, what, a senior? Old enough to drink and old enough to know who you are. But not older than twenty-two because you don't look like the fifth-year senior type. Too driven and too focused not to have a solid life plan in front of you. Let me guess, business major?"

My mouth quirks in amusement. "That's a pretty easy

guess. Try for something that's not obvious."

She shrugs. "And you're obviously not a frat boy, though you're not nerdy enough to have school as your only focus. So that means you have a hobby where all your friends are. Likely a sport, by the looks of the muscles on your muscles." I couldn't stop grinning at that, even if I wanted to. "My guess would be MMA."

For the second time in five minutes, my jaw drops. "How the fuck did you guess that?"

She grins, looking incredibly pleased with herself. "Your cauliflower ear. My gut reaction was wrestler, but you're too lean for that."

I can only gawk at her. And when I finally find the words, all I manage to say is, "Are you sure you're not just stalking me?"

She chuckles and lifts the camera up to capture a picture of the group of sorority girls a few feet away from us. "Don't flatter yourself, pretty boy. I don't have the patience for stalking. Besides, if I wanted you, I'd just take you."

My dick twitches again. *Who the fuck is this girl...*

This time when she looks at me, I can see the mischief sparking in her eyes. And with her next words, I know exactly why.

"Wanna see something really cool?"

I quirk an eyebrow at her. "Why does that question make me think 'cool' means 'illegal'?"

Her grin stretches even wider. "I plead ignorance. Come on, I'm sure you've done crazier things."

I sigh and shake my head. "You're already trouble and I

don't even know your name."

Her eyes twinkle again. "Help me with this, and maybe I'll give you more than just my name."

My body automatically jumps into action before my brain can process what the hell that might mean. And then I'm following her through the courtyard and toward one of the older buildings on the far end of campus.

CHAPTER 2
Aiden

SHE DOESN'T SAY a word as we walk down the path between buildings. I don't really mind the silence because it allows me to stay a step behind and admire her from there.

And there's a lot to admire.

"In here," she says when we reach one of the old Liberal Arts buildings. I haven't been in here since my GenEd classes freshman year, and even then, I wasn't entering through the emergency exit.

I quirk an eyebrow at where she's holding the door open and ushering me inside. "If I get expelled the semester before graduation, I'm going to be pissed."

She lets out a laugh. "Stop worrying. We can't *not* be in here, we just… *shouldn't* be in here."

I sigh. "I'll be sure to tell my lawyer that." But even still, I follow her into the empty stairwell.

We climb all the way to the top. Which ends up being nine flights of stairs.

"Jesus Christ, woman, I was not prepared for this," I pant, leaning on the railing as my quads light on fire.

Of course, she's barely even breathing. "Come on, I thought you were a big bad fighter? Aren't you guys supposed to be some of the most in-shape athletes out there?"

"I'm equipped to lift a two-hundred-pound man over my head and slam him, not to hike a skyscraper," I grumble.

She looks over her shoulder, and I catch the smirk on her lips. "It'll be worth it, I promise."

Motivation unlocked.

When we finally reach the top, we step into a narrow hallway, at the end of which we find another stairwell. As we scale the steps, I look around in confusion. "Wait a minute, the elevator only goes to the seventh floor in this building. What does this lead to?"

She yanks open the door at the top with a grin. "The best view on campus."

And sure enough, we walk out on the roof and find exactly that.

"Holy shit," I breathe.

I walk out and look around, taking in the view of not only the entirety of the college campus, but of the Philly skyline beyond that.

"What is… how did you…?"

"It's not hard to find places like this, you just have to want to explore a little," she says as she walks past me. It's not a "finished" roof, which means there's no railing, and that we're definitely not supposed to be up here. But there's enough of a lip that she can get settled right up against it and start adjusting the settings on her camera.

"Why do I get the feeling you've done a lot of exploring

like this?" I ask in an amused drawl.

She shines a grin at me over her shoulder in answer. Then she lifts the camera to her eye and the click of the camera sounds as she starts to capture the breathtaking scenery stretching before us.

I stand back and let her work. I'm mesmerized by the Center City skyline even from where I'm standing, so it's easy to give her a few minutes for her art.

But when she calls to me with a quiet *come look*, it takes no effort to tear myself away from the incredible view and walk toward an even more incredible view.

She looks at me with a sparkle in her eyes that I can't help but admire. I've always felt like the most attractive thing about a person is the passion with which they do something they love, and this girl definitely loves what she's doing.

I step up beside her, staying slightly behind. "You get another National Geographic-worthy shot?"

"Something like that," she says with an appreciative chuckle. Then she holds the camera out for me to see.

Sure enough, the picture on her screen is fucking stunning. It's a little after 4:00, which means we're just about in the golden hour and she has the perfect lighting for some stunning landscape photos. The remaining daylight is softer and redder than during the day, and is perfectly complimenting the fall colors all over the city.

"Beautiful," I murmur. Though I don't think that's entirely aimed at the picture on the camera.

I let my gaze trail over her hands, over the ink tattooed on her arm, and along the line of her neck. "What's your name?" I finally remember to ask her.

She turns fully to face me. "You first, pretty boy."

I extend my hand with my classic, dimpled grin. "I'm Aiden." She clasps her hand in mine and takes a step closer. "What about you, troublemaker? What should I call you?"

Her green eyes shine up at me as her close proximity sends a shock through my system, and it's all I can do to suck in a breath and wait for her answer.

"It's nice to meet you, Aiden," she practically purrs. "I'm Danielle."

I tilt my head, still holding on to her hand in mine. "You don't strike me as a Danielle. Sure you're not giving me a fake name?"

She grins, looking pleased with my catch. "And why would I want to give you a fake name? You planning on seeing me again?"

I let my thumb trace over her hand where I'm touching her. And then I flash her a grin of my own, saying, "I don't know about again, because the only thing I'm thinking of right now is how stunning you look with that camera in your hands, and how much I'm enjoying doing illegal shit with you."

She laughs and finally pulls away from me. But she doesn't go far, she just pulls the strap over her head and hands me the camera.

"Here, you try. The settings are already there, just point and shoot."

I lift the strap over my head to make myself feel slightly less stressed about dropping what is clearly a several-thousand-dollar camera. Then I raise it up and look through the lens at the city.

I snap a few pictures of the skyline in the distance. Then of the bell tower in the center of campus, and the courtyard where I first saw her.

As soon as I'm trained on a closer target, I start noticing people walking around below us. So I twist the lens to test how far I can zoom in—and it's pretty damn far, because a couple holding hands immediately comes into focus.

I snap a picture at the moment the girl rips her hand out of the guy's grasp.

When I shift my focus elsewhere, I manage to snap a picture of a group of freshman girls giggling and whispering about the frat bros that are strutting around the courtyard. Then another of the resident stoners drooling over the food trucks, and another of the engineering majors curled around their many textbooks.

"People over landscapes? Interesting," I hear murmured in my ear.

I lower the camera and twist slightly to show her the last picture I took.

"You have a good eye," she says thoughtfully as she grips it with one hand and flips through the recent shots. She laughs when she sees the moment I captured the girl pulling away from her boyfriend. "You *do* have a good eye. You even managed to catch trouble in paradise."

"That's not that hard to do, since we're on a college campus," I say with a chuckle. I hand the camera back and face her fully. "So what's your name, really?"

She pulls the strap over her head again before looking up

at me with a pleased grin. "It really is Danielle." When my eyes narrow in suspicion, she sighs. "Okay, I don't go by Danielle. Only my dad calls me that. Everyone else calls me Dani."

I nod and let my gaze roam over her again, slowly and from head to toe. "I like it," I drawl. "Definitely suits you."

"Oh yeah?" she asks, shifting closer to me. "Why's that?"

I take that as permission for more contact, so I reach for one of her belt loops and tug her closer. She bites the edge of her lip to contain what is clearly a smile. "It's both badass in its masculinity, and sexy as fuck in its femininity," I tell her. My finger trails the hem of her jeans, along her skin and light enough to make a shiver run through her. "It totally fits the whole vibe you're giving off. It might not live up to your FBI profiling skills, but I think I have you figured out, Dani."

She tips her chin up to make eye contact with me, letting me see her emerald eyes turn black with desire. *Fuck*, this girl is sexy. She's completely unashamed of not only herself, but of what she wants.

"I think you did okay, pretty boy," she murmurs, her gaze dropping to my lips when I let out a small chuckle.

"I thought the whole reason I gave you my name was so we could move past the nicknames."

She shrugs, her stare darting from my lips to my eyes and back again. "I like how it sounds. *It fits the vibe you're giving off*," she mimics with a grin.

I grip both of her belt loops this time and tug her even closer. "Smartass," I growl. I drop my hands to her hips and squeeze lightly. "You've definitely got that vibe, too."

"Oh, most definitely," she whispers as she tilts her mouth

up to me.

I can't focus on anything else anymore. My grip tightens on her hips, and I lower my head, glancing one last time at her eyes to make sure I'm not doing something she doesn't want.

But her eyelids have lowered, and she's pushing up on her toes to initiate the contact. I let slip a small groan when her lips graze mine in a fleeting moment of contact. I think she smirks at the sound—at the control she already clearly has over me—and then she's back again.

Unfortunately, the second one is even less of a kiss than the first one.

"*Hey!* What are you two doing? You can't be up here!"v

"Fuck," I breathe, looking past her to see who just caught us. Sure enough, there's an older, overweight man standing in the doorway to the stairwell.

"Oh shit," Dani says on a laugh. "Come on, we have to go." She pulls me in the opposite direction, away from the security guard.

"Where are we going? There's only one way down from here and he's standing in front of it!" I let out a groan, but let her drag me anyway. "I knew I was going to get expelled today. I had a feeling. Goddamnit."

Dani continues pulling me after her. "You're so dramatic. Come on." When we reach whatever point she's looking for along the edge of the roof, she turns back to me. "Do you trust me?"

My mouth drops open in shock. "Based on the twenty minutes I've known you? Sorry, sweetheart, that answer's not looking good."

She rolls her eyes again, but a smile twitches at the corner of her lips. "Just come on. You're fine."

"You sound like my coach when he's trying to convince me pain doesn't exist," I grumble. But I follow her to the edge anyway.

I hear bleeps on a walkie talkie behind us. "There's no place to go, kids. Might as well make this easy on yourselves and just hand yourselves in," the security guard calls as he strides over to us.

But the second Dani throws a leg over the edge of the roof, the vibe in the air changes.

"*No!* Don't do that! Oh my God, you're not going to *jail*, you'll just get fined! Jesus Christ, *don't jump!*" I look over my shoulder to see the security guard loping in slow-motion toward us.

"Dani…" I start nervously, unsure of what she's doing. *Is there a second ledge? A ladder down? What the fuck is this nut job doing?*

"Come on, you have to climb over before he reaches you," she says from where I can only see her head peeking over the ledge. "Just trust me." And then she lets go and disappears from my view.

"Jesus fucking Christ, my heart's not built for this kind of stress," I grumble to myself as I step closer. "Lock me in a cage with a man who wants to kill me and I'm cool as a cucumber. But toss me in with a crazy hot chick who I really want to fuck, and all brain cells go out the window." I peek over the edge and see a second ledge, just as I suspected. "Or off the roof, apparently."

"Just come on," Dani hisses from where she's standing. It's not a ledge like she's hanging onto the edge with only one foot to maneuver, it's more like a drop to a second narrow roof that runs this length of the building. There's enough space that when she turns toward wherever she's going, she actually *bolts*.

With a few muttered *fuck fuck fucks*, I throw my leg over the ledge. Taking one last glance at the advancing—but still shockingly far away, out-of-shape security guard—I let go and drop down.

"Over here," Dani whispers. From where she's, *once again*, hanging off the roof.

But sure enough, when I make my way over to her, a fire escape comes into view.

"How did you find…" I trail off when I realize it's a pointless question. I shake my head instead. "Never mind. Move over, I'm coming down."

She flashes me a grin—giving me a look that clearly says, *now you're getting it*—and disappears down the steps.

"*Hey!* Come back here, you two!"

I look sheepishly at the security guard right before I drop down to the ledge. "Sorry, man. I gotta go with the lady."

I follow Dani down two levels, sending multiple *thank God*'s to whatever gods are out there that I don't have a fear of heights. Because despite the fact that we're climbing down an enclosed fire escape, we're still *seven stories up* on a building that clearly hasn't been used in years.

"In here," she finally whispers as she disappears through an unlocked window.

But when we drop into the empty hallway, we hear the

security guard yell into his walkie talkie, "They stopped on the seventh floor! Somebody catch them on the way up!"

"Shit." Dani looks around frantically. She grabs my hand and moves to open a classroom door, then promptly shoos me inside. But before she follows me in, she looks thoughtfully at the entrance to the stairwell that's right next to our classroom.

"What're you doing? Get in here," I hiss.

"Shut up and get in the supply closet," she hisses back.

"I'm not leaving you to go into a closet," I whisper with a glare. "I can already hear the jokes coming."

She gives me a look of annoyance. "Don't worry, I'll be back in a second to soothe your fragile masculinity."

"Trust me, sweetheart, there ain't nothing fragile about my masculinity."

At the sound of a door slamming nearby, both of our attention jumps to the stairwell. I let out a very *un*-masculine sound of distress when Dani bolts toward the door.

She opens it and pokes her head out so she can listen. "They're in the stairwell," she whispers. Then a determined look appears on her face, right before she glances around her.

And then slams the stairwell door loud enough for even the dead to hear it.

"Are you *insane*?!" I hiss. "Now they're going to know we're here."

She gives me another exasperated look.

"Not quite, though it's good to know you're not the getaway partner I've been looking for. You suck at this."

I glare at her, speechless for probably the first time in my life.

But I catch a smile on her face as she shoves me back into the classroom. "Go, closet, now," she barks like some war general.

We're almost to the supply closet when we hear voices outside the classroom. I quickly push Dani inside, but leave the door slightly open so we can hear what the security guards are saying.

"Where'd they go?"

"I saw them go down two floors on the fire escape. I know they're on this floor."

"Yeah, but we also heard the door to the stairwell slam. They probably climbed down another floor before we could get up here."

"Goddamnit, there are like ninety classrooms just in this section of the building. They could be anywhere."

"Come on, Carl, they're just a bunch of kids. Were they doing anything illegal?"

"You mean being on a blocked-off and hazardous roof isn't enough?"

"Not enough to make me keep climbing steps. I'm hungry, man, don't make me tired, too."

"Screw you, Rick, you're lousy at security."

"In this case, I'm okay with that."

After a few more grumbles, we eventually hear them walk off. And after another minute, we hear the ding of the elevator.

And then… silence.

Silence except for the sounds of my heavy breathing and Dani's giggles.

"I can't believe you're laughing right now," I say on an

exhale. "My heart's beating so fast."

And when she looks up at me, her laugh trailing off, her blown out pupils let me know she's feeling exactly the same kind of adrenaline high that's currently making my heart race and my cock harden.

Slowly—but not tentatively—she places her palm on my chest. Her breaths start to come quicker. Mine do too. It's like the air that was already thin in this closet is suddenly sucked out, and we're left with only each other's breaths in a too-small space.

In the end, she makes the first move. She grips my shirt in her fist and pulls my lips to hers, immediately plastering her body against mine and letting out the sultriest moan I've ever fucking heard.

I open my mouth to her wandering tongue with a groan. My hands grip her hips, holding her close to me so I can feel the way she starts to grind.

"*Fuck*, Dani," I manage to gasp. I weave a hand into her hair and tilt my head to kiss her deeper—harder. I want to absorb as much of this woman's essence into my skin as I possibly can.

"I want you," she whispers against my lips as she pushes me back against the wall. And immediately after that, I feel her reach down to start fumbling with my slacks. She manages to get my zipper down as she breathes, "*God*, I need you."

I drop my head back against the wall with a groan when I feel her hands reach under my boxer-briefs and wrap around my cock. Nothing about this woman says *hesitant*, so why would this be any different? Her grip is hard, and sure of herself. She starts to jack me with a pressure few women would feel comfortable with, especially a first time.

"Fuck, you can't keep that up," I choke out when I feel my balls start to tingle.

Dani smirks at me and doesn't stop what she's doing. "And here I thought you would be a big alpha guy that can control his load. I'm disappointed."

That forces a growl out of me. I knock her hand away and then, in the same motion, reach up to wrap my hand around her throat. Her eyes go wide at the contact, and then wider still when I use my grip to back her against the opposite wall.

I lean forward to whisper in her ear. "Trust me, Dani, disappointment is the last thing you're about to feel." And before she can respond with anything snarky, I slam my lips back to hers and *devour* her.

"You're going to flatten your palms against the wall, and you're going to keep them there while I eat my fill. If they move, you won't like the punishment." I pull back a little farther so I can get a better look at her expression. "Understood?"

I'm still holding her in place with my grip on her throat, so I can see every reaction that flits across her face. I can tell she wants to sass me. She wants to take the control back.

But I can also tell she likes me owning the power dynamic.

"Yes, sir," she whispers with a sly smile.

And I swear to God my dick turns to stone at the sound.

"Good," I growl. "Do it." When she slowly moves to press her palms to the wall behind her, I give her throat an appreciative squeeze. And with a final bratty look, she widens her legs and licks her lips.

I fall onto her with another kiss. Part of me is waiting for her to disobey my commands, but she doesn't—she keeps her hands away from me even as she returns my kiss with equal fervor.

"Good girl," I whisper against her lips. At that, she lets a whimper slip, and I grin when I realize she likes to be praised.

I want to find out if she likes the opposite end of that spectrum, too. But I'm too focused on getting her pants undone so I can pull them down to her knees, leaving her legs trapped together and her unable to move. And the whole time I continue to devour her mouth, my tongue brushing over hers in a sensual, but desperate, caress.

Then I slowly, so slowly, let my hands start to drift from her jeans around her knees, up along the soft skin of her thighs, to her panties that I've left on for the moment. My touch brushes across the thin lace of the crotch area, just for a moment, and it's enough of a tease to pull another whimper from Dani's lips.

I grin at the sound. I expect her to shut it down with a glare, or something that lets me know she doesn't appreciate being vulnerable, but I get the opposite. A sensual smile slides across her lips and she pushes herself farther into my hand, an unspoken plea to *take*.

I can't remember the last time I was so eager to give a girl pleasure. To taste her on my tongue and feel her come apart on my cock. I'm salivating over the thought of stripping Dani out of her underwear.

So I do just that. I tuck my fingers under the lace on the side and slowly peel them down. They fall down and bunch around her knees with her jeans.

And when I tip my chin down to finally take in the sight

of her, I can't stop the groan that rolls through me at the sight of her perfect, pink pussy.

"Fuck, you're gorgeous." I can't take my eyes off her. "Do you taste as good as you look?"

She leans forward to nip at my bottom lip before soothing the hurt with her tongue. "Only one way to find out," she purrs.

That pulls another groan out of me. *I'm going to devour this girl.*

"Remember, no touching," I remind her.

And then I drop to my knees. Because I can't wait another second to put my mouth on her.

Her pants bunched around her knees inhibit how much of her I can reach, but I don't mind. She can spread her legs enough that I can reach her clit, can slide my tongue along the slit of her pussy, and that's as much as I need. With my hand, I reach up to stroke her drenched entrance. And when she lets out a moan at the feeling of my finger sliding inside her, a switch flips and I become ravenous.

I echo it with a groan of my own, latching onto her clit and circling it with my tongue. I can't get enough of her drugging taste, of the way she's squirming against my face and pushing her hips into me.

She looks like she wants to take her hands off the wall, but for some reason, she's still obeying my instructions.

Not quite a brat, then. Maybe she likes being told what to do?

I slide my finger out so I can slide two back in. Then I test my theory.

"Grab my hair with one hand and ride my face," I order.

"Kinda hard to do when my pants are holding my legs

together," she gasps.

Okay, maybe a little bit of a brat.

Without a word, I rip one of her combat boots off and push the leg of her jeans farther down, just enough so I can bring a single leg out of confinement.

She immediately takes that as an opportunity to throw her calf over my shoulder and pull my face back to her. Then, with one hand weaving into my hair, she drops her head back to the wall and starts to ride my face.

At the sight of her shamelessly chasing her pleasure, I let out a groan. "God*damn*, Dani." Then I'm back to devouring her because nothing in this world could stop me from tasting her again.

I circle her clit with my tongue, soaking up her taste and teasing her in the process, and then I suck hard at the same time I slide my two fingers inside her again. She lets out a moan at that, and I feel her leg flex behind my back so she can press her hips harder against my face.

After a minute or so, I hear her breath hitch. Her grip tightens in my hair, so I know she's close. She's just not quite… there.

And *fuck* if this isn't my favorite part of eating a girl out. They all have their own formulas, and different things that turn them on. I'm the lucky bastard that gets to figure out what those things are. I get to read her body, touch her in different ways, taste her over and over again, until I uncover the secret she's hiding.

And right now, Dani's still hiding from me.

I change the path of my tongue, then the pace of my

fingers, but I still don't hear the telltale hitch in her breath that tells me she's about to explode.

I take a guess and slide my pinky down to the little rosebud hidden between her round cheeks.

Ah, there we go. There's that gasp I was waiting for.

"Dirty fucking girl," I growl, taking my mouth away from her just long enough to issue a taunt. My fingers continue moving inside her, my pinky still circling her entrance with her own wetness. "Are you going to let a stranger finger your ass? Is that how horny you are?"

As intended, my words cause her to look down at me, a glare creasing her perfect features. Her lips pop open, likely to snap at me with something, but I use that as my opportunity to pull the orgasm from her. I slide my pinky inside her ass at the same time that I lean in to suck on her clit with the pressure I noticed she likes.

She fucking explodes around my fingers.

"Oh my *Goddddd*," she groans, tightening her grip in my hair as she shudders through the pleasure. "Don't stop, don't fucking stop—"

Like there's a chance of that. Watching Dani come on my fingers and mouth might be the hottest thing I've ever seen.

When she slumps against the wall, I let my fingers slow, then begrudgingly take my mouth away from her. She tastes so good that I'm already dying for another hit. But she's pulling at my hair and urging me to my feet, so that will have to wait until next time.

"Let me taste," she gasps, taking a fistful of my shirt and pulling my lips to hers. And just the fact that she *wants* a taste is enough to make me groan into her mouth.

I sink a hand into her hair at the base of her neck and angle my head, deepening the kiss and sliding my tongue across hers. When I feel her hands drift from where they're clutching my shirt, to my still-open slacks, and finally down to cup my hard length, I realize she's just as impatient for me as I am for her.

"Fuck, you're huge," she breathes. She squeezes once before her lip ticks up in a grin. "I should've known your arrogance has to come from somewhere."

I chuckle and start to trail kisses along her jaw and under her ear. "Just wait until you see how I use it," I whisper against her skin.

"So much talk," she murmurs, arching her neck to give me more access. I take it, searching for that spot that will make her crazy.

I don't bother responding, instead pushing my hips into her hand as I lick and nip along her skin. When I finally find the spot at the base of her neck where it meets her shoulder, when I hear her suck in a breath at my bite, I let out a grin at my victory.

Then I'm gripping her hips and spinning her to face the wall.

She gasps at the motion but brings her hands up to brace herself.

Her flannel is still on so I can't see the arch of her back—despite the fact I would love to trace the lines of it—but with her pants half off and her legs spread, I've got a great view of her ass.

"Goddamn, this ass is perfect," I groan. My hands drift

from her hips, over her plump cheeks, down to her thighs. For a moment, all I can do is stare at the sight before me.

"Aiden," she whines, pressing farther back into my hands.

"Fuck, say my name again," I beg, falling onto her so I'm plastered against her back. And I go right back to kissing that spot I figured out she likes.

"Fuck me and I will," she breathes.

Welp, there goes my self-control.

I push my pants and boxer-briefs over my hips and pull the condom out of my wallet. It only takes me a second to roll it on, then I'm gripping her hip with one hand and pressing the tip of my cock against her slick entrance. When she whines and arches a little harder, it takes everything in me not to slam inside and fuck until release.

"Aiden," she gasps desperately.

I press into her with a slow slide.

"Oh my *God*, you're not going to fit," she says breathlessly. I can't even bring myself to tease her; I'm too busy choking on my own breath at the tight squeeze of her around me.

"Too much?" I manage to grit out.

"*No.* Don't you dare stop."

I drop my forehead to her shoulder as I punch the rest of the way in. She sucks in a breath at the sensation, but it's one of ecstasy, not of pain. Especially because she immediately arches her back for more.

"Greedy," I murmur. Then I pull back slowly and push back in.

"Holy shit," she breathes. "*What the fuck.*"

I don't respond. I'm too busy fucking my way in and out

and slowly losing my mind in the process. I don't think I've ever wanted to come as quickly as I do right now.

But somehow, I hold back. It might have to do with Dani's hands grappling at the wall, or her hips arching harder into my hands and silently begging for *more, more, more.*

So I give it to her. I increase my pace, driving harder, driving *deeper* on every stroke, until the only sounds in the closet are of flesh slapping against flesh. And when I finally feel like she's gotten used to my size and my pace, I take us to the next level.

I force myself to still the movement of my hips, pushing all the way inside her before I pause and press my lips against her ear to say, "I want you to bring your legs together. I want to feel you squeezing around my cock. Can you do that for me?"

She must be too far gone because there's no sign of her usual cockiness when she nods quickly and says, "Yes, yes, give me more. *Please.*"

At the sound of that word on her lips, I groan and drop my face into her neck. Then I kick her feet together and plaster my hips against her ass, so I'm all the way inside while she's tightening her muscles around me.

"*Fuck,* that's tight," I choke out.

I pull my hips back and drive in as deep and as hard as possible, pleased to hear her suck in a breath and utter another *oh my God.* I follow it up with another hard thrust, and then another. At this point, I'm holding back my release with a sheer force of will. Thankfully, my punishing drives seem to do their job because it doesn't take long for Dani to start panting and her hands to start squeezing into fists against the wall. When

I feel her cunt start pulsing around my length, I move one of my hands from her hip up to her hair, winding the soft strands around my fingers so I can tug her head back and press my lips to her cheek.

"Want to come, Dani?" I taunt. "Should I even let you? Or should I come in this pussy and make you walk away unsatisfied?"

"If you don't make me come, I swear to *God*—"

But I don't let her finish because suddenly I'm moving my other hand around her hip and down to her clit, sliding my fingers across the drenched feel of her and propelling her into another orgasm when I bite into that spot on her neck. I can *feel* her explode around me.

"Good girl," I groan into her skin when I feel her muscles ripple around my cock. "Come for me, just like that."

It feels like it takes minutes for her release to fade. At least, that's how long it feels like I have to hold my own back. I grit my teeth and continue fucking into her, wanting to wrench as much pleasure from her as possible before I give into my own.

Eventually, her muscles go limp. I take that as my sign that I can let go and give into the urges that have been screaming at me for the past ten minutes.

"Don't move," I growl in her ear. "I'm going to come and you're going to take it." And then I'm doing exactly that. I'm fucking into her and filling the condom that I suddenly wish wasn't between us.

When I eventually float back to earth, I realize we're both panting, trying to get our breaths back. Dani's slumped against the wall, and lets out a content hum when my hips finally slow.

I can't stop myself from nuzzling into her neck.

"Perfect girl," I murmur without thinking.

I feel it the second the words snap her out of this haze. She doesn't necessarily pull away, but she seems to slip into something that seems almost like a façade.

She rolls her hips against mine and purrs, "Guess you weren't all talk after all."

I pull out of her with a wince. It only takes me a second to slip off and tie the condom, and by the time she turns around, I've already discarded it in the trash can in the corner of the closet.

Between the two of us, I'm the one wearing more clothes, but you'd never know that based on the level of confidence that Dani straightens with. Despite the fact that she's only wearing one boot and her jeans are hanging off one leg, she looks every bit the siren that I knew she'd be the second I spotted her.

Bending over to reach for her pants, she smoothly tugs them back on in one motion. Then she goes for her boot, laughing and saying, "I can't say I expected my Jesus lady photoshoot to end like this, but I'm not complaining."

I let out a snort. "I should hope not. You're the reason we're even in this closet."

She looks at me with a smirk. "Don't act like you didn't enjoy breaking the law with me."

"On account of my fifth amendment rights, I refuse to answer that question."

With her clothes fully righted, Dani starts to look a little restless. Like she's eager to get out of here. And before I can even attempt to slow her down—to ask for her number, her last name, *anything*—she's pushing the closet door open.

"Well, this was fun," she says without looking over her shoulder. "I'll see you around, pretty boy."

I'm too stunned by her sudden departure to go after her. When I realize that she's actually leaving, it takes me a second to right my own clothes and zip my pants back up. Then I'm ripping the classroom door open and rushing after her into the hallway.

Only, there's no one there. I'm left with only the echoes of the door to the stairwell slamming shut.

"Hey, Mom," I greet after blowing into my parents' house. I press a quick kiss to her cheek as she makes dinner. "How was your day?"

"You mean my day of a retired stay-at-home mom with nothing to do?" She gives me a knowing chuckle, continuing to slice the vegetables she's got on the cutting board in front of her.

I take a seat at the counter of their gorgeous, massive kitchen, quirking an eyebrow at her. "If you're implying that I think you have nothing to do, I think you might just be getting defensive, Mother."

Now it's her eyebrow that rises. "Oh yeah? So you *don't* judge me for not going back to work after you kids grew up?"

I keep my smile plastered on my face, despite the fact that I know she can see right through me—she's a mom, of course she can read me like a book.

"I can *not* understand it and still be supportive of it," I admit stiffly. Gesturing around the Pinterest-perfect mansion, I say, "God knows you don't *need* to work anymore. Not with

Dad doing as well as he is."

She looks around the kitchen and open floor plan living room, as if seeing it for the first time. By some definitions, my parents might be considered rich, not wanting for anything and perfectly comfortable in their lifestyle, which means Mom never had to go back to work after my older brother and I were born. Instead, she took over the kid and house chores and is now content to live the happy life of a retiree, reading books and having lunch dates with her girlfriends.

I don't understand it.

"I like my life," she says honestly. "I like taking care of your father, and I like being a housewife. That's all there is to it." I must still look baffled because she sighs as she goes back to chopping the vegetables. "Oh, honey. I know you don't understand how someone wouldn't want to work or travel everywhere or have a bunch of hobbies, but believe me, I was busy enough for two lifetimes when I worked as a doctor. I loved my job, but it's okay to want an easier life, too."

I wince and reach for the plate of carrots that still needs to be peeled. "I know, I'm sorry. I'm not judging, I promise. And I'm sure I'll understand one day. Just… maybe not today."

She shines the kind of love-filled smile that only a mom could give. "I know, sweetheart. Believe it or not, I was just as full of life at your age as you are. I thrived on hard work, I loved being busy outside of it, and I rarely ever said no to things. I wanted to try to do everything."

She gives me a tentative look, and I know before she even continues what she's going to say—and why she's approaching it gently.

"The only thing I've never understood is your aversion to including dating into that mix," she says softly.

I tense at the subject change, then force myself to roll my eyes in an effort to move on from this particular topic. "I'm twenty-three, Mom. I'm hardly at the age where I start feeling desperate to settle down."

Ignoring my silent cue, she continues on. "It's not about *needing* to settle down. Relationships can be just as exciting as everything else that you do—they might even make your life *more* exciting, having a partner to do it with." She hesitates again. "I know the Matt breakup was hard, but it's not like he tried to change you or—"

"I don't want to talk about Matt," I snap, sharper than intended. But the last thing I need is my mom telling me what she does or *doesn't* know about the one relationship I ever had, the one that made me swear off meaningful friendships and relationships equally. Because he *did* try to change me, and he *did* inspire my view on dating.

But nobody knows that. And nobody needs to, because I never want to get that close to another person again.

Mom winces at my tone, and I immediately regret snapping at her. I know she's just trying to understand.

"I'm sorry," I sigh. "I just... *really* don't have an interest in dating right now. I've got too much going on with work, and I'd much rather focus all of my energy on that rather than a guy that doesn't know what he wants to do with his life. I can't relate to that."

She smiles at me, though it's a little sad this time. "I understand. Your passion is one of the things your father and I love most about you."

"What do we love about our darling daughter?" I hear from behind me, the tone just as love-filled as my mom's smile was.

"Hi, Dad," I say, forcing the tension from my shoulders and standing up to give my dad a hug.

"Hi, Danielle," he says warmly.

Hearing the name that only my dad calls me brings a smile to my face, and I squeeze him a little tighter for it.

"So what are we blowing smoke up our daughter's ass about now?" he asks Mom, rounding the kitchen counter to press a kiss to her cheek. And just as it always does, the minor gesture brings a pink flush to her skin, the love shining so brightly in her eyes that at first glance anyone would think they're newlyweds. Not that they've been married for almost thirty years.

"I was just telling her that her passion for life is one of the things we're the proudest of," my mom replies, returning her attention to the cutting board.

"Did you doubt that?" my dad asks in confusion. "I would've thought we make that abundantly clear. Pretty sure the entire neighborhood is sick of hearing me brag about you." He perks up when something occurs to him, his energy immediately taking on a bragging quality. "My fearless daughter, fighting against the status quo and always looking for the next adventure. And *especially* after that article that just came out about the protests at the Lincoln Memorial. Honey, those pictures were *incredible*. I have them plastered all over my office. Easily some of the best work you've ever done."

Any concern I had over my parents not approving of my adventurous lifestyle immediately dissipates at the sound of my dad loving that *I'm* passionate about the things I love. I worked damn hard to get those pictures, threw myself right into the middle of those protests, and then spent days editing them to make sure they were perfect. My work as a photojournalist is important, and it can be risky, so I take pride in the work that I do. Being admired for it is the biggest compliment I could ever receive.

"Thanks, Dad," I reply with a smile, returning to the carrots in front of me. "I heard a rumor that there might be another one planned in a few weeks, so I'm hoping Larry sends me back for that one, too. It obviously helps that I'm single without anything tying me down and can travel anywhere at the drop of a hat."

"Take advantage of that while it's still true," Dad says with a chuckle, pressing a kiss to my hair. "It won't be long before someone scoops you up."

Suddenly, a certain blonde-haired boy flashes through my mind at that mention.

I force the thought away as quickly as it appeared.

Turning back to the carrots on the cutting board in front of me, I ask instead, "Going back to the topic of work. How's it going, Dad? How's business?"

He lets out a heavy sigh that would sound tired if I didn't know how much he values work-life balance. "Busy. I'm turning clients away left and right nowadays, just because I don't have the capacity to take on so many cases."

"Why not hire more lawyers?" I ask, lifting my head to give him a look of confusion. "Your firm could probably be so much bigger than it is. Your name is already huge from the work you did back in New York. I bet it would be so easy to grow the firm with more people and more cases. What about that woman Annie that you said was really good? Couldn't she run another branch in New York?"

My parents share a knowing look, and even though it's quick enough that I shouldn't catch it, I do, and it immediately makes my mouth run dry.

It doesn't matter how many times I have this conversation with either of my parents, I always end up on the outside looking in.

"I agree, but I'm trying to slow down, not speed up," Dad replies. "I'm getting closer to retirement, so I need to look at who I'm going to sell the firm to, not how I can make it a bigger monster to hand off. It's already a successful company—I'm okay with coasting a bit until retirement."

I just barely keep the wince off my face at that word. *Coasting.*

"Work isn't everything, baby girl," my dad says softly, correctly reading the look I'm trying to hide. "I can be proud of you for being an incredible worker and still think there are equally satisfying things out there in the world."

"I know, I know, I'm sorry," I mumble quickly. "It's what Mom and I were just talking about. I don't mean to push, it's just a natural gut reaction to… well, to push."

"Ah, so that's why your mother was blowing smoke up your ass," Dad says with a chuckle. "Now I see what I walked in on. Yes, we are incredibly proud of you for how hard you work. But we also understand the benefit of slowing down to enjoy the rest of life's beauties."

"I'm sorry, I'm not familiar with that speed."

Dad lets out a knowing chuckle. "Trust us, we know. You've been on the go from the second you learned how to crawl. We had to use one of those kid-leashes on you a few times when you were little, since you never learned how to stay in one place."

I roll my eyes. "Alright, alright, I get it. Slow is good and retirement suits you both. Now tell me what trip you two are planning next so I know when I need to house sit?"

My not-subtle change of topic works effortlessly, my parents' excitement over their upcoming Caribbean cruise trumping any discomfort I feel over acknowledging that being constantly busy isn't the most important thing in life.

Regardless, I let them chat excitedly about their vacation while the three of us prepare dinner. It makes me happy to listen, and happier still to see how enamored they both are with each other as they do it. I don't miss Mom's looks, or Dad's kisses, as the two of them move around each other with the practiced ease of a couple in love. And not just in love, but a couple destined to be together. A couple that has been madly in love for almost thirty years, and withstood things that other couples would wilt in the face of.

My parents' marriage is the kind that all should aspire to match.

So then why have I always felt like there's a piece of it that I don't understand? A piece that makes me want to stay single and focus on myself?

Those thoughts continue to roll around in my head the entire time we prepare dinner.

They roll through my head *even more* when my brother walks through the door, with the reason for his own sacrifices bundled warmly in his arms. Mom descends on her granddaughter before the hat is even taken off of her adorable, bald little head.

"How's my sweet girl?" my mom coos as she lifts her granddaughter out of Tommy's arms. "How's my sweet, beautiful, perfect girl?"

I meet my brother's gaze across the room, both of us rolling our eyes at the baby voice. Except, Tommy follows the motion with a smile and a look of happiness that couldn't be more obvious if he tried.

"Sorry we're late," Rachel says in a breathless voice. "I had to substitute at the elementary school last-minute, so everything's been a little crazy today. I had to take Jenny to the babysitter instead of her coming to us."

A delighted giggle sounds through the kitchen as Mom taps my niece's nose. "You could've called me. You know I would've come to pick her up for the day. Any excuse to spend time with my grandbaby."

Rachel looks slightly guilty at that. "I know, but since you had dinner planned for tonight, I assumed you'd be busy prepping during the day. I didn't want to bother you."

That finally pulls Mom's attention up. "Nonsense. I'm never too busy for you or Jenny. At least call me next time and if I can help, I will." She waits for Rachel's relieved nod before turning back to the smiling infant in her arms. An equally large smile spreads across Mom's face at the sight. "So how was it at Greenside today? I heard their new principal is driving the

PTA up the wall lately. Although God knows the principal that was there while Dani and Tommy were in school was no better."

Rachel lets out an exasperated breath. "Oh my gosh, I thought I was the only one that can't stand her. That makes me feel so much better. It's like she's *trying* to be difficult!"

I shift awkwardly where I'm standing against the counter, feeling suddenly uncomfortable with the overly domesticated conversation. Not because I don't like kids—if I didn't think Mom's eyes would shutter with sadness, I'd steal Jenny from her immediately—but because I can't relate to it. Both my parents and my brother live the perfect, 1.2 kids and a white picket fence kind of life where all conversations revolve around babies, mortgages, and neighborhood gossip.

Mine revolve around taking pictures in sometimes-risky environments and looking for the next shot of adrenaline when work doesn't deliver and life gets boring.

"So what's going on, Dani-Fanny? Fight any drunk assholes lately?" my brother teases, likely sensing my discomfort. Being six years older than me, we were too far apart to be really close when we were kids, but we've always been solid enough in our relationship that we could read the other better than anyone else.

Something I'm immensely grateful for right now.

"You know, I've dealt with so many of those recently, I can't remember who my last victim was," I answer with mock-seriousness. "Although there was a massive Russian guy at the bar the other night that was very loudly shitting on Americans who needed to be put in his place."

"Oh dear God…" I hear my dad grumble from behind me.

Tommy only laughs and slings an arm around my shoulder. "Wish I could've seen that. It's been a while since I've witnessed what you're capable of out in society."

"You could always come out with me one night," I offer casually. Hesitantly. Because I miss my brother, and it feels like I haven't seen him without a wife or a baby in almost two years.

Tommy winces as he pulls his arm back. "Sorry, D, nights are my time with the baby. At least for now." Guilt morphs his expression as he looks at me, and his voice is hopeful as he asks, "Maybe when Jenny gets a little older? Or you could always come over to the house. I brewed this new beer that I think you'll like." His expression becomes excited, the same way it always does when he talks about his beer-brewing hobby. "It's way too sour for my taste, but knowing you eat Warheads like Tic Tacs, you'd probably love it."

Externally, I plaster a smile onto my face. Internally, I deflate. Not because of his answer, but because no matter how many times I ask, a part of me always hopes it will be a different one.

And lately I've felt more and more desperate for it, for some reason.

"Sure, that sounds fun. You know I prefer Jenny's silent company to your new shitty dad-jokes, anyway."

He lets out a loud, relieved laugh at that. "You're still an asshole, Dani."

"Alright, enough with the language," Mom scolds, handing the baby to Rachel. "She's going to be repeating everything before you know it, and then you'll be screwed." She hustles over to the oven just as the timer goes off. "Dinner's ready. Everyone can take a seat at the table."

A few minutes later, once everyone has heaped food onto their plates and Mom has finally settled into her seat after getting everyone else comfortable, Rachel turns her attention to me and asks, "So Dani... any upcoming trips for you?"

I chew a bite of potatoes thoughtfully before answering, "A few local ones for work. Beyond that, only idea I'm tossing around is popping over to Finland in December. I've been dying to see Lapland and the Northern Lights."

My idea is met with only understanding nods. My family is more than used to me randomly picking a place in the world and traveling there on my own. This particular location is one of my tamer ideas. They learned a long time ago that I don't respond well to worried looks—and definitely not to being told I *shouldn't*.

"That sounds so fun," Rachel says with a smile. "You'll have to send us pictures of the reindeer if you go." She hesitates a moment, pushing the potatoes around on her plate, before asking quietly, "Your brother says there's a resort in the Bahamas that you loved. Do you remember what it was called?"

"Yeah, in Nassau. Why? You guys planning a vacation?"

Rachel and my brother exchange a look. "Yeah, I think we want to fit a trip in with the three of us before... things get a little crazy."

I look at my brother in confusion. "What's getting crazy? Work?"

Tommy's still looking at Rachel as he answers. "Not exactly," he says quietly.

My parents and I only stare at him expectantly.

"Umm," he starts, then swallows roughly. He stares at his wife for another moment before turning to us and announcing bluntly, "Rachel's pregnant. Again."

All eyes snap to Rachel, and then to the five-month-old currently laughing and tossing peas all over the floor.

"Oh my God," my mom whispers. And then... "Oh my *God!* Oh my God, congratulations!!" Before anyone else can react, she's jumping up from her chair and launching herself at her daughter-in-law. "You're having another baby!"

Rachel lets out a choked sob as her arms wrap around my mom. "I *know.* God, I'm going to have two under two. Am I completely insane?"

"Oh honey, you're going to be amazing," my mom says as she pulls back, tears shining in her eyes. "I'm so happy for you."

Dad and I finally overcome our shock. While he stands from his chair and approaches Rachel with a hug of his own, I'm looking at Tommy and saying, "Well done, bro. Guess the swimmers are doing what they need to."

"Dani," my mom hisses in scolding.

I wince and stand from my chair, rounding the table so I can punch my brother in the arm. "In all seriousness, congratulations. That's amazing."

He aims a relieved but nervous smile my way. "Thanks, Dani. It's no Finland, but..."

Rolling my eyes, I punch him again. "Yeah, the North Pole is way better than a baby. You're an idiot."

Except, I understand what he's trying to do. And I give him a tiny, thankful smile that only he can see for it.

He knows I can't keep up with this level of adulting. That I don't understand settling down like this. He says baby, and I hear *I can never go out for a beer with my brother ever again*. And he's trying to make me feel less guilty about thinking that way.

"Well, this calls for a celebration," my mom interrupts, trying to hide that she's wiping a tear away. She claps her hands together in excitement. "Everybody, keep eating your dinner. I'm going to make my famous apple pie to celebrate."

Around the table, everyone bites down on their smiles to hide them from my mom. At the fact that her solution to good news, *any* good news, is to whip up something sugar filled.

I hold on to the warmth in my chest for the rest of the night, and carry it all the way home with me.

The thoughts from before dinner are still rolling through my head when I finally get home to my cozy, one-bedroom apartment that night. Not just the news that I'll have another niece or nephew to spoil, but also the fact that Dad wants to retire, that Mom thinks I should try settling down with someone—that my brother, who already has, doesn't even have time to get a beer with me anymore.

None of those things sound even remotely appealing to me, even after a little distance from the conversation.

I shake the distracting thoughts away and instead dive into editing my current work project, an event where I took pictures of a new statue being unveiled at a historic site. I spend hours going through the footage, falling so deep into my work that I don't look up from my computer until I notice birds chirping and the sky lightening.

I let out a groan when I look at the time, stretching my arms in the air and cracking my spine that I haven't straightened in way too long. I love getting so lost in the story I'm trying to tell that I forget about everything around me. It's one of the main reasons I love photography. When I'm on-site taking pictures, it's my job to capture the story unfolding—I throw myself into the varying emotions of the people, the different features of the setting, the essence of the moment. And then, with editing, I get to highlight the details and weave the pictures together to tell the story in an album. It's the greatest creative outlet I've ever experienced.

I debate pausing for breakfast, but I'm so far gone in the images that I decide I'm not ready to stop yet. Instead, I scroll through a few pictures that I haven't edited yet, for one reason or another. I pause on one in particular.

It's the image of a younger man, likely in his early twenties, with dirty blonde hair and a smile that rivals everyone else's. I can't tell what he's staring at in the picture, but the shot I've captured is one of him beaming at something in the distance. With his lips turned up and his blue eyes focused on something, he seems every bit the playful, gleeful portrait. It only takes me a few minutes to edit the picture and bring out his best features.

The shot is enough to remind me of another smiling man. One I left inside a college classroom with no way to contact me and with no hope of further contact.

I'd be lying if I said I didn't regret that. If I said I didn't regret leaving him there on his own, with no hope for reaching out again. Regardless if it's him or I making the contact. When it happened, I just knew I had to get out of there. I had to create some space between us, because the time we did share was already too much for me to handle. I've never once been so eager to see someone again. The fact that I wanted to see *him* was a red flag that I needed to bolt out of there.

Still, that leaves me with questions and *what ifs.* Enough that when it's 5:00am a week after said encounter, I'm still thinking about whether or not I did the right thing leaving a guy who was so obviously worth taking another shot at. Someone who seemed like they might understand the casual thing.

And without my mother hovering over me, without her pressuring me into trying dating for real, for just one moment… I let myself consider it.

I let myself think about what it would be like to give him my number. To answer when he calls, and schedule a time to see him again. Not just to have sex, but to spend time with each other. Doing what? Going to the movies? Having dinner at a nice restaurant? What would it be like to hold his hand through all of that, and let him stay the night at the end of it? To make me breakfast in the morning so we can do it all over again?

What would it be like to date him?

I can almost picture it. Can picture how much he would make me laugh through the date, and how much fun I would have shocking him with my spontaneous idea to go skinny-dipping in the LOVE park fountain after dinner. It would be a fun night. It would be a fun *relationship.*

But fun doesn't last. Fun isn't sustainable in a serious relationship, because as people get close to each other, as lives are woven together, it's not just one person that certain decisions affect. It's two. Which means compromises need to be made, and soon those compromises become big sacrifices.

Before long, my more *risky* activities are being frowned upon, and I can no longer jump on every crazy and fun idea that pops into my head. Before long, I'm passing on the more dangerous assignments, or traveling less so I can stay close to home. Before long, I'm not the same person I am today, not doing the same things that used to make me happy.

Suddenly, I'm flashing back to visions of a boyfriend upset about how I yet again snuck into a dangerous place to take pictures. To arguments about how photography should be a hobby, not a career. To the night when I finally agreed to give it up, and to—

I snap myself out of that memory with a quick shake of my head. The last thing I need is anger simmering in my veins while I do the job I—thankfully—never gave up. That, to this day, still brings me more joy than any man ever brought me.

Even if one of them did come awfully close.

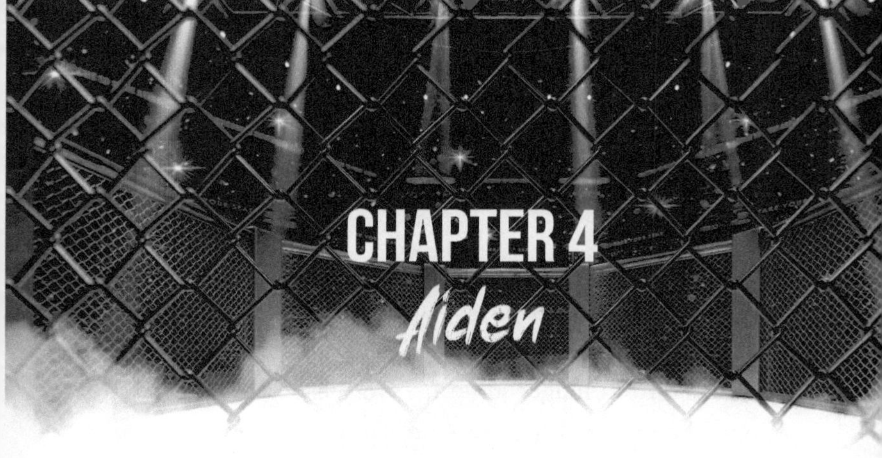

When I walk into my dad's house, I throw my backpack by the door the same way I've been doing for the past decade and yell, "Pops, I'm here! Where you at?"

He comes lumbering around the corner from the kitchen and throws himself in the well-worn recliner in front of the TV with a grunt. With as much of a greeting, he throws his feet up and turns the TV on before asking, "How was school?"

I take my usual spot on the couch with a tired sigh. "Fine. Ready for this semester to be over. How was work?"

This time I'm surprised to get an answer when he says, "We got a new building booked today. Construction starts in three months. Should be a good location to have on the company's resume."

My eyes widen in surprise. It's been a while since my dad's company has signed a good construction, so this is huge. "Holy shit, Dad. That's awesome, congratulations."

Another grunt. For as long as I can remember, he's never been a man of many words, so it's hardly a surprise that he doesn't go into much detail about a job that is likely huge for his company. Instead, I let him have his content silence, and simply watch the rerun that he's currently got up on the screen.

"You got any fight prospects?" he asks a while later.

I let out a sigh as I drop my head back on the couch. "Not really. I feel like I've fought everyone I can in the local amateur circuit, so I'm not sure what else Coach has planned for me. I'd say going pro is next on the roster but I'm not sure I'm ready for that, either. Feel like I'm stuck in limbo or something."

He mulls that over for a second before he responds. Dad's always been supportive of my sport choice, bragging to anyone that will listen on the construction site that his son is a well-known Philly MMA fighter, so he knows as much about the sport as any fighters do. With it just being the two of us as I was growing up, he always made it a point to devote all of his attention to anything I was ever interested in—whether that be baseball, lacrosse, or even rugby for a short time in college.

He's the definition of a supportive parent. The only one I've ever had.

At the thought of the mother that I've never known, a cold feeling comes over me. The same one that always makes an appearance when I think of the woman.

Dad and I never talk about her. Sometimes I think he wants to, but only in the way that he'll answer my questions if I have any.

It's clearly not a secret between us that her abandoning us before I even turned a year old has fucked me up. As much as I don't want to admit it. But it's hard to not hate a woman that hurt my dad and left her own child all in one fell swoop. All because she *wasn't ready to settle down.*

Her words, and the only thing my dad has ever said about her leaving.

He'll never admit it, but he's fucked up over her leaving, too. I was too young to remember the heartbreak part, but I can see that he was in love with her just by the way his eyes go hazy anytime the topic of moms and wives come up. And even though they never married, he's clearly convinced she was his soulmate. There's probably even a part of him that believes the pregnancy wasn't an accident—that it was fate trying to tie them irrevocably together.

Except, you can't hold someone down whose biggest fear is *being* tied down.

I obviously don't remember her, so I don't know how hard she tried to fight that fear after she got pregnant. Something tells me not very hard. Because a woman who could leave her own child—and then, in twenty-one years, never *once* say another word or send a birthday card—likely isn't one that cares too much about fighting for the right thing.

I got over my anger a long time ago. When I was a kid, of course I had some days where I couldn't understand why I didn't have a mom like the other kids did, but they were few and far between. For as long as I can remember, it was simply understood that it was Dad and I. Always has been, always will be. We didn't need anyone else.

Instead, I became almost numb to the idea of women in my life. Well… long-term women, at least. *Women* I like.

I just don't expect them to stay.

It's one of the reasons why I've never had a serious girlfriend. Even in high school, when I first started coming into myself, it never appealed to me to put my heart and trust into another woman. One look at my dad and I know loving my mom would've been the biggest mistake of his life if he hadn't gotten me out of it.

I prefer to keep things surface-level with the women I meet. Not that I only want them for sex, because that's not the case, but the charming, ladies' man part of my personality is such a comfortable default, and so effective when it comes to keeping things casual, that I don't think I even know how to be anyone else. I probably couldn't deepen a connection even if I wanted to.

Which leaves me with flirting, fucking, and then hoping like hell they aren't looking for anything serious.

I've even perfected the art of gently steering the situationship when that seems to be happening. I love women, and I want them to have nothing but positive interactions with me, even when I'm setting a boundary that might hurt their feelings. Because that's the last thing I've ever wanted to do.

I just don't want to get attached to them and risk having them leave me.

I'm snapped out of my thoughts when Dad says, "Coach'll come up with something. Even if we gotta fly you out to the West Coast to get some competition, we'll make it happen."

That makes me frown in confusion and raise my head up. My dad's hardly poor as a construction manager, but with me in college and my only job being a measly part-time internship, funds aren't exactly flowing right now. The fact that he's offering something that big just speaks to how much he supports my fighting career.

"I don't have to go to California for competition," I argue. "I mean yeah, it's where the most fighters are, but I don't exactly want to get in the habit of flying out there every time I'm in need of a fight. At that point, it would make more sense to move."

"So then do that," he murmurs.

Just the thought of that is enough to make my blood freeze. Leaving my dad out here on his own? No thanks, nothing is that important.

I let out a forced chuckle. "Don't be so eager to get rid of me, Pops."

No answer. Then again, I wouldn't expect one. He's so used to my humor that he rarely reacts to it anymore.

"Mind if I crash here tonight?" I ask tightly. I'm feeling weirdly lonely this week, and I don't really feel like going back to my college apartment that I share with a never-there senior who overstudies during the day and works all night. The idea of watching a football game with my dad and falling asleep on the couch sounds way more appealing than being by myself.

I obviously get an affirmative grunt as my answer. Letting out a breath of relief, I settle farther into the couch and turn my attention to the TV, letting a content smile creep across my face.

The next morning when I walk into the gym, I'm greeted by the sight of Jax tossing Tristan across the mat.

"Dude, what the fuck has gotten into you?" Tristan moans,

straightening from an almost violent foot sweep takedown. "Why do you have so much energy lately? You only get this way after you've won a fight or gotten a promotion or something."

The blonde Viking only grins in response. "Sounds like someone is looking for an excuse for when I kick their ass."

Tristan glares at his best friend. "Hardly," he says drily. "Consider it a check-in so I know what's going on with you." He rubs his lower back and grumbles, "And so I know when to prepare myself for your alpha moods."

I shake my head with a chuckle. People often assume fighters are just barbarians that want to beat up everyone they can get their hands on, but that couldn't be further from the truth.

Most fighters hate sparring hard. Punching others in the face means *getting* punched in the face. No one ever thinks of that part.

Or of getting thrown across the mat.

"Alright, first person to three takedowns buys lunch," Tristan growls, crouching into a wrestling stance and starting to circle the still-grinning Jax.

"You're on, asshole."

When I leave them to make my way to the other end of the gym, and by the time I push the door to the locker rooms open, all I hear is Tristan's shout of surprise, followed by Jax's raucous laughter.

"Fucking children," I hear a female voice mutter from the hallway.

I'm still laughing under my breath when the door opens again. A massive, tattooed stranger steps into the changing room, someone I've never seen and that definitely doesn't seem like he's been to this gym before. His hair is buzzed and his lips are turned down into a scowl, making him the epitome of unapproachable.

Still, it's not in my nature to ignore anyone. "Hey," I offer, lifting my chin at the new guy.

He only glares in my direction as he rips one of the lockers open.

Mentally shrugging off the interaction, I turn toward my own locker. God knows we've had enough people pass through here that don't stick, I'm hardly going to give more of my energy to the ones that clearly don't mesh with the gym vibe. I simply grab the equipment I need for today's workout and throw the rest of my gym bag into the locker.

When I eventually leave angry boy in the locker room, everyone's already gathered on the mat for today's jiu-jitsu lesson. Tristan and Jax in particular are already sweating as they wait for Coach to start class.

"So who's buying lunch?" I whisper with a grin as I approach the two of them.

Tristan aims a glare at his best friend. Jax simply lets a shameless grin slide onto his face, looking every bit the gleeful winner as he says, "I feel like going to Huda for lunch today. I'm in the mood for a good sandwich."

"You're lucky I like Jehuda's food enough to take you there," Tristan grumbles.

We go through a warmup like normal, our noon class filled with the pro fighters as it usually is, and then we're working jiu-jitsu drills with our partners.

I give Max my usual *we're partners* look, and grab him for the exercise that we're starting with. It only takes a few reps to get the hang of the move, to get comfortable enough that I start chatting.

"So what're we doing this weekend? Want to go to Maxi's?" I grin when I realize something. "I want to go to Maxi's with Max."

My best friend rolls his eyes at the same time that he throws my legs over his shoulder and passes to my side. "Since when are you so dead set on partying on Temple's campus?"

"I like the music," I mumble half-heartedly.

"Liar," he accuses. Then he's resetting us to the starting position and starting all over again. "You're searching for that chick you met last week on campus."

At the reminder of Dani, my limbs go stiff. Yes, I've been hoping to run into her, but I'm not consciously trying to see her again. That would be insane. I'm a 22-year-old guy, for God's sake. It's practically required of me to be young and single.

"I don't know what you're talking about," I grit out, combating his move and flipping us into a different position. "I just like the vibe over there."

I don't miss the eye roll that my best friend gives me. It's his usual *I'm over your shit* look that he gives me whenever I'm pushing one of my schemes too far.

"Dude, if she wanted to see you again, she would've given you her number," he says, resetting us to the original position.

And as much as I want to smash him, I also know he's right.

"You would be doing the same thing if a chick had blown

your mind," I grumble.

"Aiden and Max," a voice barks from the other side of the mat. We turn to our coach, a guilty look already on our faces. "Anything you'd like to share with the class?"

"No, sir," we mumble, properly chastised.

We don't speak for the rest of the class—or at least, we don't speak about Dani. I doubt I'm capable of staying silent for a full hour.

Once we're done drilling, we spend twenty minutes doing live rolls and implementing the moves we learned during class. By the time we're done, I'm drenched in sweat and gasping for breath.

"I swear Coach's classes get harder after people fight," Max pants, bent over and bracing on his knees. I can only nod in agreement.

We take the time to stretch out and cool down. By the time we're ready to leave, I look around at the slowly emptying gym. "I have to get to class in a bit, want to grab some food with me before?"

Nodding as he grabs his gym bag, Max replies, "Alright, but I'm picking the place and I refuse to hear you talk about your disappearing Cinderella for the next hour." He quirks a judging eyebrow at my glare but after a moment it forces a grumbled *fine* out of me.

"Burgers it is. Let's go, I'm starving."

Twenty minutes later we're standing in line at our favorite burger bar, waiting for our orders to come out. I open my mouth to say something but at Max's knowing glare, it snaps shut again.

"I wasn't going to talk about her," I grumble. "I just wanted to ask if you've ever had to run from security guards."

"Yeah, which you're asking about *because* of her. You're not sneaky."

I let out an exaggerated sigh. "Fine. Then I just won't talk at all."

"Hardly a punishment, dude." A pause. "But yes, I've had to run from security. That memory is the reason I never take Remy up on her offers of tequila shots. I tend to feel threatened by authority when I drink it."

Chuckling, I turn to scan the restaurant. My gaze bounces from staring impatiently at the kitchen, to the other patrons, and then to the entrance as the door opens.

And I suck in a startled breath at what I see.

"Dani," I breathe.

Max lets out a loud groan. "Dude, *come on*—"

"No, I mean… she's here." I jerk my chin at Dani entering the restaurant, my voice low and my eyes wide.

She looks just as hot as she did the last time I saw her. Skinny jeans and a tight tank top that shows off a sliver of her stomach, with a pair of well-worn Converse finishing off the look. Her black hair is down, same as last time, and the strands look so soft and shiny that my fingers start to twitch from the memory of wrapping them around my fist. Taking hold of them as I take her from behind, as I—

My train of thought is cut off when she turns and spots me.

And then a gorgeous smile spreads across her face, a delighted twinkle appearing in her eyes.

"Aiden," she greets me, walking immediately toward me.

"Fancy running into you here."

"I was hoping I would eventually," I admit before I can stop myself. "But I thought it would be on campus. Temple's crazies aren't good enough for your pictures anymore?"

She lets out a chuckle, leaning against the table in front of us. "Those were just practice shots. I had some real work to do last week. Although there *are* some interesting characters over there." With the way she's looking at me, I know she's including me in that category. And it's enough to drive a bolt of pleasure through my chest.

"That sounds like you missed me, Dani," I tell her with a grin.

She shoots me a grin of her own but doesn't respond.

"God, I can practically smell the sex between you two," Max comments. He gives me an almost apologetic look. "Now I understand why you won't shut up about it."

"Dude," I groan, dragging a hand down my face.

Dani only chuckles at the knowledge that she blew my mind. She gives Max a once-over, completely shameless about the fact that she's clearly checking out my best friend in front of me. Yet, there doesn't sound like there's any innuendo when she sticks her hand out and offers, "I'm Dani."

He shakes it with an appreciative look. "I'm Max. Nice to meet you."

She cocks her head and studies him in a completely different way. "You fight too, don't you?"

Max and I share a look. "How does everyone always know? Are we wearing signs I don't know about?"

"It's the easy confidence," Dani explains. "Men who know

how to handle themselves physically don't act the same as the ones that overcompensate and walk around with a chip on their shoulder." She pauses, then adds, "Also the ears. The ears give it away."

I rub my ears, the one thing I'm slightly self-conscious about being the cauliflower ear that jiu-jitsu has caused.

"I think they're sexy," she assures me with a wink and heated gaze.

My hand drops, a grin stretching across my face as my usual arrogance returns. "Yeah? I know an abandoned building right around the corner that we're not allowed into, want to go check it out with me?"

"Wish I could, pretty boy," she says softly—in a voice that sounds like she's letting me down easy. *Fuck.* I generally have a rule with my women that's the equivalent of a no double-texting rule, which is: *no double offers.* I'll chase once, but never twice in a row. It's bad enough that Max told her I've been thinking about last week ever since it happened.

My stomach sinks in disappointment. That was supposed to be my way in. Now, I have to force myself to act cool—and indifferent—when in reality, all I want to do is beg her for her number and convince her to go on a date with me so I can hang out with her and fuck her again.

Instead, I heave a dramatic sigh. "Fine, I guess that means I'll be crying myself to sleep tonight, sad and alone. Maybe someday I'll figure out how to get over you."

She lets out a laugh at my answer, which sparks hope in my

chest. *Maybe she'll ask me out instead? I can't be the only one that enjoyed last week and wants more.*

"How about we go find some poor security guards to outwit, instead?" she asks cheekily, cocking her head. "Maybe Friday night?"

I smooth my expression into one that looks almost lazy. "Sure, I could make time for that."

Just then, our names are called for our to-go lunch order. Max automatically moves to grab it.

"Let's say Moriarty's at 9," Dani says.

"Sounds good," I agree. I hesitate, glancing down at the phone in her pocket. "Want to take my number so you have it?"

She shakes her head with a coy smile. "No. Because I don't need it, and you don't get mine yet. If you don't show up, I'll just go home with someone else instead."

I think my eyes widen in surprise but I'm too thrown off by her brazenness to really notice. I even allow myself to mutter, "Damn, girl. That's cold."

She huffs a laugh at that. "So make sure you show up then."

"Yes, ma'am," I drawl appreciatively. Turning to Max as he returns with our order, I nod my head toward the exit to signal that we're leaving.

He reads my unspoken message and turns to Dani to say, "It was nice meeting you, Dani."

"You, too," she says with a kind smile.

Max starts to walk toward the exit but before I follow him, I take two quick steps until I'm standing directly beside her.

Until I can lean down to press my mouth to her ear.

"Do I get your number before or after I make you come? Because I have plans to do a lot of that on Friday, and I fully expect to earn it."

I only wait long enough to feel the shiver run through her at my words, then I'm following behind Max.

CHAPTER 5
Aiden

WHEN I WALK into Moriarty's on Friday night, I feel more excited than I've felt in a long time about a date. I tell myself it's because we've technically already gone on a 'date,' but deep down I know it's because of Dani. I've met confident, successful women before, but never one like her. And it makes me excited that it's so damn easy to like her and get along with her.

I scan the restaurant, my gaze bouncing from the tables to the bar, and it only takes a second to decide that Dani is definitely not a sit-down-and-have-dinner girl. After letting the hostess know I don't need a table, I walk over to the bar and take a seat at one of the stools.

"What can I get you?" the bartender asks when he stops in front of me.

It's an Irish pub, so it's not hard to decide on a Smithwick's while I wait. "Actually, can I get two double shots of whiskey, too?" I add.

"It's that kind of night, huh?" he asks with a knowing smirk.

With a chuckle, I respond, "Not exactly. But I have a

feeling the girl I'm waiting for is a whiskey girl."

"You would be correct," a voice purrs behind me.

I almost don't want to turn around, that's how much I'm enjoying the shocked and impressed expression on the bartender's face. I wait until he gives me a look of approval before I turn to face Dani.

"Hey, dirty girl," I murmur so only she can hear.

"Hey, pretty boy," she responds with a teasing smile. She takes a seat at the bar next to me before I can ask if she wants to move to a table, and then nods at the bartender for another Smithwick's.

"No table?" I still ask, angling my body so I'm still looking at her.

"Nope," she says, facing forward and getting comfortable. "Sitting at the bar is easier because it takes away the need for that awkward kind of forced eye contact. This way, I don't have to look at you if I don't want to."

I can't help it—I chuckle. "It's a good thing my ego is rock-solid because you are definitely not good for it."

She shoots me a playful grin at that. "Yeah, I'm sure commenting on the awkward side of a first date totally overshadows the ego-push of me screaming your name last week."

I don't miss the way the bartender's eyes widen in shock when he overhears Dani's comment as he slides the beers over to us. Nor can I help the smug smile that stretches across my face when his gaze slides to me.

"You're right, I'll probably live," I concede. Looking over her outfit, I'm struck with a momentary flash of awe—somehow, she's even hotter than I remember. She's wearing a dress this time, though it's black and paired with the same combat boots I saw her wearing that first day on campus. Her black hair, as it always seems to be, is left to hang to her waist and tempt me into wanting to grab it. Memories of doing exactly that pop into my head, and it's all I can do to take a huge swig of beer in an attempt to cool down.

"So," I start instead, wanting to focus on something other than how badly I want to fuck this girl. "Does this mean I need to abandon all usual first date etiquette, or just the dinner date at a table part?"

"Let's just skip the usual awkward bits." She shoots me another coy smile. "Technically we already know each other as intimately as you can know a person, so I'd say we can skip the other stuff."

So much for distracting myself from my hardening dick.

"So no questions about what you do and if you're close with your parents," I choke out. "Got it." Then I take another big swig of my cold beer.

"Exactly," she says in a pleased tone as she slides one of the shots of whiskey over to me. Lifting hers in the air, she says, "To the ideal kind of date: no expectations, none of the awkward bits that come from them, and to it ending exactly where every good date should end."

And then I watch in amazement as she throws the shot back.

This is already the greatest date ever.

Then I down my own shot.

I want to ask her a million questions. I want to know who

the fuck this girl is that blew into my life out of nowhere and blows my mind every time I see her.

"So what do we want to talk about?" she asks casually, crossing her legs under the bar. All it does is bring her closer to me, close enough that her foot is now stroking along my leg every time she bounces it.

"Well, since we're not doing the cliché first date questions, let's just do the fun ones," I suggest. "How about the question game?"

She quirks an eyebrow. "The question game? Isn't that just called conversation?"

"Kind of," I say with a chuckle. "You take turns asking questions, anything you want, but you can't repeat any of them. My friends love this game. Although for some reason, they refuse to play it unless they're on a couch."

Dani shrugs and waves the bartender down for two more shots. "Sounds fun. Let's do it. Couch can wait for next time."

"Next time, huh?" I ask with an amused quirk of my lips. "Already planning a next time?"

"You can thank your big dick for that," she says with a grin.

I can only blink at that. "I take it back. You're great for my ego."

Chuckling, she gestures for me to begin. "Alright, pretty boy, ask your question."

"What do you do for work?" I blurt out immediately.

There's that playful eyebrow quirk again. "I thought we weren't doing any cliché first date questions?" she asks.

"Doesn't count as cliché if I really want to know the answer," I say with a shrug. "It'll be the only one, I promise."

She still looks skeptical but she answers anyway. "I'm a photojournalist," she says, confirming my suspicions. I knew she was too good at taking pictures for it to not be her job. "My boss sends me on assignments, usually local but sometimes around the country, to photograph current events."

"Was the crazy Jesus lady an assignment?"

She gives me a scolding look. "I believe it's one question at a time, is it not?" I only grin guiltily, but she answers anyway. "She was not. That was just for fun while I was waiting for another assignment."

"How often do you get assignments?" I can't help asking.

Dani aims a good-natured kick at my leg beneath the bar. "Naughty boy," she murmurs. "You're not playing fair."

I lean forward to bring my lips to her ear. "Something tells me it would be more fun playing with you if I bend the rules a little," I murmur in a deep voice.

She sucks in a breath at my words, and it takes everything in me not to immediately drag her off that barstool.

"Go ahead then," I concede. "Ask your question."

Desire still sparking in her eyes, she asks, "Who was your celebrity crush as a kid?"

For a moment, I can only blink in surprise. "That's your question?"

She shrugs, the corner of her lips twitching. "If we're staying away from first date questions, I'm going to ask the fun ones instead. You said anything goes."

That's true, I did say that. So, racking my brain for a moment, I answer with, "Mila Kunis, I think. Even when she was in That 70's Show, I was obsessed with her." I give Dani a once-over as something occurs to me. "Actually, with the black hair and kiss-bitten lips, you're kind of like a badder version of her. Like a tattooed version." My gaze drops to those lips and suddenly all I can think of is how they would look wrapped around my cock. *Fuck,* I should've gotten her on her knees the first time. She probably looks like a dream when she's—

"Down, boy," Dani murmurs, brushing her foot against me once more. "That comes later."

My eyes snap back to hers. Despite her teasing words, I can see she's just as eager to follow my train of thought as I am.

But as soon as that thought hits, so does the thought that as soon as I take her to bed, our date will be over. And I'm not ready to let that happen yet.

"What's the coolest trip you've taken?" I ask, eager to keep the game going. "For work or pleasure, doesn't matter."

"I backpacked across Europe by myself for six weeks after high school," she answers, a shadow of something crossing her face before immediately being wiped away by the exciting memory of the trip. "I had saved all my money in high school so I decided to spend most of it on train rides and hostels after I graduated. Best decision I ever made."

"Not a single part of me is surprised that eighteen-year-old Dani took a solo trip that big," I say with a chuckle. "Was that a before college kind of thing?"

I realize my mistake when Dani tsks in disappointment. "Okay new plan. Forget the game. I don't like these rules."

"Tough luck, pretty boy, game stays in play." She leans forward to prop her elbow on the bar, tapping her finger against her lower lip. Yet again, my gaze zeroes in on her mouth.

"Why fighting?" she asks finally.

"Ooh, a normal question? You're flirting with first date etiquette. I might start thinking you actually want to date me." I add a teasing edge to my words by shooting her a wink, feeling pleased when it makes her smile and roll her eyes.

I twirl the beer bottle on the bar top, absentmindedly looking behind the bar as I contemplate my answer. "Why fighting? Well I wrestled in high school—hence the cauliflower ear—so MMA wasn't totally out of the blue. I liked how competitive wrestling was but at the same time, I kind of wanted to try something a little more combative. A little riskier, with higher stakes. MMA was the logical choice. Philly's a fighting city so I knew it wouldn't be too hard to find a good MMA gym. I signed up for a gym membership before I even signed up for college classes."

"And do you want to make it a career?" Dani asks.

I give her a knowing look at the rule break, even though I'm secretly giddy over the fact that she wants to know more about me. "That's your freebie," I tell her, playfully chucking her under the chin. I wait until she predictably rolls her eyes before I answer the question.

"I don't know," I answer honestly. "I love the sport more than anything, and I definitely want to go pro soon, but I'm not as dead set on getting into the UFC as some of my teammates. I mostly just want to push myself as far as I can go. If that means I get good enough to make it a career, then so be it. But it's not a life or death dream."

I watch Dani mull over my answer. "I like that," she says. "It probably makes it a lot easier to deal with the pressure, too."

I nod in confirmation. She turns her body to fully face me, a movement that's not lost on me—she went from not looking at me to giving me her full attention. "Can I come watch next time you fight?" she asks.

"Of course," I answer immediately–and slightly too eagerly. Then I'm grabbing under the barstool she's sitting on and pulling her closer to me in one hard pull. Close enough that I can brace my foot on the rung of the stool and my arm along the back of it. "Wanna be one of my groupies, Dani?"

"Hmm," she hums, leaning into me now that she's closer. Her finger lazily traces over my jawline, her touch leaving a trail of sparks on my skin. "I'd be such a good groupie, too. Tell me, Aiden, how many girls have offered to suck your dick after they see you fight?"

My breath leaves me in a rush. "I lost count after a while," I lie breathlessly. Right now, all I can think about is *her* sucking my dick after a fight.

Her grin is radiant. She's teasing me, and I'm getting lost in it.

"Your turn," she murmurs, finally pulling her finger away from me.

"My—?" I ask in confusion.

"To ask a question," she says with a chuckle. She knows exactly how far she's woven me into her spell. And she's shameless about it.

I have to blink my brain back online, just so I can remember what the fuck I'm supposed to be doing that's not fantasizing about taking this girl to bed.

"Uh, favorite animal?" I manage to ask. Then I wince when

I realize how stupid that question is.

"Aw, you're not very good at this game, are you?" she asks, patting me on the arm. But there's a smile tugging at her lips and I think she might not hate the question after all.

"Don't underestimate my unassumingly simple questions," I defend. "I used to be a psych major—maybe I'm secretly analyzing your personality with them."

That smile is definitely about to take over her face. "Let me guess: you took one psych class as a freshman and realized the major is for the birds."

"It took two, thankyouverymuch."

She finally lets out the laugh she's been holding in. It's the first I've heard it, and *God* I want to hear it again. It's one of those laughs that comes from the belly, that is so genuine, you can't *not* smile when you hear it. And when she drops her head to my shoulder and shakes with it, a smile does creep onto my face.

I feel her hand brace on my hip, gripping my jeans as she gives into the laughter for a moment. I embrace it, enjoying the subtly sexy smell of her, the incredible feel of her body pressed to mine. Her essence is so intoxicating that even the usual pleasure I get from making someone laugh pales in comparison to it.

When she eventually pulls away, a pleased look on her face, I bring her attention back to the topic at hand. "Alright, out with it," I scold playfully. "Rules of the game say you have to answer any question I ask."

She looks thoughtfully over my shoulder as she contemplates her answer. Then she seems to perk up as she says, "A honey badger."

I frown slightly at that. "Because you're… ferocious?"

Dani shakes her head, that knowing smile still planted firmly on her face. "Not just that. They also prefer the bachelor/bachelorette life."

My frown deepens. "You like being single?"

She shrugs. "Sure. Don't you?"

"I mean, yeah, but I'm a guy. I'm genetically engineered to want to fuck my way through the city, especially at my age." I narrow my eyes in an exaggerated way that lets her know I'm joking. "Don't you have some inherent need to tame some poor guy and trick him into taking care of you?"

Her grin doesn't lose steam at my comment, it actually gains some. "I'm perfectly capable of taking care of myself. The only thing I need from men is orgasms, and that's just because the ones I get from a partner are unfortunately better than the self-induced ones. But I can still be single while I do that."

"I can't tell if that was a compliment that I can make you come, or an insult that you only want me for my body," I say in a flat voice.

She lets out a loud laugh at that. "If all I wanted from you was your body, I would've pulled you directly into the alley when I got here."

"Fine, then my body and my amazing sense of humor."

Chuckling, she shakes her head. "Okay but in all seriousness, are you really looking for a relationship? Because that's not why I'm here. And the reason I didn't give you my number before."

"No, I'm not looking for a relationship," I answer honestly.

"I have too much going on with school and fighting and my job search, so a girlfriend is the last thing I have time for." I take a big swig of my beer as I mentally add, *and women don't tend to stick around anyway.*

I don't say that, though. This isn't even a real first date, so dropping *that* kind of honesty bomb is not what the doctor ordered here.

Instead, I turn my skeptical—but teasing—gaze back to Dani. "But if that's the case, then you're definitely too good to be true. You want to have fun and fuck? With no expectations? That sounds like a friends with benefits thing."

The look she gives me is amused. "I don't know you enough to call you a friend."

"There you go basing me down to my body again. I think now would be a good time to give me another one of those ego-boosts."

She lets out a snort at that. Then something occurs to her, because she turns her attention fully toward me again and asks, "What's *your* favorite animal?"

"A quokka. We suck at this game."

"Those cute little marsupial things?" she asks with a confused rise of an eyebrow. "They look like raccoons, right? Why that one?"

I can't help the cocky grin from appearing on my face, or the way I gesture at myself. "They're the happiest animal in the world. And the cutest, because there isn't a human on this earth that could argue with that fact *or* stop themselves from playing with them. It hits close to home, ya know?"

And *fuck* do I love making her laugh. I mean, I love making everyone laugh, but with Dani it's a special kind of victory. Like she only does it when she really means it.

"We really do suck at this game," she agrees as she takes another sip of her beer. "I think we've broken every rule multiple times. Maybe we really should try the couch next time."

The idea of having Dani on a couch—instead of a storage closet or a barstool—is enough to make my dick start to harden again. I had gotten it under control during our teasing, but it's right back to half-mast at that comment.

She turns back to me, completely oblivious to my inner struggles. "Okay, let's pretend I didn't reciprocate that last question. My turn. What's the craziest place you've ever had sex?"

"You mean besides a supply closet after I just ran away from two security guards?" I ask with a quirked eyebrow.

She sighs. "If that's the craziest place you've ever done it then this might not work out, pretty boy. I need someone more adventurous than that."

"That's not adventurous enough?" I ask in mock outrage. "I'm pretty sure we were trespassing in that building, which means we were breaking the law being in there. Plus, public sex is also illegal, so technically that's a double whammy. Can't get more adventurous than that."

She gives me a knowing look. "You can, and I'll bet you have." Then she cocks her head as she studies me. "You strike me as a public sex kind of guy."

A grin stretches across my face. "Yeah? Why's that?"

She shrugs. "You just have that 'the world is mine and I do what I want' kind of vibe."

"What a coincidence, I have that tattooed across my lower back."

She lets out a giggle, the sound so feminine that it makes my dick twitch.

"I'll tell you mine if you tell me yours," I tell her with a grin.

"Count of three then."

"One..." We speak at the same time, both of us starting the countdown with mischief in our voices. "...two...three!"

"A bear cave on a mini golf course."

"On my high school soccer field."

My mouth drops open. "You did *what?!*"

"You were a soccer kid?" she asks with a laugh. "Oh my God, that's amazing."

"You had sex on a mini golf course?" I hiss.

"That's what I said," she whispers back, leaning her head closer to mine. "You know we're in a bar and don't need to use inside voices, right?"

I ignore her, too busy trying to understand her thought process to react to her sarcasm. "Are you *crazy*? How did you know a kid wouldn't catch you?"

She rolls her eyes and leans back, then takes a sip of her drink. "I'm definitely crazy, but I'm hardly a psychopath. I wouldn't have done it if there were people around."

My eyes are still as wide as saucers. "So then what, it was abandoned?"

She simply nods and drinks more of her beer.

"Where is there an abandoned mini golf course?" I ask, still utterly confused.

"You're really bulldozing this question game," she says with a sigh.

"We ran straight through that game and into another dimension when you admitted you had sex on a kid's playground," I clap back.

Aiming a glare at me, she replies, "What about you on a soccer field? Plenty of kids could've caught *you* there."

I let out a snort. "Yeah. Kids *my own age*, who would've congratulated me for banging the hottest senior in school when I was just a sophomore."

Now it's her jaw that drops and her eyes that widen. Then… she bursts out laughing.

"Oh my God," she gasps on a giggle. "And I thought my game was good. That's amazing."

"Trust me, your game is just fine," I mutter, taking a drink of my own, nearly-forgotten beer.

A massive grin stretches across her face. "If I nailed you then I guess it has to be."

At that, I drop my arm along the back of her barstool and lean in close, close enough that my lips graze the shell of her ear and I can hear the way her breath catches. With my foot still resting on the back rung of the stool, she's caged in.

And she knows it, because a shiver runs through her.

"I don't remember you being the one doing the nailing," I murmur, my nose lazily tracing her cheekbone. "If I remember correctly, *I* was the one nailing you against the wall."

Another shiver, this time with the added reaction of her knuckles turning white as she tightens her grip on the beer bottle. And when her chest starts to rapidly rise and fall with her breaths, I make a game time decision.

Pulling away from her, I wave the bartender down. "Can I close out my tab, please?"

"Always so polite," Dani says with a laugh. But the sound is breathless, some of her cockiness fading in the face of the growing heat between us.

I lean over to whisper in her ear again. "Say that again in five minutes when I'm disrespecting the fuck out of you in the back alley."

Her breath catches again, the sound louder this time. "Is that a euphemism?"

A grin slides across my face. "Funny. Not tonight—but good to know you're into that. Tonight, I want to feel how wet I can make that pussy before I fuck it."

"Oh my God," she whispers, finally giving up the last of her public-Dani persona.

And slipping into the one I suspect few have seen—the blissed out, lust-drunk Dani that only comes out to play when she's ready to give up the reins.

The bartender slides the check in front of me, winking as he says, "Have a good night, you two."

I scribble my signature and pocket my card, ignoring his comment because I'm too eager to get Dani outside as quickly as humanly possible. I grab her hand and drag her off the stool and out of the bar.

There's an alley beside the bar that stretches the length of it and connects to another alley running behind the row of buildings. I take a quick glance along the street to make sure no one will see us disappear, and then tug Dani into the alley.

Despite all my joking about liking public sex and the thrill of getting caught, I don't have any interest in getting arrested for public indecency. So I move us all the way to the end of it, deep into the shadows where you can't see us from the street.

And then I push Dani against the brick wall and take her lips with a hunger I don't think I've ever felt before.

She moans into the kiss, her arms winding around my neck and her lips opening to invite my tongue inside. I squeeze her hips and press her harder against the wall as I happily tangle my tongue with hers.

Fuck, she tastes like whiskey and the best night of my life.

Because she's wearing a dress, it's entirely too easy to run my hands from her hips to her thighs, until I'm gripping the end of her dress and pulling it up to her waist. I waste no time sliding my hand down the front of her thong. She's soaked, and the feeling makes me groan into our kiss.

"Dirty girl," I mutter against her lips. "I haven't even touched you yet and you're wet. What are you going to do when I fuck you?"

"I don't know, let's find out," she gasps, pulling me closer to her body.

"I want to play first," I growl, rubbing circles on her clit. "Be quiet and don't give us away."

She tries. I know she does. But the second I sink a finger into her, a moan slips out of her that would undoubtedly attract attention if there was anyone near the alley.

So instead, I put some space between us and tug her panties down her legs, momentarily dropping to my knees so I can pull them off her feet. Then I'm standing up and crowding her against the wall again.

"You're not very good at being quiet," I tell her, kissing and nipping along her neck. "You know what that makes me want to do?"

"I'm sure you're about to tell me," she says breathlessly.

I don't tell her. I show her.

I reach down and wad her thong into a ball, then I stuff it into her mouth. Not deep enough to truly gag her, but enough to make her eyes drift closed and to elicit a deep, sexual moan from her lips.

"Keep that in there so I don't have to fill your mouth with something else. As much as I'm dying to get your lips around my cock, I'm too desperate to get inside you to spend the time choking you with it right now. Understood?"

When she quickly nods her assent, I take the opportunity to hike her leg around my waist and grind my hips into her pussy. She drops her head back to the brick wall with a whimper, proving that my makeshift gag will do what it needs to keep her quiet.

"Good girl," I murmur. "Just like that, keep quiet for me while I work my fingers in here." And then I'm dropping my hand between her legs again and sliding my fingers through her slit.

She makes another sound, but the fabric is keeping her quiet enough that I can tease her a bit and spend a few seconds circling her clit before driving my finger into her at the same time that I take her mouth again. With her panties in her mouth I can't really kiss her, but it doesn't stop me from pressing my lips against hers and trying to weave my tongue into her mouth to meet hers through the silk.

The kiss is awkward and bumbling and the hottest thing ever.

Not to mention, the second I sink a finger inside her, she lets out a moan that even my mouth and the strength of the fabric in her mouth can barely contain. They do, but it's a close call.

I pump my finger inside her. When her chest starts to heave with her breaths, my attention drifts down to her barely-contained breasts. The more she squirms, the lower her dress slips, and in the end it only takes a quick tug of the fabric to lower it under the swell of her breasts. I let out a groan when the tight points of her nipples are exposed.

"Fuck, these are so pretty." Those are the only words I get out before I'm falling on her like a starving man, suctioning my mouth around the tip before nipping gently. By the time I switch to the other one, she's writhing against my mouth and trying to grind down on the finger that's still slowly fucking her.

When I begrudgingly straighten and remove my mouth from her skin, I sink another finger inside her. The sight of Dani like this, so lust-drunk and desperate, is too perfect not to absorb. So I take my free hand and move it to her throat, just so I can tip her head back and get a full view of her wide-eyed gaze.

A sound catches my attention and when I take a quick glance to our right, an idea starts to form in my mind. I let a grin stretch across my face as I pin Dani's neck harder against the wall, and drive my fingers deeper inside her.

Leaning forward to press my lips against Dani's ear, I whisper, "You were almost right earlier, Dani. I do like public sex. But do you know why?" When she only whimpers in response, I grip her jaw and turn her head to face the couple that I can now see making out not far from us. They've turned into the alley to hide in the shadows, but they're not quite close enough to really see us yet. Which is why I feel safe taunting Dani and pressing the pad of my thumb to her clit, coaxing her orgasm even closer.

"Because I like the idea of getting caught. Of someone watching as I make you *mine*."

And then I curl my fingers inside her and do exactly that.

I watch as her eyes roll to the back and her head drops to the brick wall behind her. She shudders around my fingers, the orgasm rolling through her body, and then she's collapsing in my arms with weak gasps of air through the silk in her mouth.

Reaching up to tug it out of her mouth, I press a gentle kiss to her lips. She sighs happily and takes her time kissing me back, her nails digging into my shoulders as she comes down from her intense release.

"Good girl," I whisper against her mouth. "You think you'll be able to stay quiet while I fuck you or do I need to gag you again?"

And just like that, the lust flares in her eyes again. Her chest starts to rise and fall in quick breaths, and I have my answer without needing a word.

I make an exaggerated tutting sound, shaking my head in mock disappointment. "Talks such a big game, and can't even stay quiet through a little orgasm," I taunt.

When her eyes flare with anger and her mouth pops open to scold me, I stuff the fabric back in her mouth.

"The only sound I want to hear from you for the next five minutes is the sound of your moans while you come on my cock," I growl. Then I'm hitching up her dress again and unbuckling my pants, suddenly desperate to get inside her. It only takes a second to roll a condom on and then I'm pressing her into the wall again and lining up at her entrance.

"Remember, you have to stay quiet. We can't have them knowing how desperate you are, can we?"

And when my words cause her eyes to drift shut and her head to drop back to the brick, I drive in with one hard stroke.

"*Fuck*," I grit out, dropping my forehead to the wall beside her head as I suck in a breath. "I thought I imagined how fucking tight you are." I take a few seconds to compose myself, only pulling back when Dani starts to squirm and whine in my arms. I use that as an opportunity to collar her throat again, more so wanting to bring her attention back to me than actually cut her air off.

"What did I say about the sounds I want from you," I growl, squeezing once to make my point. "I'll fuck you when I'm ready, and not a second sooner."

She's far enough gone in her pleasure that she doesn't fight me, she just nods and wraps her leg tighter around my hip. And as much as I know she wants to start rolling her hips, she stays where she is and waits for my movement.

Eventually, I pull my hips back so only the tip of my cock is inside her. Then I'm driving forward with a grunt and seating myself as deep inside her as possible.

She mumbles something into the gag, something that sounds like *Oh my God.* And that's enough to make my dick jump and make me want to pound into her until she explodes.

So I do just that. I start to thrust, *hard,* until she's scratching at my shoulders and whimpering into her makeshift gag. If she was any louder I'd cover her mouth, but as it stands she just sounds like she's hyperventilating.

I grind against her clit on every thrust, wanting to get her as close to finishing as possible before I pull my final card. And when her breaths start to hitch and her leg starts to tighten around my hips, I think I'm at that point.

Grabbing her chin, I forcefully turn her head to the side again. In the next second my lips are against her, whispering directly into her ear at the same time I'm driving pleasure into her body.

"Are you going to scream when you come? Are you going to let the drunk couple know that you're at the end of this alley being fucked against the bricks? I bet they would freak out, dirty girl. I bet they wouldn't expect to see you losing your mind and screaming for more. Are you going to give them a night they'll never forget?"

My words are enough to catapult Dani into an explosive orgasm. And, anticipating her scream, I clap my hand over her mouth to further muffle the sounds she lets out as she comes.

The second her cunt starts to violently contract around my dick, I have no hope of lasting. I drop my forehead to her temple with a groan and empty into the condom. She's too hot for her own good, and I don't have the willpower to give her a lasting session in public. So I begrudgingly come inside her as her own orgasm dies down.

The second I have my breath—and my wits—back, I quickly tug the silk from her mouth so she can breathe again. I tuck it into my back pocket without fully realizing what I'm doing, though the gesture definitely feels right. She doesn't seem to mind, either. She just looks at me with a loopy smile, tightening her grip on my neck, as if she's afraid I'll move away as soon as our tryst is over.

"I guess next time we won't have to wait for the mini golf course to be abandoned before you fuck me," I say breathlessly, my forehead still pressed against her temple. I don't even know if I'll see her again, I just know I don't want this to be the last time.

But she seems to like my casual *this isn't the last time* vibe, because she laughs and squeezes me tight for a second. Then she's unhooking her leg from my hip and pushing me back a step so she can right her clothes. I'm left to pull the condom off and tug my own pants back up.

"So... will there be a next time?" I ask, cringing at the tinge of desperation in my tone. It's not that I only want to fuck her, it's just that I'm not used to pushing women for dates after I've made them come hard enough to lose their minds. And I *like* Dani. I want to see her again.

"Maybe, pretty boy," she teases, tugging her dress down and taking a step toward the alley entrance.

"Wait, I don't even have your number," I blurt out, giving up on all dating games.

"Are you sure?" she asks, a sly grin on her face as she backs toward the street. Then she's turning around, passing the shocked-looking couple at the end of the alley who is only now realizing they weren't alone. Dani doesn't acknowledge them though, she just strides by them and disappears around the corner.

I let out a string of curses under my breath as I tug my pants into place and button everything up. I'm still whirling from my experience with Dani and I'm pretty sure my brain isn't working right after that orgasm so I'm a few seconds behind on the uptake.

Unfortunately, that's all it takes for her to get away. Again. By the time I'm rushing into the street, she's already long gone. I don't see her anywhere.

I let out another set of curses that would make a sailor blush. *Fuck. Fuck fuck fuck.*

I'm digging my fingers into my hair in frustration when I feel my phone buzz.

Confused, I pull it out of my back pocket and come face to face with an unknown number.

UNKNOWN

Tonight was fun. Let's do it again sometime.

A grin slowly stretches across my face. *That little minx. When did she get her hands on my phone?*

But I don't care that she stole my phone and somehow programmed her number into it.

I'm too ecstatic about the fact that I have her number.

CHAPTER SIX
Dani

I LET OUT an impatient huff as I lean back in my office chair.

I'm waiting for an approval on an assignment I really want, and being entirely impatient as I do it.

Instead of trying to distract myself with more mindless internet browsing, I decide to pull up the app I use to find random travel bartender gigs. I started using it when I realized how sporadic photojournalism can be, when I needed some supplementary income to hold me over between assignments.

As a twenty-three year old girl living on her own, I can use all the money I can get.

But before I can even open it, I see a text from an old friend of mine.

BOBBY

Any chance you're available to work a shift tonight?

I let out a grateful breath at the offer.

I look around my room, contemplating what I need to do for the next hour. On a whim, I open some of the old pictures I've been meaning to edit. It's a folder of my extracurricular events, some events that I took pictures of as a hobby. When I pull up the latest one, I come across the last pictures I took of a crowd.

They're the pictures of Jesus-lady. Which immediately makes me think of Aiden.

I scroll through the pictures he took, tamping down on my smile when I notice the focus of his shots. Almost all of his pictures are people-focused—specifically, of college kids. Every picture I review is one of a student and their college experience.

He's got a good eye for it. In only a few minute span he's captured academic life, a relationship, and plenty of different cliques. I could print any of these as a representation of the college experience.

At his memory, my brain starts to go down a rabbit hole of Aiden experiences. Of meeting him, of our time together, and then of my subsequent date with him at the bar.

He's… the ideal fuck buddy. And not just because he knows how to fuck, but because he's detached enough to understand why a woman might not want a longer term commitment. A lot of young men just assume women want relationships, but Aiden seems like he might actually understand a woman wanting a partner for orgasms only. That he might actually want a situationship of his own.

I scroll through the pictures until I reach the one that I secretly took of him before he even approached me. It's one of him with his water bottle in his hand, looking out over the college campus as if he's ready to take the next step. Like he's ready to move on from college and take the world by storm.

He looks… confident. Not just because he's well-dressed in slacks and a button-up in the picture, but because he looks like he knows he's in the right place. Because he looks like he wouldn't question why someone might be taking a picture of him.

The memories of that night, and then of our first date—

I shake the intrusive thought from my head the second that word comes to mind. I don't *date*. We just went out for drinks.

Fuck buddies don't date.

Reminder firmly embedded in my mind, I let myself go back to the memories of my time with Aiden, making sure to linger the most on the physical moments. Those thoughts are enough to drag me away from my current thought process. Instead of thinking about how I want to edit a picture, I'm thinking about when I want to see Aiden again. Of when I want to say yes to another offer, to a night where I can make him laugh and feel his body against mine.

On a whim, I grab my phone and send a text.

DANI

Feel like keeping me company tonight?

The answer takes some time to come through, making me question our last encounter. Making me question if he was as interested in us as I thought he was.

Which then makes me annoyed that I'm even questioning myself. I don't doubt myself over *men*.

But then my phone beeps.

AIDEN

What did you have in mind?

My exhale is one of relief. I knew after our last date that I wanted more of him, but putting my number in his phone wasn't exactly a surefire way of seeing him again.

DANI

I'm covering a bartending shift at a friend of mine's bar tonight. Join me at the end of the night?

His answer comes immediately.

AIDEN

Done. Send me the address.

I'm standing behind the counter when he appears. He's

wearing jeans and a light grey Henley, the shirt tight enough that I can see his muscles ripple as he walks in. His dirty blonde hair is styled to look perfectly messy, and with his hands in his pockets showing off the ease with which he walks into the now-closed bar, his entire stance screams his self-confidence.

Yeah, that boy is hot as fuck and he knows it.

He grins when he sees me, those damn dimples making me want to give him anything he wants.

I force myself to shake the traitorous thoughts away. "Hey, pretty boy," I open with instead, letting a flirty smile appear on my face. "Come here often?"

He takes a seat at the barstool in front of me and aims an equally flirty look my way. "Never been. I'm just following this sexy woman around in the hopes that I can see her naked again."

I slide a PBR and a shot of whiskey across the bar. Then I raise my own shot of whiskey in the air and say, "Play your cards right and you might."

He quirks an eyebrow at that but doesn't say anything, he just downs the shot before reaching for his beer. He looks around at the empty bar, then back to where I'm standing behind the counter. His eyes travel the length of my body, taking in my black lace tank top and cutoff denim shorts. When he peeks a little lower and sees my thigh-high fishnets, I can practically *see* the lust flare in his eyes.

Just as slowly, his eyes travel back to my face. And when he meets my gaze, I can already tell where this night is going to end.

"So," he drawls in that perfectly-arrogant voice. "What is

this place? And what do I have to do to get another shot, this time ideally poured directly into my mouth?"

I snort. Then I pour him another shot—in his glass.

"I used to work here with a guy I was seeing. I liked the woman that owns the bar so I kept working here even after I ended it with the guy. Although, I can't say the ex lasted here much longer—he was too big of a spoiled brat to hold a job down."

Aiden snorts. "You're not exactly giving him a glowing recommendation here." He takes another sip of his beer, then aims a thoughtful look my way. "So is that your type? Rich boy who's just looking for the next fun thing?"

"I guess so," I admit with a shrug. "That was the circle I grew up in. Plus they're usually hot and guaranteed to not want anything serious, so it's a fairly safe bet." He nods in understanding, as if I just gave him the answer he was already expecting.

I cock my head and study the man in front of me. "What about you? What's your type?"

"Female," he says simply. Shamelessly. "Rich, poor, smart, dumb, I don't really care. Every woman has something to offer so in my book, every woman is special and worth getting to know."

Chuckling, I shake my head as I pour each of us another shot. "You are *such* a charmer."

Aiden shrugs, looking completely unapologetic. "I love women, what can I say?"

"Ever have a serious girlfriend?" I ask, suddenly curious. For some reason I can't picture this friendly guy settling down to focus on one girl. But maybe I'm wrong—maybe Aiden's rebounding from a long-term relationship.

"Nope," he says, completely unabashed in his answer.

"No?" I repeat, and the surprise is evident in my voice.

Taking the shot glass that I slide across to him, he swirls it in front of him while he answers. "Never had any interest in tying myself to one woman," he says honestly. "Not that that means I *never* want to settle down, I just… haven't really wanted to so far. I enjoy being single."

I'm not really sure how to respond to such honesty, so I stay silent and let him say whatever it is I can see him working up to.

"I like one *particular* woman, at the moment," he admits, and I stiffen in alarm. "She's sexy as fuck and one of the most interesting people I've ever met." He gives me a blatant once-over before smirking. "Definitely my favorite flavor."

And just like they always do, those words put me immediately on edge. I force an eye roll to cover up my internal panic. "Alright, let's not get ahead of ourselves. There will be no R words used to describe this… situation. No one is liking anyone beyond what they can offer in the bedroom. Understood?"

Aiden gives me a shameless grin. "What if we're not in a bedroom? Does a pool table count in this scenario?"

This time I really do roll my eyes, but there's a smile tugging at my lips.

He is such a flirt.

"Pool table, bedroom, at the foot of the Rocky statue, doesn't matter. None of this goes beyond sex."

Aiden's jaw drops with an audible gasp, and I almost laugh at the outraged expression on his face.

"You had sex at *Rocky's feet?*" he whispers in mock-horror. "How could you desecrate his memory like that?" When I only chuckle in amusement, he glares at me. "Monster," he hisses. "You're the worst Philadelphian ever."

At that, I do laugh out loud. "Calm down, Rocky's fine. But yes, same rules apply."

He sighs, all traces of humor sliding from his face. "Yeah, okay, I get it. Nothing goes beyond the bedroom. Message received."

My eyes narrow in his direction. "Is that going to be a problem? I thought we were clear on this, Aiden."

He gives me a skeptical look. "Stop worrying. We're clear, I want the same thing anyway." He studies me for a moment, looking like he's trying to figure out how to ask something. And when he asks it, I'm not even surprised at the question.

"I know why *I* don't want a relationship, but what's your excuse? Why are you so opposed? Parents end up divorced or something?"

"Does it matter?" I mutter, not really wanting to have this conversation. It never ends up the way I want it to, because no one ever agrees with my theory.

"I'd like to understand," he answers with a shrug. His tone is casual enough that it makes me sigh and throw back my shot, which prompts him to do the same. But then he's right back to watching me like I'm the most confusing person he's ever seen.

I lean back on one hand and think about his question. Typically this conversation is risky with men, because their reason for asking is usually that they want to understand my reasoning—and then want to try to convince me otherwise. But something tells me that's not why Aiden's asking. He's genuinely curious.

"Alright, but let me ask you something first," I start. *Fuck it, if we're going to talk about this then let's dive headfirst into this clusterfuck of a topic.* "Your parents are divorced, right? You grew up with your dad?"

"Not sure you can be divorced if they were never really committed to you, but yeah, they're separated," he says tightly.

"What about the rest of your family? Or friends of the family? Anyone happily married?"

He gives me the respect of thinking about my question for a moment. But then his answer comes, and it's the same one I always expect and always get.

"Okay, yeah, most people in my family have been divorced. The ones that haven't are happy, though."

"Happy? Or content?" I press. "How do you know they didn't just settle? Or maybe they're just terrified of divorce?"

That makes him frown. "I can't speak to what kinds of relationships they have behind closed doors. They *seem* happy."

I nod in understanding. "Would you say you're just as happy as they are, even being single?"

"Yeah, but I'm young. I doubt I wouldn't be lonely if I was single at their age." His frown deepens. "That's your argument? That every relationship either ends in divorce or simply settling? That's a depressing way to live, Dani."

I sigh. "That's not the whole argument, I'm just trying to paint the picture." I scoot to the edge of the counter so I can uncross my legs and drape them on either side of Aiden's seat. I'm not touching him, but the close proximity forces us to focus solely on each other. His gaze never moves from my face.

I let out another sigh, this one heavier. Sadder. "Now

picture the other end of the spectrum. Picture a couple that's blissfully happy, two people that are disgustingly in love with each other and have been happily married for years. Do you know anyone like that?"

He contemplates the question for a moment before answering, "I think my high school English teacher had a relationship like that. She would always light up when her husband called, even after twenty years together." He frowns again. "I don't understand where you're going with this."

"Just one more question," I assure him. Taking a deep breath, I ask, "What did she do before she taught high school?"

"I think she was a professor at Columbia. If I remember correctly."

I give him a knowing and sad smile. As often as I have this conversation with people, and as many times as I go through these questions, I'm always hoping for someone to prove me wrong. And yet, they never do. "You just proved every part of my argument without even knowing what it is."

Aiden gives me a look of confusion. "That love ends with either divorce or bliss?"

I shake my head and answer softly, "That even when love does somehow result in something other than divorce, it still comes with massive sacrifices."

Aiden still doesn't look convinced. I sigh and look around the bar. "Look, most people that don't want a relationship are scared of them because they end in heartbreak or pain more times than not. I get that. And it's a logical argument, even though I can't imagine being scared of that risk. What gets me is that if, by some miracle, it doesn't end in divorce, or it doesn't become a relationship where both people are 'settling,' it still doesn't end well. For the 1% of relationships like your teacher's, love still pulled her away from something monumental, something she loved and probably worked half her life to achieve. How could love possibly be so great if, by diving into it, you have to choose between your passion for a person and your passion for a job? Or a place, or a friend, or anything else? How often does love come *without* a massive sacrifice?" I shake my head, my frown etched on my face. "See, that's why I'm good without it. Because in no situation does love ever work out the way we want it to. As a positive."

Aiden sighs and puts his hands on my thighs, rubbing absently. Already we're so in tune with each other that he touches me without realizing, simply to keep us connected. The thought should terrify me, but for some reason… it doesn't. Whether that's because I trust he's accepted my terms for us, or simply because I'm just that comfortable with him, I'm not sure. But right now, maybe because of this conversation, I have no desire to question or stop it.

I can see him working through what I just said. He's trying to piece everything together and make it fit with what he knows about me. "What are your parents like?" he asks after a moment. "Tell me about your family."

I sigh and lean back on my hands, letting Aiden's touch ground me as I open up.

"My parents have been married for almost thirty years," I start. "I've never seen a couple happier in love than them. My dad is a lawyer, my mom is a stay-at-home mom after a medical career. My dad was successful, too. Still is, but it's nothing compared to what he was when I was born." I look beyond Aiden at the empty bar. "I watched my parents do the same exact thing. My dad was one of the best criminal defense attorneys in the city before giving it up and opening a local practice for family law. My mom was a top neurologist before giving it up to become a stay-at-home mom. She *loved* her work. Both of my parents gave up impressive, massively successful careers that they were obsessed with because they wanted to spend more time together and with their kids.

"And it's not just my parents, either. My brother and his wife are the same way. They have a great marriage, but they also gave up a big piece of their lives for each other. He turned down a massive promotion at his work doing medical sales that would've allowed him to turn his beer-brewing hobby—the hobby that used to be the first thing to bring a smile to his face—into a legitimate business. All because he didn't want to travel as much as an executive role would've required him to. And his wife? She gave up her job as a full-time teacher and became a substitute so she could spend more time with their new baby. And I'm not saying that I'm anti-family, or anti-babies, or even that I put my job above everything else. I'm just saying, serious relationships take you away from the things you *love*." I shrug and finish softly, "You've seen how I live my life—every day is a new adventure. I do crazy things all the time, a lot of which guys I've been with haven't approved of or even tried to get me to give up. Even my job being potentially dangerous has been a dealbreaker. But I *like* having an insane, spontaneous life. I can't imagine giving that up for anything. I don't want to have to choose between my passion for life and anything else. Even if that makes me a selfish bitch."

I smile sadly at Aiden. "The way I see it, love either ends like your parents, or my parents. And I have zero interest in either situation."

Aiden mulls over my words, his hands continuing to rub my thighs as he thinks. Eventually he asks, "Are you sure an ex has nothing to do with it?"

I give him a hard look. "Not in the way you're thinking, no."

Aiden's look is equally knowing. Eventually, I sigh.

"Okay, so an ex was the one that kickstarted this whole theory. We were young and in high school and he was the first boy I ever loved." I frown at the thought. "Or, that I thought I loved. Looking back at the things I did—and almost did—for him, there's no way it was love."

"So you *are* a scorned lover," Aiden teases. But when I aim a glare at him, he winces and says, "Okay, not a joking matter. Got it."

"He might be the one that first opened my eyes to it, but the proof comes from everything else I just told you. I'm not bitter because of an ex, I'm just… not interested because of the reality of relationships."

He's quiet for another moment. Then, "That's still a lonely and depressing way to live, Dani."

I let out a heavy breath, even though his reaction isn't any different from what I usually hear. Is my theory so crazy? I've never found anyone who agrees with me. Am I so content by myself or is everyone else just eager not to be alone?

"Do I seem depressed to you, pretty boy?" I ask instead.

The corner of his lip finally twitches into an amused smile. "Not exactly."

"So then why does it matter?" I scoot closer to the edge of the bar top, draping my legs over his hips. "I would've thought a 22-year-old guy would be the last person I'd have to explain the benefits of being single to. I thought you'd be happy to find a girl that just wants to fuck." I cock my head and raise a hand to his hair, running my fingers through it as I study him thoughtfully. "Is this going to be a problem? I can't do this if it doesn't stay casual, Aiden."

He quirks an eyebrow and pauses his movements on my thighs. "Hardly," he says dryly. I almost laugh at his tone. "I'm just trying to understand you. Is that so bad?"

A smile twitches at the corner of my lips, even as I mentally heave a relieved breath at the way this conversation ended. "The only thing you need to know about me is how to make me come. That's the foundation of this arrangement."

He leans away from my touch so he can stretch an arm across the back of the barstool next to him, his lips lifting into a grin and making him look every bit the self-assured pretty boy I know him as. "Do I need to remind you that I already know how to do that?"

And with a single word, I issue a challenge and safely move us back into comfortable territory.

"Yes."

His eyes immediately darken with a familiar hunger, and he reaches for my hips, already starting to tug me off the bar top and into his lap. But I stop him with a hand on his shoulder. Confusion flickers across his face, but when I grab his whiskey and take a big sip, then curl my hand behind his neck and pull him forward, that desire comes right back to life. And when I brush my thumb across his lower lip in a silent order, he opens without any hesitation.

I part my lips and let the whiskey slowly trickle into his

mouth.

A second later his lips crash against mine.

"Why are you the hottest thing I've ever fucking seen," he growls, pulling me off the counter and settling me in his lap. I let him this time, because I'm equally desperate for his touch.

He leads the kiss, sinking one hand into my hair to angle my face the way he wants me. Even the way he nips my lower lip, the way his tongue licks into my mouth, everything tells me he's eager to take over. That he wants to *own* me like this.

I happily hand over that power. As much as I enjoy control, I'd much rather sit back and enjoy the pleasure he wants to dish out.

And *God*, does this boy know how to deliver.

That's very quickly proven when, after only a minute, Aiden's kiss has so thoroughly overwhelmed me that I start moaning into his mouth and shamelessly rocking against his cock.

"Dirty girl," he whispers against my lips. His hands guide my hips as I continue to writhe in his lap. *Fuck*, I can't seem to stop. "Are you going to come in my lap before I've even taken your clothes off? Just from my tongue in your mouth and my cock rubbing against that needy pussy?"

I'm too far gone to answer. All I manage to do is whimper and tighten my arms around his neck as I continue rolling my hips over his.

"Alright then," he drawls, pulling his hands away from my hips and letting them settle on the back of the barstools again. "Use me. Come all over yourself. Show me how desperate you are for my cock, Dani."

His words trigger an almost immediate explosion. All it

takes is for me to grind down again once, twice, three times before I'm gasping at the force of the pleasure rolling through me.

Aiden snaps forward to capture the sound in my mouth. Feeling the hungry slide of his tongue against mine only prolongs my orgasm, and my hips continue to rock against him as I ride it out. Eventually I slump forward with a sigh.

"Beautiful," he whispers, his gaze roaming over my face.

I force myself to straighten, then to hop up on the counter again. "Go lock the door," I tell him.

He doesn't even blink at the request, he just stands up and does as I ask.

I shoot a quick glance at the bar behind me to confirm I'm mostly done closing up. Bobby has left me to lock up enough times that I know no one will come in for the rest of the night—making what we're about to do a lot easier—but I also don't want to shirk my duties in favor of a gorgeous dick.

Even if it's a gorgeous, massive, talented—

My train of thought is cut off when Aiden grabs me around the waist and hauls me over his shoulder. I let out a shriek of surprise, even though I shouldn't be—I knew my whiskey-trick would bring out the aggressor tonight.

After a few steps I'm dropped to my feet and immediately spun around. I barely make note of the pool table in front of me before a hand between my shoulder blades is pushing me down onto the table.

"You're too hot for your own good," Aiden growls from behind me. He swats my ass through the denim shorts. "It pisses me off."

I smile into the green fabric and arch my hips a little more, press back a little harder. He lets out another angry growl when he grips my hips and grinds into my ass.

"These sexy little thigh-highs would drive any man to madness," he muses, reaching down to snap the top of the fishnets against my skin. I let out a moan at the bite of pain, and he does it again on the other side.

"Then you have this tight little crop top that puts your perfect tits on display and makes it almost impossible to focus on anything else." His hands smooth along my legs and over my stomach, coming to rest just below my breasts. At first I think he'll just cup and knead them like most young guys seem to do, but I should really know better by now. Aiden doesn't fuck like a young guy.

He fucks like he knows exactly what I crave, and will do anything to give it to me. So I shouldn't really be surprised when he tugs the fabric of my crop top up over my breasts. And then goes right for my nipples with a hard pinch.

I let out a deep moan at the sensation.

He soothes the pink tips with a gentle caress, and then he's moving on to the rest of my pleasure points. But not before pressing me farther down, until my now-sensitive nipples are rubbing against the coarse material of the pool table.

Fuck, he's good at this.

It registers that his hands are now back on my hips, his touch reverent as it travels along my sides and over my waist. "And these short shorts…" he murmurs in awe. Being bent over like this, I know he can see the bottom curve of my cheeks, can maybe even see a little bit of my pussy from his vantage point. "Every time I'm with you, all I can think about is taking your pants off and getting my cock as deep inside you as possible."

He unleashes a stinging slap on my exposed ass cheeks. "It's distracting."

"Oh my God," I moan into the table. *I'm going to come so quick like this.*

All of his movements seem to become angry now. He spanks me again, ignoring my moan as he reaches around to hurriedly unbutton my shorts and tug them down. They barely make it over my ass to the middle of my thighs when I feel him freeze.

I know exactly what he notices, and I smile into the table as I shamelessly wriggle my hips.

"*Fuck*, you're like every man's wet fantasy come to life," he says in an awed tone. His hand soothes over my bare ass. "This is why you came in my lap, isn't it? Because you've been behind the bar all night with no panties and your jean shorts rubbing against that needy little clit?"

I chance a look over my shoulder just so I can catch a glimpse of the sheer hunger and amazement in his eyes. He doesn't even notice me looking—he's too focused on the sight before him.

But then he's not, and he's dropping another angry slap onto my ass. I couldn't keep from moaning again even if I wanted to.

"Dirty girl," he mutters. He spanks me again. "*Filthy* girl."

"Aiden, please," I whimper. "Please fuck me. I can't take it."

His gaze finally snaps to my face. "You'll come when I let you come and not a second sooner." Only, I think he's just as desperate to fuck as I am because his hand travels down to the zipper on his jeans.

"Take the shorts off," he orders in a tight voice. I comply immediately, bringing my legs together so my shorts can slide down. Then I reach to pull them the rest of the way off.

I've just dropped them onto the pool table when I feel Aiden's hand on my hip and hear the crinkle of a condom wrapper. I swear that sound is enough to turn me on all over again because I automatically whimper and push my hips back to take him inside me.

He spanks me in scolding. "Wait," he growls. But that becomes nearly impossible when I feel the tip of him pressed against my entrance. You'd never know I just had an orgasm five minutes ago because it feels like I'm about to go crazy if he doesn't start fucking me right this second. At the very least, I'm about to start begging.

Sure enough, the words come unbidden up my throat. "Aiden, please fuck me. *Please.* I need you inside me, I need you to fill me up. I need—"

I choke on the words when he slams inside me with one hard thrust. And then he begins to fuck me.

"I know what you need," he says in a tight voice, his thrusts nonstop and punishing. "I know exactly what your body begs me for every time we're together. Do you really think I won't give it to you?" His hands slide up my sides until they're cupping my breasts, alternating between squeezing appreciatively and giving my nipples a hard pinch.

My moans become louder the more he plays with me. By the time he moves on from my chest, my nipples are so sensitive that the first scratch against the coarse fabric of the pool table makes me gasp and contract around Aiden's cock.

"*Fuck* yes, that's what I was waiting for," he hisses, his

thrusts increasing in intensity. "See, baby? I know what you need."

My orgasm is already rising like a tidal wave by the time his hands shift to another grip. They move up to my shoulders, where he can both hold me down on the table and use the grip as leverage to fuck me harder. Which he does. And which immediately catapults me into an explosion.

"There it is," he groans, enjoying the vice grip of my pussy clenching around him. "*God*, you feel amazing."

I barely hear him over the roaring in my ears, over the pleasure completely taking over my body. All I can do is let the sensations roll through me.

When he feels me go limp on the table, his hips slow slightly. He massages my shoulders for a brief moment before gently caressing along my back. He even drops a kiss to the skin below my ear that he knows makes me shiver. And when it does, and when my breath catches once again, I know he did it intentionally.

"We're not done yet, Dani."

I let out a whimper at the words, but even still my pulse starts to race as he gathers my hair in his hands. When he tugs my head back and lifts me onto my forearms, once again starting to fuck brutally into me, I know it's not going to take him long to make me come again.

"I want one more," he growls. "Give me one more, Dani." Then his other hand slides over my hip and down to my clit, and the pleasure ratchets again.

His fingers brush across me, faster and faster, both his touch and his thrusts beginning to feel desperate. Like he needs me to get there *now*. And that thought is confirmed when he pulls my hair hard enough to lift me higher up, onto my hands.

The new angle now has him hitting my G-spot with every snap of his hips.

"Oh God, oh God, that's gonna make me come so hard, oh my *God...*" I babble. Between his fingers stroking me outside and his dick hitting me inside, I am very rapidly being driven toward an orgasm even bigger than the last one.

"*Yes*, that's what I wanted to hear," he hisses excitedly. "Give it to me, Dani. Show me who fucks you."

If my last orgasm was an explosion, this one is an atom bomb. Pleasure explodes into every inch, every cell of my body. I'm lost to the world, lost to everything that isn't *this bliss* taking over me. And I can't do anything but let it happen.

When it finally abates an eternity later, I'm slumped on the pool table with Aiden breathing heavily against my back. He must have come because he's not moving anymore, he's just limp and trying to catch his breath.

"You're going to ruin me for other women," he groans in my ear.

And it must be the pleasure-coma that makes me say it, because after our sensitive conversation earlier, the last thing I should be doing is encouraging him. And yet, I can't stop myself from responding with a breathless, "Ditto."

I feel his smile against my shoulder but he must sense I don't want any affection from him because he pulls away without another word. He doesn't kiss me, doesn't touch me, he just straightens and begins to right his clothes.

I lift up and do the same.

"Do you need help closing up?" he asks as he zips up his jeans.

I wince when I pull my own jeans back on. Maybe no underwear was a bad idea. "No, that's okay. You can head out, I only have a few things to finish before I lock up."

He scoffs at that. "I'm not leaving you here alone. I'll just wait until you're done." He cuts down my outraged glare with a hard stare of his own. "Sorry, sweetheart, independent woman or not, I'm not leaving *anyone* to lock up a Philly bar on their own at midnight. Deal with it."

I glare at him for a moment longer before turning away with a sigh. "Fine. Wait if you want to. But if you're staying in the hopes of getting a goodnight kiss at the end of this, then you weren't listening earlier."

He shrugs but takes a seat again at the bar, settling in to watch me as I finish the final closing tasks.

It only takes me a few minutes. Especially when Aiden helps to throw the barstools up and lets me get started on the sweeping. Less than ten minutes after our conversation, I'm hustling him out the door and locking up behind me.

Thankfully, there's a taxi coming down the street right as we turn around. I lift my hand to wave it down, and when it flashes its lights in acknowledgement, I turn to Aiden to say goodbye.

"Alright, pretty boy, thanks for the ride. Call me if—"

I'm cut off when he wraps an arm around my waist and pulls me tight to his body. His lips are on mine before I can even react.

I stiffen in surprise but he patiently continues the kiss as he waits for me to return the affection. When I do, when I eventually melt against his embrace, he lets out a pleased sigh and sinks his other hand into my hair so he can pry my lips open with his tongue and deepen the kiss.

I'm still too surprised to do anything but let it happen.

When the taxi honks impatiently, I practically jump out of Aiden's embrace. I can only stare at him in wide-eyed surprise.

"I thought I said no goodbye kiss?"

"I don't accept this rule," he says with a grin. He leans forward to give me another quick peck on the mouth. "Relax, Dani, this hardly means I'm planning our wedding. I just wanted to kiss you."

I narrow my eyes at him to see if he's lying, but find only charming, playful Aiden. I sigh and give him a light shove. "Fine. But the second I see the invitations come out, I'm gone."

He rolls his eyes. "Yes, fine, message received. Now get out of here before your driver takes off without you." Then he lightly swats my ass and pushes me toward the car with a grin. "Bye, troublemaker. Maybe I'll text you sometime."

That parting comment is enough to convince me that he's not making this more than it is. After the third date is usually when men start to get ideas—especially if you stress to them that you *seriously* aren't looking for a relationship—but Aiden really does seem to just want sex.

So I give him a parting wink and reply, "Maybe I'll even respond."

CHAPTER SEVEN
Aiden

"So you're just... sleeping with her. Without sleeping. Or expectations."

I give Max a bemused look as I start to warm up for kickboxing class. "That's exactly what I'm saying."

He still doesn't look convinced. "That rarely works, dude. Look at what happened with me and Victoria: we said we were going to be friends after the breakup, occasionally fuck, and next thing I know I'm being tricked into coming over to her grandmother's 80th birthday so I can be introduced to everyone as her boyfriend again."

The memory of that particular night—of Max showing up at my apartment in a panic after he somehow managed to get away from that party—makes me laugh out loud.

"That was different and you know it," I chuckle. "Victoria was trying to get back together with you the second you dumped her. You were just too blind to see it. There was never any way of that 'friendship' staying casual."

Instead of acknowledging that I'm right, Max just aims a glare at me before turning to grab his boxing gloves.

Just then, I hear my phone buzz from the edge of the mat. I reach for it and let out a whistle when I see who's texting me. "Speak of the devil." I turn my phone toward my friends with a grin. "See? Booty call. You were saying?"

All I get is an eye roll in response.

Dani: Hey pretty boy. Busy later?

I quickly type out a response.

AIDEN

For you? Never. What's up?

DANI

I'm bartending a paintball party this afternoon for some corporate gig. Wanna come keep me company? You can bring people from the gym if you want.

I look up from my phone and catch Max's eye. "What're you doing later? Want to go paintballing with Dani?"

He shrugs. "Sure, I'm in."

AIDEN

Max and I will be there. Just shoot me the details, we'll come over after training.

Max is staring at me with narrowed eyes when I look up from my phone again. "A paintball date? That doesn't sound like sex."

I shrug in response. "Maybe she wants me to fuck her on the field. Or maybe she wants *you* to fuck her on the field." Max shakes his head at that. "Look, all we said was we're not *dating.*

That we wouldn't treat this as something heading toward a relationship. It's hardly a date when she invited *other people* to come with me. She's a fun girl, she probably just wants us to keep her company so she doesn't get bored. Nothing more to it than that."

He sighs in defeat. "If you say so. I've just never seen a fuck buddy agreement where one party *didn't* catch feelings."

I toss my phone to the edge of the mat before walking back over to the bag and getting into a ready stance. "Stop worrying so much, it'll be fine."

Just then, the door to the heavy bag room opens and the newest member of the gym walks in. He's the massive, tattooed stranger I ran into in the locker room last week. He looks just as angry as he did that day, and every day I've seen him since. Which has been a lot, because angry boy apparently lives for the gym. I haven't trained with him yet but from the glances I shoot him during class, the guy is *intense*.

"Hey, did you get that guy's name?" I ask Max in a murmur, jerking my chin in the guy's direction. "I don't think I've heard him say a single word in the two weeks he's been training here."

Max frowns thoughtfully. "I think Jax said his name was Kane. He's the one who signed him up."

"What's his deal? Do we know?"

Max shrugs and starts to stretch again. "Only information he volunteered was that he's new to the area and needs a place to train. I don't know what kind of gym he was at before, though, because dude goes *way* too hard. Like, I heard Tristan has to keep an eye on him when he teaches and partner him strategically because he's the kind of guy that hurts his partners."

"Yikes," I say with a wince. There are plenty of those fighters in the world—the guys that hear the word fighting and translate it to brawling—but it's been a while since we've had one at our gym. We pride ourselves on taking in and producing athletes—people who love this sport and want to get better while still keeping their training partners safe. MMA is no longer just human cockfighting in a cage. There's still a time and a place to go hard in training, but a regular drilling class isn't it.

"Hopefully he figures his shit out soon," I say. "Tristan and Jax only put up with that shit to a certain extent."

"Amen," Max agrees.

"Aiden. Max. Quit gossiping and get started on the bag," Tristan barks from the other side of the room.

"I will never understand where that man keeps his extra eyes and ears," I mutter as I begrudgingly pull my boxing gloves on.

Three hours and a torture session later—otherwise known as a Tristan workout when Remy has peed in his cereal that morning—Max and I have showered and are pulling up to the paintball place.

"So are we actually playing today or we're just here to do unpaid work?"

I slam the car door behind me and slide my shades on, feeling Max come up next to me. "No idea, I just know there's going to be an open bar and a Dani."

Max sighs. "So I'll take that to mean unpaid work. Got it." He looks up at the massive facility in front of us. "So she's a photographer… who also bartends kid's birthday parties? What am I missing here?"

I let out a snort at the thought of Dani working a kids' party, surrounded by screaming, sugared-up eight year olds. "Being a photojournalist is kind of hit or miss at her stage, since she's so new. So she supplements by being a travel bartender. She gets hired to bartend random shifts, sometimes as a fill-in at bars and sometimes at parties like this. There's some private corporate thing going on today."

"Ah, okay. So we're basically walking into a corporate team building event. Wonderful."

I don't miss the sarcasm in Max's voice, so I try to reassure him. "They're almost done. We're here to play with the employees, not the customers. Unless you *want* to shoot some corporate guys?"

He holds his hands up in surrender. "I don't care what I have to aim at. I just want to paint some people."

It only takes us a few minutes to find the area where the private party is being held, and a grin stretches across my face when I spot Dani behind the bar.

She's her usual gorgeous self, her black hair falling in waves over the black tank top she's wearing with the paintball shop's logo. She's focused on one of the patrons, sliding a beer over to him and laughing at something the guy says. But it isn't until she spots me that her face truly lights up.

"Hey, boys, glad you could make it. Want a drink before you help me close up here?"

Max nudges me as we take a seat at the bar, giving me a look that says *told you so.* I only heave a defeated sigh in response.

Dani watches the exchange and winks at us before whispering, "I just needed my manager to hear me say that. I need you guys to lift two boxes and then the employees get the turf all to themselves." She slides a Heineken over to me and then looks expectantly at Max for his drink order.

"Same is good for me," he responds. "Thanks. And thanks for inviting me."

"Anytime," she purrs, taking in his post-gym attire of grey joggers and a muscle tank with an obvious once-over.

Which makes me chuckle and makes Max's eyes widen.

After Dani walks away, I lean over to my best friend and murmur, "See? Casual. She wouldn't be hitting on you in front of me if we weren't just having sex."

"You two are fucking weird," he mutters, taking a big swig of his beer.

We hang out for the next twenty minutes, chatting between the two of us, but mostly watching Dani give out last call drinks and laughing with the other patrons. If Max notices I'm quiet, he doesn't comment on it, but the fact of the matter is his words from earlier today are still ringing in my head.

On average, he's not wrong. One person typically does get more emotionally involved than the other during a friends-with-benefits relationship. Personally, I've noticed it almost always starts to happen after the third or fourth date. By that point, two people have spent enough time together that they have a decent understanding of the person, and find themselves drifting either toward or away from them. I know I only ever last that amount of time with girls I've gotten involved with.

I like Dani. A lot. She's probably the most fun girl I've ever met, and the sex with her is out of this world. And since we just passed the three 'date' mark, we're at that pivotal point.

Do I want a relationship with her? Or do I want to start distancing myself before this can get too serious?

I frown at the second option. I definitely don't want to stop seeing her. Even the thought of that makes me annoyed, imagining not having her easy laugh ringing in the air or her moans pressed against my ear. Fuck that option.

And when Dani shoots me a grin and playful wink, that thought eddies completely from my mind.

Fuck pulling away, I like us right where we are.

But I can also be honest with myself about the fact that I don't feel the need to push for something bigger with her. It's not just that I have a lot going on in my life, it's that I *like* where we are. I like the casual thing. It's more fun, and way easier to navigate than a label.

Plus, I know where Dani stands. So it's kind of a moot point. But I feel better thinking through Max's question and confirming where *I* stand on things—not just where Dani clearly wants to put me.

"Alright boys, I'm ready for you now," she says coming over to stand in front of us. She gestures at the two remaining boxes of liquor that need to be carried inside, silently asking for our help. It takes no time at all to get everything moved inside.

And then she's standing in front of us, hands on her hips and a grin on her face. "There are about a dozen kids working the field right now that like to end their shift with a game, so if you guys are up for it, the field is ours."

I clap my hands together in glee. "Definitely. I can't wait to kick your ass."

A look of mischief crosses her face as she jerks her chin toward the equipment area. "Go suit up. I'll see you on the field, and we'll see whose ass gets kicked today."

"How many snot-nosed teenagers do we have left?" I hear Max call.

I peek around the stack of tires I'm hiding behind, my gaze sweeping across the field and over to the crow's nest on the opposite side. We've already taken out two of the six opponents on our way up the turf, and we're guessing there's at least two guarding the flag on the high ground.

I spot movement in front of Max's hiding spot.

"You've got someone at 11:00," I say, just loud enough for him to hear.

He gives me a sharp nod before quietly moving around the barrel he was crouching behind. I aim my gun where I saw the movement, ready to offer cover fire as Max bolts the twenty feet to the next barricade. No one fires, though, and it takes him less than ten seconds to spot the kid hiding behind the tree and take him out with a quick burst of shots. I capitalize on Max's gunfire by sprinting to the same blockade he's hiding behind, the sweat starting to trickle down my back in the thick suit.

"There's probably one more covering the flag up there, right?" he asks, his eyes darting around for the lone gunman.

"That's what I would do. There should be only two others on the field, and if I remember my competitive dodgeball days correctly, as a teenager I only ever wanted to be the aggressor. So it's unlikely they have more people guarding their flag than hunting ours."

Max nods in agreement, his body already readying to sprint toward the crow's nest.

"Let's split up and each take a side," I tell him. "I'll take left, you take right. If one of us spots the gunman, make a bird sound to alert the other."

Max's head drops back with a sigh. "Why the fuck would I make a bird sound? Do you even *know* how to make a bird sound?"

I can only stare at him in shock. "Of course. Don't you?"

He shakes his head in a way I've come to interpret as *how did we ever become best friends?*

"Just… call out if you see the guy," he says with a heavy sigh. "Good?"

"Sure, if you want to be boring," I grumble.

He doesn't even respond. He just takes off.

I let out a sigh of my own and dash in the other direction.

I'm nearing the crow's nest from the right side when I see a flash of something, immediately before hearing the *pop pop* of a gun going off.

"Kakaw, *kakaw!*" I scream in a panicked voice, throwing myself behind another stack of tires.

"Dude, I *hear* the shots! At this point the call is kind of redundant."

Peeking around the tires, I see Max aiming at a point in

the crow's nest, still as a statue and waiting for movement. A moment later, it comes.

Pop pop pop.

"Damnit!" the kid yells from his high-up spot, begrudgingly lowering his paintball gun from where he had poked his head out to level at Max. Three spots of yellow paint are splattered across his chest and shoulder.

Max lets out a whoop of joy, and then he's straightening from his crouch and walking around the tires, a look of victory on his face as he nears the ladder going up to the crow's nest.

Pop pop.

My brow furrows in confusion. *Where did that shot come from? Max never raised his gun.*

Then he turns around, his jaw slack and his chest painted in pink.

Who...?

My question is answered when I hear a sultry laugh from somewhere ahead of me. I can't see her, but I'd recognize that sexy sound anywhere.

"Didn't your mama ever teach you not to celebrate early?" Dani asks.

I can't help it. I start laughing.

"Dude, she totally got you," I cackle, doubled over with tears leaking out of my eyes. "And you're a competitor! What the fuck, man?"

Max goes from shell-shocked to annoyed in an instant. "I wouldn't laugh too hard if I were you. She's coming for you next."

That sobers me in an instant. I'm still hidden where I am,

but I don't know where Dani's shot came from and no idea where she is. I peek over the barrier to try to locate her.

And promptly get shot in the face.

"Ohhh fuck," the little teenage shit gasps from where he's still waiting in the crow's nest, watching this whole thing unfold.

"Are you fucking kidding me..." I grouse, pulling off my helmet when I'm blinded by the pink paint splatter on the face shield.

This time, Dani's laughter is joined by Max's. I still can't see her, but I settle for glaring at my best friend, ignoring the fact that I was just laughing at him for the same thing.

"Should I feel bad that I found that to be the most entertaining part of the day?" Dani asks with a chuckle, appearing from behind a barrier not far behind the crow's nest. The paintball gun is braced on her shoulder, her posture and lazy gait making her a vision of confidence. And that's not even considering the arrogant smirk on her face.

"What are you even doing back here?" I ask instead. "I would've thought you'd play offense."

She shrugs as she stops beside me. "I made defense my offense. I knew if I could take you two out, I could just grab the flag afterward myself."

And as a grin stretches across her face, she readjusts the gun in her hands and starts to back away to likely do exactly that. "Looks like I was right. Who's your daddy now, pretty boy?"

Then she turns and lopes toward the end of the field.

For a moment, Max and I can only stand there in shock.

Then…

"Holy shit, I think I'm in love," I whisper in an awestruck voice.

"Me too," I hear from the crow's nest.

Dani's already waiting for us in the parking lot when Max and I finish returning all the gear. She's leaning against her car, shades on as she scrolls through her phone, looking every bit the self-assured victor.

"Feel like celebrating your victory?" I ask when we reach her. "I promise we won't be sore losers."

She tucks her phone into her back pocket, the corner of her lip twitching upward. "What'd you have in mind? I would've expected you guys to be too tired to celebrate."

"You underestimate the energy levels of two twenty-two year old fighters," I scoff. "And their hunger. Want to come back to my place for some dinner? I'm in Fairmount, so I'm the closest one to here. I'll pick up some beer on the way and throw some burgers on when we get there."

I can tell she wants to say yes, but what comes out instead is, "I have to shower, I'm all gross after the game—"

"Shower at my place," I say hurriedly. I have no idea why I'm suddenly desperate to keep her with us, I just know I'm not ready for this day to end.

When she only narrows her eyes and stares at me, I shove my hands in my pockets and let the charmer smile slide onto my face. The one that has a 100% track record of getting me what I want.

"Come on, Dani. Hang out with us a little."

And *bingo*, I've got her. She rolls her eyes and reaches for her car handle, calling over her shoulder, "Fine. Text me your address, I'll meet you over there. And make sure you get me a Fat Tire if you're stopping for beer."

"Yes, ma'am," I murmur, sliding my own shades onto my nose and turning to Max with a grin. "You heard the lady. Let's go."

Twenty minutes later, we've all reached my apartment, and I send Max into the shower as I start to ready the ingredients for dinner. Dani takes a seat at the counter, reaching immediately for one of the beers.

"Do you cook a lot?" she asks curiously once she's popped open the top with her teeth.

"I guess so," I answer with a shrug. "You kind of get in the habit of it when you're fighting. Your diet becomes pretty limited, so it's just easier to prepare food for yourself. I'm not saying I'm Gordon Ramsey or anything, but I do make a mean chicken and broccoli."

She huffs a laugh at that, taking a sip of her beer, before reaching for the salad ingredients. She gestures for me to hand her a big bowl. Silently, we start to prepare dinner together.

After a while, I can't keep the question in any longer. "So this isn't too date-y for you?"

She doesn't even look at me as she shrugs. "Nah. As long as it's not in a restaurant, I'm good with food dates." Appearing to think of something, her hands pause their work as she shoots a quick glance at the bathroom door. "Plus, Max is here. Three people hardly makes a date."

As if saying his name summons him, Max chooses that moment to step out of the bathroom. He's soaking wet and completely naked, save for the towel wrapped around his waist.

It takes everything in me not to let the grin appear on my face when I see Dani's eyes go wide.

Max doesn't seem to notice. In fact, he's only in our sight for a second before he's striding down the hall to my bedroom to get changed.

I stay silent as Dani physically shakes herself from her reverie. It isn't until she reaches for her cold beer and takes a huge swallow that I let a chuckle slip.

"Dirty girl," I purr in a tease.

Her attention snaps to me, and for a moment I think she'll blush or try to deny it. But I should really know better by now.

She shrugs, returning to the salads. "He's hot. I'd have to be blind or dead to not be interested."

In an instant, an idea flashes through my mind. Excitement fills my veins, but I glance toward the bedroom, taking a second to consider how Max might feel about it. Except I'm perfectly aware of my best friend's... tastes, having seen them myself a few times before.

It's an easy decision, especially weighed against Dani's lust-filled look from a moment ago.

Abandoning my own dinner preparation, I wipe my hands off before walking around the counter and stepping up behind Dani. I cage her in with my hands on the counter, not quite touching her, but crowding her with my presence as much as possible.

"*Are* you interested?" I murmur in her ear, my lips just barely brushing over her skin.

I feel the shiver run through her at my question. "Just Max?" she asks, her tone breathless.

I shrug, even though I know she can't see it. Truth be told, I would prefer she not fuck my best friend one-on-one, but I don't let her know that. Because that's not the game we're playing. "If you want. But that's not what I was implying and you know it."

From my vantage point behind and above her, I can see her chest start to rise and fall with her breaths. Can hear the way she's hurrying to suck down more air.

"Think about it, Dani," I continue, running my lips over her temple. "We could both take you to bed. Make you come more times than you can count. Twice as many hands, tongues, cocks... all for you. Just imagine two men completely focused on your pleasure."

She's too turned on to stop a whimper from slipping out. At the sound of it, my dick hardens in my shorts and a growl rumbles through my chest.

I don't wait for an actual answer; I can already read her body well enough to know I've pegged her needs perfectly. Instead, I drop my lips to her inked shoulder for a teasing kiss.

"Go take a shower. And don't you dare touch that pretty pussy before I tell you to."

CHAPTER EIGHT
Dani

DINNER FEELS LIKE it takes forever. When the boys finally finish stuffing hamburgers in their mouths, I've already picked the label off my beer bottle while waiting for them to finish. Although based on Aiden's occasional sly glances, there's a good chance he's teasing me on purpose.

"Should we watch a movie?" he asks, looking at Max as he throws the last of their paper plates away. He sounds so unassuming that his next question catches me completely by surprise—despite the fact that I knew it was coming. "Or do you want to help me fuck Dani?"

Max jerks his head up to stare at his best friend. "What?"

A devious grin slides across Aiden's face. "You heard me. Dani got all kinds of turned on watching us sweat and shoot things, and now she'd like us to fuck her."

Max turns to look at me with a raised eyebrow. "Is that so?" he asks in a deep rumble that immediately sends a bolt of pleasure through my body. I can only bite my lip to stifle the moan that wants to slip out, and nod.

I swear I watch him transform from nice guy to dominant

right before my eyes. He gives me a blatant once-over, taking his time looking over every inch of my body. Then he steps up to me and grips my chin so he can tilt it up and get my full expression. "I need your words, Dani. I won't touch you like that unless you ask me to."

My answer slips out immediately. "Yes," I say breathlessly. "Yes, I want both of you. Please."

Max grins and lets go of my chin. "She begs so prettily," he says, turning to look at his best friend.

Aiden chuckles. "And we haven't even started yet."

"I have one request," I say suddenly, pulling the boys' attention back to me. They both look at me with a brow quirked in question. "When we do this, I want both of you, at the same time. I want you to give me everything."

At that, Aiden's gaze erupts with desire. He steps around the kitchen island and comes up behind me, his hands settling on my waist and his lips starting to kiss along my neck. He already seems lost in a cloud of lust because his voice is breathy when he says, "I think we can handle that."

And then there are no more questions.

I turn toward Aiden so I can run my hands over his chest as he continues to kiss my neck. He grips my hips, pulling me flush against him, and I can feel how turned on he is already. I'm completely focused on and distracted by his body against mine, when suddenly I feel the heat of a body come up behind me, a hardness pressing against my ass.

And when hands slide along my ribs to cup my tits before giving my nipples a vicious pinch, I drop my head back against Max's shoulder with a moan.

"Fuck," Aiden groans when he pulls back to look at the sight before him. He stares at his best friend playing with my nipples for a moment before saying, "Let's move this into the bedroom before I lose my goddamn mind and fuck you right here on the counter."

"I wouldn't mind that," I say breathily.

"I would," he growls. "I can't fuck you in the right positions out here." And before I can respond with anything else, he grabs my hand and drags me down the short hallway to his bedroom, Max silently following.

When the door shuts behind us, Aiden spins me around so I'm facing away from him again. For a moment, I have no idea what he wants, because he simply holds me by the hips and aims us both to look at Max. It gives me a chance to really study his expression for a moment. He doesn't seem impatient, or nervous, or anything besides *hungry*. For *me*.

"Kiss him," Aiden whispers in my ear.

And I do just that. He's already close, but I shift slightly closer until I can feel my breasts brushing against Max's chest with every excited inhale. I let my gaze travel over his face for a moment, taking in not only his expression, but also his windswept black hair, his flawless skin, and his lips, only inches from mine and begging to be licked.

He lets me look, watching me in the same way I'm watching him. And then he moves.

His lips take mine in a slow, seductive kiss. I usually expect guys his age to kiss hungrily, passionately, like they just want to up the intensity so they can get to the fucking parts. But that's not what Max does. He kisses me like he's got all the time in the world, like he'd be just as content to kiss me as he would to fuck me.

Like he knows exactly how good he is at the seduction game, and he wants *me* to be the one to beg for the next part.

It feels different than it does with Aiden. I still prefer Aiden's more intense, barely-leashed way of slow kissing, but I can't say Max's technique isn't making my knees go weak. Especially when his tongue slides lazily across my lower lip at the same time that Aiden's hands start to drift under my tank top to cup my breasts.

"You look so good between us like this," he whispers in my ear. "I can't wait to see how you look when you're taking both of us at the same time."

I can't help it—I let out a needy whimper. I try to kiss Max harder, try to beg him to give me more, but the bastard pulls away instead.

"What do think we should do with her first?" he ponders, brushing his thumb across my lower lip with a heated gaze. "Her lips do seem like they would look amazing wrapped around a cock."

My breath catches at the knowledge that Max is just as much of a dirty-talking alpha in the bedroom as Aiden.

Dear God, these two might actually kill me tonight.

"Only one way to find out," Aiden drawls, thumbing my nipples lazily.

I want to scream *yes!* and drop to my knees between them, but before I can do that, Aiden removes his hands from my shirt and slides them down my stomach until he can perch one on my hip and let the other drift farther until it's cupping my pussy through my jeans. My breath catches at the absolute *ownership* his touch brands me with.

"Or maybe we should focus on her pleasure first," he muses, pressing the seam of my pants against my clit. "Maybe we get her drunk on orgasms before we fuck her anywhere."

Max cocks his head thoughtfully. It's taking everything in me to not beg for *something, anything, please*, and when his eyes light with mischief, I know he can see it all over my face. I'm not even surprised when he continues with their teasing game and reaches for my nipples while Aiden starts to rub the seam across my clit—as if he knows, without being told, that my breasts are a huge part of my pleasure-center.

He's proven right when he brushes his thumbs over the hard tips through my tank top and my head drops back against Aiden's shoulder with a moan. A shameless grin spreads across Max's face.

"Yeah, I think that's definitely how we need to start this," Aiden confirms. His hands shift to grip both sides of my tank top as he says, "Hands up, dirty girl, let's show Max how pretty you are naked."

He barely gets my shirt off before Max is sucking a nipple into his mouth with a groan and a muttered *fuck*.

Aiden lets out a chuckle against my shoulder. "Yeah, I felt the same way the first time I saw them."

I can only weave my fingers through Max's hair and hold his head exactly where it is, a silent plea to not stop. But when my hips start to rock—forward, back, searching for *something*—a snap enters Aiden's voice.

"Let's get her on the bed."

Max pulls away with a regretful look on his face, but he moves aside to let Aiden push me toward the bed in the middle of the room.

I'm guided onto my back, clothed in only my jeans, as the two boys stretch out on either side of me. And Aiden wastes no time kissing me.

"You're so fucking perfect," he growls, kissing me in that barely-leashed way of his. When I moan in response, his tongue slides inside to brush against mine. And just as I reach for him, my hips beginning to rock again, he grips my jaw in his hand and turns me to face Max, breaking our kiss.

Max takes his turn without needing to be told. His kiss is more aggressive than last time, likely because teasing me is getting *them* just as wound up. He angles his head so he can kiss me deeper, demanding my full attention while he takes what he wants.

I barely notice Aiden's touch drifting down my stomach, down to undo the buttons on my jeans. But when his hands slide straight into my panties at the same time that he latches onto my left nipple, it becomes *all* I notice.

I cry out into Max's mouth. The sensations are overwhelming, and we've barely even done anything yet. But with Max fucking my mouth with his kiss, Aiden nipping at the hard points of my nipples, and now the added feeling of excited fingers brushing across my clit, I'm powerless to stop the budding orgasm.

Suddenly, Max pulls away. I open my eyes in a daze, confused about the abrupt lack of his kiss. Aiden must sense that I need it to stay grounded, because barely a breath later, his lips are on mine. His kiss soothes me, even as his fingers continue to stir me up.

I feel the weight on the bed shift as Max maneuvers enough to tug my jeans down my legs. He must be too impatient to get them all the way off, though, because I feel them catch around my knees. Then he's settling his weight beside me again, this time leaning down to capture my right nipple in his mouth and sucking hard.

"Oh *God*," I whimper into Aiden's mouth. Between the two of them, there's no doubt that they're going to break down my usual cocky, self-assured image, and revert me to a whimpering, babbling puddle of need. Already I want to spend the rest of the night begging.

"There's my girl," Aiden praises against my lips. His fingers slip from my clit down to my slick entrance, and he only circles once, twice, before he's sliding two fingers deep inside me.

"Aiden," I gasp. "God, *fuck*, I can't—"

I choke on the words when I feel another set of fingers on me.

"Easy, baby," Aiden murmurs in a soothing voice. He pumps into me at a leisurely pace, working in perfect sync with the fingers now swiping across my clit. With Max's mouth alternating between hard sucks and vicious nips, I'm seconds away from detonating.

And when Aiden drops *his* mouth once again to my left nipple, I instantly go off like a bomb.

Crying out as the orgasm rolls through me, my eyes drift shut and my back arches off the bed, desperately trying to get closer to their mouths. I think I even grip their heads to hold them to me, but I'm so far in another dimension that I can't be sure. I hear twin growls of approval.

I come to when I feel Aiden slide his fingers out of me. When I blink my eyes open, his drenched fingers are already nearing my mouth, a hungry glint in his eyes as he places them against my bottom lip.

I open and suck them into my mouth without a second thought.

"Fuck," I hear from my right. My eyelids droop as I look sideways at Max, watching the desire in his eyes grow as he stares at me sucking my own taste off of his best friend's fingers. His throat dips on a swallow.

Then he's sliding to the end of the bed so he can kneel at my feet and rip my jeans off.

"I need to taste her," he growls in desperation.

He barely gets my panties off before his mouth is devouring me.

I *moan* around Aiden's fingers. My eyes drift closed again, helpless to stay open as my pleasure immediately roars to life again. I savor the feeling of Max's tongue swirling around my clit, of his hands bruising me with their grip on my thighs as he holds them apart.

My eyes snap open when Aiden's spit-soaked fingers pull from my mouth and start to lazily circle my nipple again. I turn to see him watching Max, clearly turned on by the sight of him going down on me.

"How does his mouth feel?" he eventually asks, turning his focus back to me. "Do you like my best friend's tongue in your pussy?"

"*God* yes," I moan, arching harder into Max. Despite the fact that I came two minutes ago, I can already tell it's not going to take much to make it happen again.

Aiden growls his approval at my answer, and leans down to kiss me. But one hard kiss turns into a hungry, passionate one, and then suddenly he's angling my head to stroke his tongue deep into my mouth, directly mimicking what Max is currently doing between my legs.

That thought causes a needy moan to break free, and then I can't stop myself from scrabbling at Aiden's chest, across his abs, and down to his shorts where I start to frantically tug at the waistband.

He grins against my lips. "Want my cock, dirty girl? Here, let's get those pretty lips wrapped around it." He pulls away and kneels beside my head, then pushes his shorts over his hips. I lick my lips at the sight of him stroking himself inches from my face.

"Please," slips out when he continues to tease me. When he moves just close enough that my tongue can swipe at the slit, but not close enough that I can get him in my mouth.

He growls a curse at the word and immediately nudges his cock up to my lips.

"Suck me, Dani."

I eagerly pull him into my mouth. I'm desperate to give back some of the pleasure that they've given me, so I waste no time sucking him as deep and as hard as I can. I try to shift my upper body closer, gripping him with one hand and groaning when he reaches my throat.

"Jesus fuck," Aiden hisses. "Slow down before you make

me bust. I still need to get inside that ass."

I let out a moan at that, my eyes fluttering open and looking up at his face. He looks like he's in pain, yet his hips continue to thrust into my mouth. I slow down slightly, not wanting to end this too soon, even though it pains *me* to do it. With a tongue inside me and a cock in my mouth, I've never been *more* desperate to lose my inhibitions.

And yet when Max's tongue returns to my clit and two fingers slide inside me, all my patience goes out the window.

A whimper slips out, and then I'm once again sucking Aiden as hard as I can. My tongue slides along his shaft, my suction increasing with my desperation, and then circles around the head as he finally pulls away.

"If you're going to be bad, you don't get my cock," he growls. He glances down at his best friend, and for the first time he notices just how eagerly Max is working me. "Are you going to come again? Is his mouth that good?"

"Yes," I groan, digging my nails into Aiden's thigh in an effort to stay grounded as this orgasm builds inside of me. "Why are you both so good at this? What do they teach you at that gym?"

Both boys let out pleased chuckles, though Max's is muffled where he refuses to take his mouth away for even a second. His fingers continue to drive into me, and I know he's about to send me flying.

"Oh God, oh *fuck*, I'm going to—"

"Good girl, come all over his face," Aiden says in a deep, seductive purr.

And when Max curls his fingers inside me and starts

hitting that spot with perfect precision, I do.

My eyes lock onto Aiden's as the pleasure hits. My mouth opens on a silent gasp, and my nails dig even harder into his thigh. And even though it's his friend making me come, someone I'm friends with but won't ever be interested in, I feel intimately connected with Aiden in this moment. It's like his eyes are sending the message *he might be the one giving you physical pleasure, but he's doing it under my command. Because you're* mine.

The thought drives my orgasm to insane heights. It feels never-ending, each wave bringing on another, stronger wave, until finally my body goes limp on the bed. I'm still trying to catch my breath when Aiden leans down and braces a hand next to my head.

"Beautiful," he whispers, his gaze roving over my face with a tender look of awe. My pulse trips over itself at the sight, everything around us fading away for a split second as I get lost in the affection in his expression. I'm too far gone to panic over the sight of it, so when he leans down to press a gentle kiss to my mouth, I'm helpless to do anything but return it with a content sigh.

But when he pulls away at the same time that Max removes his fingers, the random moment of intimacy ends.

"Hands and knees," Aiden growls against my lips, apparently snapping out of our reverie at the same time. Gone is the look of awe—now he just looks hungry. "Go show Max how much you appreciate how hard he just made you come."

I turn over in a daze and crawl to the end of the bed. Max is standing there, still fully dressed, looking supremely arrogant as he waits to be undressed and taken care of. I'm too sated to give him any attitude, so I simply sit back on my heels and reach for his athletic shorts. In seconds, I have them pushed over his hips, with his boxer briefs quickly following.

"Fuck," he groans out when I waste no time wrapping my lips around his hard cock. Clearly my taste was enough to get him ready to fuck, a thought which immediately flames my desire again. I moan, feeling pleased when the vibration makes Max curse again.

"God*damn* her mouth is sweet," he grits out. "No wonder you almost came when she was sucking you."

I'm surprised to hear Aiden's chuckle sound from behind me. I must've been so wrapped up with Max that I didn't notice Aiden's weight shifting to settle behind me on the bed. And sure enough, his hands come around my ribs to cup my breasts.

"Just wait until I start to drive her crazy. *Then* you'll see how sweet her mouth can be."

His fingers pinch my nipples, twisting and tugging, but only for a moment before they drift back down my sides. When he reaches my hips, he tugs gently.

"Up on your knees," he commands in that deep voice that only comes out when I give him the reins. "Let me see that pretty pussy."

I do as he asks, settling on my hands and knees and giving him a perfect view of all of me when I arch my back—or as much as I can while I have his best friend's cock in my mouth.

"Fuck, you're perfect," Aiden grits out. "Look how incredible you look between us like this. Do you like it? Do you want me to fuck your pussy while he fucks your throat?"

My moan is dripping with lust as I nod eagerly.

There's a rip of a condom, and then Aiden is pushing inside me. He moves slowly, likely not wanting to overwhelm me just yet, but there's really no way for someone his size to *not* overwhelm me. I can't stop my whimper from slipping out, or my hips from wriggling as I adjust to him.

He brushes a hand down my spine, soothing me before he starts to move. "I'm going to fuck you now, and I want you to let Max in deeper. Can you do that for me?"

I'm already nodding as I look up at Max and relax my muscles, a silent invitation for him to do just that. He lets out a filthy curse as he drives more of his cock into my throat.

And then Aiden starts to move.

It's completely overwhelming, being between them like this. My brain doesn't know what to focus on: the feeling of having my mouth filled, or the pleasure that's literally being fucked into me from behind. Do I focus on Max's hand weaving into my hair to hold me in place, or Aiden's hand as it brushes over my ass cheeks and eventually slips between them?

Fuck. *Fuck.*

"Do you want to come like this?" Aiden asks. "Or will you wait until I start to fuck your ass?"

That mental image has my eyes closing on a moan—has *another* orgasm bearing down on me. And when I feel the pad of his thumb press against my puckered entrance, I know I'm not going to make it much longer.

He lets out a cocky chuckle. "That's what I thought. Let's see if I can even get my fingers in here before we make you explode." He presses one wet finger inside me, never stopping his easy thrusts.

I squeeze my eyes shut, lost in the sensations assaulting me from everywhere. I've lost the ability to suck Max, but he doesn't really seem to mind. With his grip locked in my hair, he's taken over driving into my mouth at his own pace. Giving him control allows me to focus more of my attention on what Aiden is doing behind me.

His finger slides out, to be replaced by two this time. He doesn't go easy on me, knowing I'm already too turned on, too loose from my orgasms, to need to be coddled. Plus, I'm desperate for more of him inside of me. I start to push back against his thrusts, an impatient whine leaving my lips.

Aiden lets out a laugh. "So eager," he taunts. His thrusts become punishing, his hips slapping against my skin as he stops teasing. Now, he's on a mission.

I'm already on the precipice, but when he drives both fingers deep inside me, I detonate immediately.

"There she is," Aiden croons, fucking me through my release. "That's the second time I've made you come from playing with your ass. Will you come even harder when it's my cock in here?"

Max pulls out of my mouth to give me a moment to catch my breath, and I give him a grateful smile as I try to do just that. My head drops forward, my chest heaving as I pant. I feel Aiden start to slow, eventually pulling out of me, as well.

He gently tugs my hips back so I'm sitting on my heels again, so he can pull my back to his chest and tilt my head to rest on his shoulder. "Okay?" he murmurs quietly, running soothing hands over my sides. I can only nod in answer. It feels like that's all I've been able to do since we started this night.

Dropping a quick kiss onto my shoulder, he places a hand between my shoulder blades and presses me forward again, this time keeping my hips low.

"Then I want you to suck him a little more. Just while I get inside this tight ass." His filthy words are accentuated by his fingers sliding between my cheeks again.

"Yes, sir," slips out as I settle on my hands again, my tone that of a sated and pleasure-drunk woman. I don't even realize my word choice until Aiden lets out a pleased growl.

Hearing a tube pop open somewhere behind me, I focus my attention on Max again. He's lazily stroking his cock, waiting for me to be ready to take him again.

"What do you like?" I ask him, suddenly feeling guilty that all of my attention has been on Aiden. I'm normally a lot more invested in blow jobs, and prefer to figure out what my partner likes, but I've been a little distracted tonight.

Max gives me a half-grin, like he knows what I'm thinking. "I like what you're doing," he says honestly. His gaze jumps behind me for a moment, and when it settles back on me, he admits, "But I'd love it if you'd play with my balls for a bit."

I shift forward, a knowing grin on my face as I settle onto all fours again. Max is still standing at the foot of the bed, stroking himself as he waits, but when I come close, he pulls his length against his abs and exposes his smooth balls to me. Without another word, I lean forward and suck one into my mouth.

"*God*, yes," he groans, his eyes closing and his head dropping back. "Just like that." I swirl my tongue around the sack before shifting my focus to the other one, thoroughly enjoying the way he's loving this. Enjoying the way that I can finally give him the attention he deserves.

But that feeling only lasts for a moment, because just as I'm getting swept up in the sensation of *Max,* I feel the cold drizzle of lube between my ass cheeks.

"Did you forget about me?" Aiden murmurs, his chest flattening against my back and his lips pressing against my ear, his fingers starting to work the lube into my ass. There's no discomfort, since he already had his fingers inside me, and my eyes droop with pleasure.

"Not possible," I answer with a content sigh, pulling away from Max. I lift one hand to him, though, rolling and tugging his balls as I take his length back in my mouth again. When I let a finger slip down to rub that smooth space behind his sac, I delight in the sound of his breath hitching.

"Good answer," Aiden whispers, removing his fingers. I feel the cold, lubed tip of him nudge my entrance. "Now keep your throat open and your eyes on him while I work my cock in here."

And then he's pushing inside.

He breaks through the first ring of muscle, both of us groaning at the sensation. I'm so relaxed that I don't feel the usual urge to push him out, that initial sensation that has me questioning if this is really what I want. As he presses forward another inch, all I can think of is *more.*

Max returns to fucking my mouth, his hand once again wound in my hair and his gaze holding mine as he immediately goes back to his hard, deep thrusts from before. He's not giving me the opportunity to work up to it this time.

"Take it," he growls, seemingly without noticing his order. He's too lost in what he's doing, too focused on the sight of his length sliding all the way down my throat.

I'm momentarily mesmerized by the sight of him taking his pleasure. But then Aiden pulls back an inch, before pushing back in. Even that very small movement is enough to make pleasure strike like lightning through my body, and I let out a moan at the sensation.

"Fuck yes," Aiden hisses, driving another inch deeper. His hands, which were gripping my hips, now drift down to my pussy and begin sliding a finger across my clit. The dual sensation—or triple, with Max also fucking me—is enough to make my body start to tremble. Every muscle in my body—in my throat, in my shoulders, in my ass—goes immediately limp with bliss. Which then allows Aiden to move even deeper.

"Holy *fuck*, Dani," he groans, slowly starting to fuck me. "You take cock like a dream."

And then his pelvis hits my skin, and Max's abs hit my nose. And I'm *blissfully* full.

I let out such a deep moan at the feeling that the vibration must work straight through Max, because he mirrors it with a groan of his own, his head dropping back.

"Fuck, she really does," he breathes, fisting a hand in my hair and holding himself deep before he starts to urgently fuck me again.

Aiden lets out a lazy chuckle behind me, the slight grind of his hips equally lazy. He only pulls out an inch before pushing back in, giving me a chance to get used to the size of him.

I let out a quiet hum of appreciation.

"Ready for more?" he asks, still circling my clit and overwhelming me with distracting sensations.

And when he takes that hand away and the pleasure doesn't drop an inch—in fact it multiplies, the need to be *fucked* becoming suddenly urgent—I give him a needy moan.

He lets out another knowing chuckle. "You're so fucking filthy," he says in an appreciative tone.

And then he reaches forward to push my head all the way down on Max's cock before starting to fuck my ass with hard, punishing thrusts.

I just about explode with ecstasy and surprise.

If his fingers were still on my clit I definitely would have, but as it stands, the dual sensations cause my eyes to widen and my body to immediately shudder with pleasure. For a few moments, it's all I can do to swallow around the dick in my throat, my vision blurring with tears, and take the ass-fucking I'm being given.

It's the hottest thing I've ever experienced.

"Such a good girl," Aiden praises, pulling my mouth off of his friend's cock. I suck in a greedy breath of air, completely uncaring about the drool hanging from my lips. "Want to come yet?"

"Yes, please, *please* let me come," I plead shamelessly.

"I love when you beg," Aiden says, using his same grip on my hair to yank my head back so my back arches and my ass gets pulled right into his lap. "And you do it so prettily." Then he slides his hand around my hip and zeroes in on my clit again, his thrusts once again turning punishing.

"Come for me," he growls in my ear.

My lips pop open, my eyes widen, and I *explode.*

"Fuck yes," he hisses, fucking me through my orgasm. He ignores the way my nails dig into his arm, never once letting up on the way his fingers slide across my clit. It isn't until I shudder from oversensitivity that he pulls it away.

"Goddamn that was hot," I hear said in a breathless voice. It doesn't come from behind me, and when I open my eyes and find Max staring at us with a tight jaw and a hungry gaze, I realize I momentarily forgot about the third in our party.

He doesn't seem to mind, though. He simply stands at the end of the bed, slowly stroking himself, and waits to be tagged back in.

Which Aiden immediately does.

Gently pulling out of me, he nudges me in Max's direction. "Go on. I'm sure Max is dying to fuck you after that."

The look on Max's face clearly confirms that thought. I shakily straighten up on my knees, but he immediately reaches out a hand to help stabilize me. I grip the offered hand with a grateful smile.

I don't notice Aiden toss him a condom, but I see Max catch it before gently tugging me toward him.

He takes my spot in the center of the bed, stretching out on his back and positioning me to straddle his hips. I can't stop myself from reaching for his rock-hard, spit-slicked cock any more than I can stop the bolt of arousal that runs through me at the sudden thought that I'm about to have not one, but *two* men inside me.

That arousal ratchets when Max tears the packet with his

teeth in his desperation to get it on. If I ever forgot the level of alpha in this room, that move would single-handedly be a reminder.

He rolls it on in a single, practiced move, and then he's reaching for my hips to pull me over him.

"I could barely get two fingers into you earlier, you think you're going to be able to take my cock?" he asks in a persona I've only ever seen glimpses of.

It's the kind that makes a shiver run down a girl's spine right before she starts crawling.

"I'll take both of you and beg for more," I manage to counter, leaning forward so my hands rest on his chest. My fingers automatically flex on the marbled muscle.

He lets out a smug chuckle and positions me over him. I can tell he wants nothing more than to punish my bratty response by fucking up into me, but because I'm not his girl and he doesn't know me, he puts me in control instead. He lets me lower myself onto his length, visibly struggling with the sensation.

"Fuck, you feel good," he eventually grits out, his grip on my hips tightening.

"Then again, maybe I'm not the one that's about to start begging," I tease, but my voice doesn't have its usual edge, because being filled with Max's big dick has made me a little breathless.

Max must regain some of his control because he huffs a rough laugh at that. He lifts me up slightly, just enough that he can start slowly thrusting into me. "Let's return to this conversation in about five minutes once Aiden and I have fucked a few orgasms out of you."

Aiden chooses that moment to reappear. I feel the heat of his body press against my back, and his hand slide around my neck to the front of my throat. He tips my head back until it's resting on his shoulder.

"How many do you think we can get out of her?" he muses in a silk voice, tracing my pulse with his thumb. "Or better yet, how many until she's limp and babbling nonsense?"

An arrogant grin slices across Max's face, even as he continues his lazy thrusts up into me. "That's not going to take much."

"Fuck you both," I try to snap back, but I'm already too drunk on pleasure to sound convincing.

"That's the goal," Aiden chuckles, pressing his hips against my lower back and making a shiver run through me at the promise of him joining in. "Are you ready?"

"Yes," I respond, and this time I'm definitely breathless.

Still, Aiden's touch is slow and teasing as his opposite hand drifts down my spine. My breath catches when he nears my ass—and rightfully so, because he doesn't stop when he reaches it. He simply swipes his fingers between my cheeks until he can start to circle the area right above where his best friend is currently fucking me.

"God, you're going to be so tight with us both in here," he says in an awed voice. He continues to play with me for a moment, completely ignoring my annoyed growl, but then I feel his fingers removed and hear the sound of a cap snapping open. Only a second later, he's back and stretching me open with his lubed up fingers again, slipping one and then two fingers easily inside me.

"Dude, hurry up," Max growls, his thrusts snapping a little harder with his impatience. "You can fuck her ass anytime. I'm dying here."

I let out a breathy laugh, digging my nails into his chest as I lean farther forward and arch my hips harder into Aiden's touch. I have to take a deep breath before I can say, "Normally I would tease you for that, but I'm kind of feeling the same way right now."

Aiden's fingers pause in their movements. "If she's able to form full sentences, clearly we're not doing our jobs right."

Honestly, I'm buzzing with too much impatience, with too many sensations, to even respond to that. I can only wiggle my ass in his direction. And when nothing changes, I let out a whine. *"Aiden."*

I expect him to laugh, or tease us both, but something in him must have moved this moment from playful to heated, because suddenly he's gripping my throat again and pushing into my ass. There's no gentle waiting period this time, not when he's already made me take him once. This time, he fucks into me with a single, hard thrust.

"Oh my *God,*" I gasp. I knew this would feel good because I've always enjoyed anal, but this is *so much more* than I ever could have imagined. I've never felt as full as I do right now, or so desperate for the pleasure that I can already feel tingling in my body. It's like now that they're both inside me, my mind has been wiped clean of all thoughts but one: to be fucked into the orgasm of all orgasms.

As if sensing that, Aiden slowly pulls out and pushes back

in. He waits until Max starts to move as well, and then he starts to time his thrusts to happen opposite his. They're never inside me at the same time, which I think is their way of gradually warming me up to the feeling of having both of them fill me. And when they feel me sigh with pleasure and sink into their touch, their pace starts to quicken.

"Play with her clit," Aiden tells Max in a tight voice.

Wordlessly, Max does as instructed. He lets go of my hip with one hand and presses his thumb directly on my clit, immediately settling in with the hard, fast circles he somehow already knows I like. It's enough to make a whimper slip from my mouth, because now I can feel my release bearing down on me. With Max fucking up into my pussy as he plays with my clit, and Aiden punishing my ass, I'm about to lose what's left of my mind.

Aiden's hand comes around my neck, gripping my throat and pulling me up so I have to brace high on Max's chest. I feel his lips press to my ear, though the sensation is a distant one.

With one hand around my throat and the other tightening on my hip, his thrusts start to intensify, every drive of his hips landing harder than the last. I start to pant in desperation.

"Want more, dirty girl?" he whispers. And the feel of his lips tickling my ear drives another bolt of pleasure through me, even before his words register.

"Yes, yes, *yes*," I gasp.

There must be a silent communication between the boys because in the next second, their movements change. Instead of fucking me with opposite timing, they switch it up so they're now filling me at the same time. When Aiden thrusts, Max does too.

And I've never in my life felt so *full*.

Suddenly, I'm overwhelmed with so much pleasure that there isn't a sound I could make, a direction I could move, where I wouldn't be completely helpless in the face of their passion. I merely give in and let myself be carried away by it.

Aiden must sense it too, because in the next second he growls into my ear, every bit the apex predator. "Enough playing. I want you coming on our cocks in the next thirty seconds or I'll put you on your knees and come on your face without letting you finish." Then he bites into the curve of my neck to hold me in place as his fucking becomes frenzied.

Fuck. Thirty seconds? I don't even need five.

Because his words and the feelings surrounding me are enough to push me over the edge.

Not push—drop kick.

I think I let out a scream but I'm not sure because I'm being pulled under by a rip tide of sensations. I'm being battered by them from every direction, and every time I think I've hit the peak, I get rolled over by another wave. And then another, and another, until all feeling has been ripped from my body and I feel like I can't breathe. Eventually I go limp, too tired to figure out up from down.

When the pleasure-high finally dies down, I realize the guys have already come, and are gently fucking me through the last of my world-ending orgasm. While Max's hands rub along my thighs, soothing me, Aiden has an arm wrapped around my middle so he can pull me back into his chest and lave sweet kisses along my neck and shoulder.

"Beautiful," he's murmuring. "You're so fucking beautiful."

It's enough to make me drop my head back onto his shoulder and all but purr in contentment. He uses that as an opportunity to grip my jaw between his fingers and turn my face to his, to devour me with a kiss that's equal parts possessive and adoring.

"Perfect girl," he whispers, pressing a final, gentle kiss to my lips.

Then I'm being lifted off of Aiden—and Max—and being laid on the bed. Sleep tugs at my eyelids, but I'm conscious enough to recognize that Aiden is the one that brings a warm cloth over to wipe me clean, at the same time that Max appears in the doorway with a glass of water.

"Thank you," I croak, my throat still sore from what I assume was my screaming. He gives me a kind smile and then backs toward the door.

"I should get going," he mutters, aiming a nervous glance toward his best friend. But Aiden just claps him on the shoulder with a tired smile and gives him a nod, and then both of them are leaving the room together.

And I'm drifting off to the sleep to the memory of two boys giving me more pleasure than I ever could have imagined.

CHAPTER NINE
Aiden

I let out a pleased chuckle at the text. Not just because of the message itself, but also because I secretly love the fact that she's texting me only a day after I last saw her.

And that she texted first.

DANI

That's what I thought. Are you home?

AIDEN

No I'm out at Graffiti. Wanna join for a night cap?

DANI

It's a testament to how hot you are that even using that phrase doesn't lessen my attraction to you...

DANI

I'll be there in 15

I look up from my phone, all earlier doubts banished from my head and a giddy sort of excitement filling my chest. I don't realize I have a stupid grin on my face until I meet Max's gaze and he knowingly rolls his eyes.

"Lucy and Jax are on their way," he comments, taking a sip of his drink. "And speaking of Jax, apparently Remy and Hailey are coming tonight, too. So we'll get to witness the shit show of Jax and Hailey publicly together for the first time."

I'm momentarily distracted by that thought because he's right, it'll be interesting to see those two together. Jax has been protective of Hailey from day one, and it's got nothing to do with her being Remy's little sister and Jax's best friend. None of us ever thought of them as a couple but it makes sense now that I think about it. He's been slightly *too* protective of her lately.

"Am I right in assuming Dani's coming out?" Max asks, shaking me from my thoughts.

I turn my attention back to him as I take a sip of my drink. "Yeah. She's on her way."

He nods. "Cool." Then he glances at me hesitantly before asking, "Are *we* cool?"

At that, I startle. "What? Of course we are, why wouldn't we be?"

He shrugs, but I can tell he's slightly uncomfortable. "Just making sure. I know you said you two aren't serious but... I didn't want you to think I was moving in on her or something. You know, after last night." He glances up at me, waiting for my reaction.

"Because we both fucked her?" I blurt, so surprised by the question that I can only blink in confusion. "Dude, it was my idea. How could I be mad at that?"

Again, he shrugs in answer.

His concern makes me narrow my eyes in suspicion. "*Do* you want to move in on her? Is that what you're telling me?"

His eyes widen immediately. "No! I mean, she's great and all, but... not really my type. And she's yours. Regardless of what you say," he adds, cutting me off with a knowing look when I open my mouth to contradict him.

I sigh in defeat. "Alright fine. She feels like mine. But I *liked* sharing her with you. I don't know if we'll ever do it again, but I definitely don't regret creating a situation where, between the two of us, we made her come hard enough to pass out in my bed immediately afterwards." We both share a smug smile at the memory, although I ignore the pang that comes with the second half of that memory—the part where she left as soon as she woke up an hour later. That she *always* leaves the second she wakes up.

I shake the thought and focus back on my best friend. "So unless you're planning on trying to lock her down—which, yes, make me slightly ornery—then we have no problems here. I promise."

He studies my expression for a moment, trying to spot if I'm lying. And I let him look.

Finally, he gives me a tight nod and turns back to his beer. "Okay then. We're good. Carry on with the best lay of your life."

"Who's the best lay of Aiden's life?" a voice pipes up behind me.

I turn to see Lucy striding up to us with a big grin on her face. She's got her trademark look on tonight: a black harness over a tank top, and her blonde hair pulled back in a ponytail to show off the shaved lines on the side of her head. She and Remy are the two main girls at the gym, and I swear there's something in the water because they both are way too confident about fucking with the rest of us.

Something Lucy proves when she plucks the beer from my hand and drinks half of it in one gulp.

"By all means, take my drink, I didn't want it at all," I comment dryly.

"You've got that nice cushy job lined up after you graduate, I think you can afford to buy me a drink," she says with a laugh, taking another big swig.

I look to Jax for an assist, since he's the other person in our group with a "cushy" corporate job, and therefore the first person everyone usually looks to when it comes to buying a round of drinks.

But he merely holds his hands up in surrender. "Don't look at me, I've never been able to win this fight. Just buy her the drink, I promise it'll make everything easier."

Lucy gives him a victorious grin before turning back to me. She waits for Jax to leave for the bar to get his own drink before asking, "So… who's this 'best lay' you were talking about when we got here?"

"I believe that title would be mine," says an amused voice from behind me.

Sure enough, Dani chooses that moment to step into the fold. Lucy looks absolutely giddy at the sight of her, and it doesn't take a psychic to figure out what she's thinking.

That I rarely ever bring the girls I'm fucking to hangouts with my friends.

You know, separate worlds and all that.

I preemptively cut off whatever Lucy is about to say—none of which would work in my favor, if the look on her face is anything to go by. Instead, I turn to Dani and plaster my usual charming grin on my face. "Someone's sure of themselves," I tease.

Except, Dani's just as good at this game as I am, which means she isn't phased by my mask in the slightest. She just raises an eyebrow and asks, "Are you saying there's *another* girl who can make you come hard enough to start moaning God's name?"

I reach forward and lazily stroke a finger across her collarbone, enjoying the shiver she has to suppress at my touch. "I'm not the one that was screaming for God last time, sweetheart," I murmur.

Lust flares in her gaze, and for a moment it's just the two of us in the entire bar. I can see her remembering the last time, memories of last night flashing between us. And it doesn't even matter that Max was there, too, because right now even he doesn't exist.

But then her question registers, and I pull us back from the whirlwind of desire that we could so easily get lost in. I sweep her dark hair over her shoulder and tell her, "But no, there's no other girl that can do what you do. And believe me, they're trying," I add with a playful smirk. The comment is enough to make the corner of her lips twitch with a suppressed smile, which makes me think she easily sees through my lie: that there *are* no other girls in my bed.

Then I raise an eyebrow and ask, "What about you? How's your roster look?"

"Fuller than it's ever been," she breathes.

And I see the lie for what it is, the same way she saw mine. The lie that proves that even though this thing between us is casual, it's consuming enough to make us want to give it our full attention and not muddy it with other people. Even though we both could, if we wanted to.

We just… don't want to.

When we separate, it's with the unspoken agreement now sitting comfortably between us. I sneak a quick glance at Dani to see if there's any part of her that's freaking out about it, but all I see is a warm smile on her face. Which immediately makes a relieved breath whoosh from my chest.

She turns away from me, and directly into Max's line of

vision. He gives her a tight smile in greeting.

"Hey, Max," she says, nothing but her usual friendliness in her voice. It's enough to immediately remove the nervous lines from his own face, and he gives her a genuine smile in return.

"Hey, Dani. Want a drink? Aiden's buying."

Her eyes light up gleefully. "Ooh, yes please. I'll have whatever you're drinking."

And just like that, we're back to being three friends. Even if it is on my dime.

I turn away from them, wanting to give them a few minutes to settle into their own comfortable peace. I suddenly remember that Lucy was the one that instigated that whole conversation, and wince at how much she just heard. I open my mouth to say… I have no idea what, but something that's along the lines of *don't make this a big deal.*

Only, she's not listening. She probably hasn't been listening for a while, because when I finally face her, she's looking away from our group, a downright giddy smile on her face.

And when I follow her line of sight, I know why.

Jax is a few feet away from us, wrapped so tightly around Hailey that you almost can't see the tiny blonde from his massive stature. He's kissing her in a way that could only be considered a claim.

"I'm going to throw up in about 0.3 seconds if you two don't cut that shit out right now," an annoyed voice grumbles from beside me. I look over, surprised to see Remy there. She and Hailey must've come in while I was lost in Dani.

Hailey's cheeks pinken with a blush. "Sorry, I didn't mean to force that in your face," she mumbles. She lets Jax wrap an arm around her shoulders as they step up to join the group.

Remy sighs at that. It's no secret that she's not a huge fan of watching her best friend maul her little sister, although a part of me thinks there's something else that's making her hesitant about their new relationship. I don't know either of their personal lives' well enough to know what it could be, though, so I stay out of it and offer only my charm and wit as a buffer.

"So it *is* true," Lucy exclaims with a grin. "I always knew you scaring the guys away from her was a little suspect. Guess now we know why."

Jax just glares at her. "Tell me you'd want your sister dating any of the assholes at the gym."

That makes Lucy wince. "Okay, fair point."

"Hey, we're not assholes," I say in mock outrage. I throw an arm around Max's shoulders. "We're gentlemen of the highest caliber."

At that, I hear a snort behind me.

"I'm not sure the word 'gentleman' could apply to any part of your life," Dani says with a laugh. "I could pick some other words, but not that one."

Everyone's eyes widen as Dani steps up beside me. And where my first reaction should probably be discomfort—since they're all likely having the same reaction to my bringing a girl out as Lucy did—I feel none of that.

All I feel is pride that I get to introduce this super cool girl to my friends.

Jax is the first to speak. "Sorry, I didn't realize you were with our group."

And right away, I can tell there isn't an ounce of Dani that feels like an outsider in this environment. She easily reaches her fist forward for a fist bump. "I'm Danielle. Just call me Dani."

Jax's lip twitches in an almost-smile at the greeting, and then gives her a fist bump. "Nice to meet you, Dani," he says. Then he jerks his chin at me. "I assume you're here with the dimpled asshole?"

Dani lets out an exaggerated sigh, as if she actually hates being here.

All it does is make my dick twitch with excitement.

"Yup," she answers with a sigh. "Not sure how I got roped into his orbit, but here we are."

I let a pleased smirk form on my face. "You weren't sad about our situation last night, sweetheart."

The admission that I'm sleeping with Dani—and that I brought her out to meet everyone—is enough to make the whole group's eyebrows rise in surprise.

Remy's the one who voices the question that everyone's thinking. "How did you two meet?"

Dani immediately grins, and I can tell she's way too excited to tell the story of our meet-cute. "I met him on Temple's campus when he helped me run from a security guard. We ended up having to—"

I shoot forward to wrap an arm around her and slap my hand over her mouth, plastering my chest against her back. "Aaaand that's enough story time," I growl. "That big mouth of yours is going to get both our asses in trouble." Because as much as I don't mind my friends knowing that I have a claim on Dani— even if it's just that I'm fucking her—I don't really need them knowing the details of my relationship with her. Something about those details makes me feel protective, possessive even, and like I want those memories only for myself.

Dani must not feel the same need because she tugs my hand from her mouth and smirks at me over her shoulder. "Oh please. You love my big mouth." Her grin widens as she wiggles her ass against me. "And my ass."

The memory of the last time I took her ass—and the fact that I wasn't the only one in this group witnessing it—is enough to bring a slight warmth to my cheeks. Because the last thing I need is a public erection in front of my friends, yet Dani and her bold words are definitely about to push me in that direction.

The sight of me blushing makes my friends roar with laughter. "I like her," Remy says with a chuckle. "We need more women to keep these guys in line. It's about time this asshole found a Daddy." She grins at Dani, who grins back, and the female bond is formed instantly and visibly.

The sight of that connection makes an excitement grow in my chest that I've never felt before. I refuse to think it has anything to do with my friend group accepting the girl I'm seeing, or that I place any stock in that fact. I somehow convince myself that I'm just excited to see my friend—Remy, in this case—befriending someone else. There's nothing else in play here.

Even still, the last thing I need is those two bonding enough to start ganging up on me. There are already too many feisty women around here as it is.

So I shoo Dani over to Max, attempting to distract her

with him. Which works, because they immediately settle into a conversation about their favorite whiskeys. And even though I want to join them, I realize I like the sight of them talking. I'm glad they've become friends, especially after Max's questioning earlier.

I turn back to my gym friends, busting on Jax for his new relationship and grinning at how uncomfortable Remy is, despite the fact that she's trying to be supportive. But I'm happy for him. I'm happy he's happy, which, seeing the way he looks at Hailey, is the understatement of the year.

For some reason, it makes my gaze travel back to Dani.

Where a guy with hooded eyelids and a visible sway is currently crowding her from the side Max isn't sitting on.

I cock my head and study the interaction, taking in the way he's leaning in, the way she's looking at him with a high, skeptical eyebrow, and the way Max's gaze is narrowing in the guy's direction.

I watch as the drunk guy gives Dani a leering grin, then gestures at the bar, likely offering to buy her a drink. When she doesn't answer, just gives the Dani-est *are you fucking serious?* look, he forces a laugh and does it again, and I know he's starting the pushy asshole routine.

Max turns in his seat toward me, then shoots a silent *want me to step in?* look. I quickly shake my head.

"Aren't you going to do something?"

Turning to my gym friends that I forgot I was still standing with, I find everyone silently staring at the same interaction I was just watching. Lucy is grinning, Remy is giving me a questioning look, and Jax, with his arm still tight around

Hailey's shoulders, just looks confused. Like he can't believe that I won't protect my girl. Because he would immediately and undoubtedly jump on the fucker if someone was getting aggressive with Hailey. Tristan too, even though Remy is more than capable of handling herself in every way.

Dani doesn't need to be protected by anyone.

So instead, I chuckle. Then I gesture toward the interaction—I'm positive with awe shining in my eyes—and say, "Are you kidding? She'll do ten times more damage to that guy than I would. I would only slow her down if I stepped in."

Jax's still-confused gaze tracks back to Dani. And when my point is proven by Dani fisting her hand in the drunk guy's shirt after what was probably his fifth time trying to convince her to go out with him, his jaw drops in understanding. And some awe of his own.

I merely sigh and make my way over to the scene. "Alright, I'm taking her home before the fist fight starts."

Jax's voice is shell-shocked. "Would she really—?"

Dani's knee comes back as she prepares to hit him in the dick. "Yup," I answer dryly.

I catch her around the waist and pull her back before the knee can land. "Can't take you anywhere, troublemaker."

"*He* started it," she yells, struggling to get out of my grip. "Fucker can't take no for an answer—hey!"

Her shout is cut off when I spin her around and toss her over my shoulder. Then I turn to my friends, a huge grin on my face, and give them a salute before saying, "I think our time here is about up. Have a good evening, everyone."

"Spoilsport," I hear muttered from over my shoulder.

CHAPTER TEN

TEXTS

DECEMBER 1

10:12PM: AIDEN

You up?

10:13PM: DANI

Now who's sending cliché booty call texts?

10:17PM: AIDEN

Well you answered in under a minute, so who's the one desperate for sex here?

10:24PM DANI:

Still you

10:26PM: AIDEN

Ok fair

10:26PM: AIDEN

Interested?

10:31PM: DANI

Yea. But I have to leave for Boston early tomorrow so I can only come over for a quickie

10:32PM: AIDEN

How quick we talking?

10:32PM: AIDEN

Because I can do that

10:35PM: DANI

You're an idiot. I'll be over in 15.

DECEMBER 4

4:31PM: AIDEN:

How was Boston?

9:41PM: DANI

Kicked my ass. I've been running on fumes, I only just got home.

10:01PM: AIDEN

Shit that's insane. Feel like some food and company?

10:21PM: DANI

I'm pretty tired, I think I'm just gonna crash. Hit me up this weekend, I'll be back to normal by then.

10:28PM: AIDEN

Sounds good. Gnight.

10:31PM: DANI

Night, pretty boy

DECEMBER 10

7:51PM: DANI

Heyyy

7:52PM: AIDEN

Heyyy back

7:53PM: DANI

Whatcha up to?

7:59PM: AIDEN

Just finishing up at the gym. You?

8:03PM: DANI

Nothing really. You never texted me.

8:05PM: AIDEN

Lol phone works both ways, Dani

8:05PM: AIDEN

Is this your way of asking if I want to hang out?

8:08PM: DANI

...maybe

8:12PM: AIDEN

I want to hear you say it

8:12PM AIDEN

Say 'Aiden I am in dire need of an orgasm and only your perfect, magical dick can satisfy this urge'

8:15PM: DANI

Fuck off, you'll never hear me say that to a man. My vibrator works just as well.

8:22PM: AIDEN

I'm waiting

8:28PM: DANI

You're an idiot

8:32PM: DANI

Come over when you're done

8:33PM: AIDEN

Yes ma'am

DECEMBER 11

11:21AM: AIDEN

Fuck I can't stop thinking about last night. I keep getting a hard-on in study group.

11:40AM: DANI

I still don't think my legs have regained feeling in them

11:42AM: AIDEN

Please excuse me while I bask in that particular ego-boost

11:45AM: DANI

The next time you tell me I'm not good for your ego, I'm going to send you a screenshot of this conversation

11:48AM: AIDEN

How about you keep just stroking my ego

11:52AM: DANI

I prefer to stroke other things

11:54AM: AIDEN

I'm okay with that too

12:04PM: AIDEN

How's your day going?

12:09PM: DANI

Good. Just finishing up some editing.

12:09PM: DANI

Your semester still isn't over? I thought you'd be done for winter break.

12:11PM: AIDEN

Finals review. I'm done this week, thank god.

12:15PM: DANI

Ah

12:18PM: DANI

And next semester is your last?

12:20PM: AIDEN

Yeah but technically I only have my internship, so it's not like the class kind of semester. I'm just working.

12:24PM: DANI

Oh ok. Makes sense.

12:29PM: AIDEN

Did you ever consider going to college?

12:33PM: DANI

For a split second. Then I realized I hate classrooms.

12:38PM: AIDEN

I can only imagine how much you would argue with some of these professors

12:42PM: DANI

I definitely wouldn't be getting A's

12:45PM: AIDEN

Haha

12:47PM: AIDEN

What are you doing for Christmas? Any fun plans?

12:52PM: DANI

Nothing too exciting. I spend Christmas Eve with my parents and then Christmas Day we get the entire family together for the usual festivities.

12:53PM: DANI

You?

12:58PM: AIDEN

Kinda same. Minus the big family, since it's just me and dad. But we always spend Christmas Day together drinking beer and watching the 'best of' fights.

1:01PM: DANI

That sounds like a lot of fun

1:03PM: AIDEN

It is. Between you and me, it's my favorite day of the year.

1:05PM: DANI

Lol I won't tell

1:07PM: DANI

Get back to studying. Text me when you're done finals and can celebrate.

1:09PM: AIDEN

Yes ma'am

DECEMBER 13

2:43PM: AIDEN

I'm DONEEEEE

2:58PM: DANI

Lol congratulations. Wanna celebrate?

3:00PM: AIDEN

I would like nothing more than to celebrate this academic achievement by putting my face between your legs. You around?

3:03PM: DANI

I'm home. Come over.

DECEMBER 19

9:12PM: AIDEN

Hey you around?

9:46PM: DANI

No I'm out Christmas shopping with my mom

9:47PM: DANI

You around tomorrow?

9:49PM: AIDEN

No I have plans with my dad

9:52PM: DANI

Ok well let me know if you have some free time this week, I'll pop over before things get crazy with Christmas

9:56PM: AIDEN

I can do that. Enjoy your time with your mom.

DECEMBER 22

2:28PM: AIDEN

What do you call a snowman with a six-pack?

3:12PM: DANI

I'm not sure I want to know

3:14PM: DANI

What?

3:15PM: AIDEN

An abdominal snowman

3:18PM: DANI

I'm annoyed that that made me laugh

3:20PM: AIDEN

Have a good day, Dani

DECEMBER 25

12:38AM: DANI

I miss you

8:29AM: DANI

That got cut off. It was supposed to say 'I miss your dick'

10:03AM: AIDEN

Lol too much eggnog?

10:05AM: DANI

Way too much

10:08AM: AIDEN

How was your Christmas Eve?

10:15AM: DANI

Besides the copious amounts of alcohol? Pretty boring

10:16AM DANI

How have your Christmas festivities been?

10:18AM: AIDEN

Can't complain. It's just me and Dad so nothing too crazy. It's nice.

10:25AM: AIDEN

Do you have a big family?

10:39AM: DANI

Kind of. I only have one brother but between his growing family and the fact that my aunt has quadruplets, my average-sized family is almost outnumbered by babies.

10:41AM: AIDEN

Jesus that's a lot of kids

10:43AM: DANI

Tell me about it

10:56AM: AIDEN

Do you want kids?

11:09AM: AIDEN

Never mind, that was a stupid question

11:21AM: DANI

I do like kids, I just can't imagine wanting to be a single mom. I'll stick with the cool aunt title.

11:25AM: AIDEN

Now that I can definitely picture

11:42AM: AIDEN

Merry Christmas, Dani

11:59AM: DANI

Merry Christmas, Aiden

DECEMBER 29

3:32PM: AIDEN

Hey dirty girl

3:52PM: DANI

That nickname doesn't really work when we're not in the middle of sex

3:55PM: AIDEN

Agree to disagree

4:00PM: DANI

What's going on?

4:08PM: AIDEN

Are you around for new year's?

4:10PM: DANI

No, I'm down in Key West for the rest of the year

4:13PM: AIDEN

Ah ok

4:14PM: DANI

What're you doing for it?

4:17PM: AIDEN

Nothing crazy. I hate being out in the city so Tristan and Remy are throwing a party. Wanted to see if you were around for it.

4:21PM: DANI

I wish. I appreciate the invite though, that sounds like a lot of fun.

4:25PM: AIDEN

Have fun on Shit St. Try not to get Duval-faced.

4:27PM: DANI

Cute

JANUARY 1

12:02PM: AIDEN

Happy new year, Dani

12:02PM: DANI

Happy new year, Aiden

JANUARY 4

8:52PM: DANI

Please tell me you're around tonight

9:02PM: AIDEN

Oh thank god I'm not the only one who's desperate. I'm coming over.

9:04PM: DANI

Hurry

JANUARY 10

4:12PM: DANI

I have a favor to ask

4:15PM: AIDEN

Well this is unusual.

4:16PM: DANI

Can you give me a self-defense lesson?

4:19PM: AIDEN

...

4:20PM: AIDEN

What happened?

4:25PM: DANI

It's not what you think. I was just thinking that I'm curious to know if I'm approaching fighting all wrong or if my instincts are right.

4:28PM: AIDEN

Please tell me you didn't punch someone last night.

4:30PM: DANI

I plead the fifth

4:31PM: AIDEN

God. I should probably hesitate to give you any of this knowledge.

4:33PM: DANI

But you'll still do it, right? Because you like me?

4:35PM: DANI

Plus I'll reward you for it. Immensely.

4:37PM: AIDEN

Le sigh. I don't have a chance against you, do I?

4:38PM: DANI

None.

JANUARY 16

3:21PM: AIDEN

Come over for fight night on Saturday

4:06PM: DANI

That was aggressive

4:08PM: AIDEN

Come over for fight night on Saturday pleeease

4:10PM: DANI

Lol

4:11PM: DANI

Ok fine

4:13PM: DANI

Will anyone else be there?

4:15PM: AIDEN

Just Max

4:22PM: DANI

Is this your way of propositioning another threesome?

4:26PM: AIDEN

Not exactly what I had in mind

4:31PM: AIDEN

Do you WANT another threesome?

4:33PM: DANI

Not really. No offense to Max, I just think I'm more the one on one type.

4:34PM: AIDEN

I think I might be the same

4:36PM: AIDEN

But I'll be sure to let him down gently

4:40PM: DANI

So just fights then

4:41PM: AIDEN

Just fights. It'll be fun, I'll cook some food and we'll make bets.

4:43PM: DANI

You gamble on the fights?

4:44PM: AIDEN

Dollar bets against each other. Nothing crazy.

4:46PM: AIDEN

Although we do have a whiteboard for it. Max is notoriously atrocious at calling fights so he always tries to change his bets halfway through the fights. You'll have to help me keep him accountable.

4:47PM: DANI

Lmao I can do that

4:49PM: DANI

I'll see you on Saturday

4:50PM: AIDEN

See you then, Dani

JANUARY 27

10:22PM DANI

Hey

10:36PM AIDEN

Hey, troublemaker

10:37PM: DANI

How are you?

10:39PM: AIDEN

Good. Just got home from the gym.

10:39PM: AIDEN

You?

10:44PM: DANI

Working at the bar

10:46PM: DANI

It's completely dead in here. I'm bored.

10:49PM: AIDEN

Want me to come down there to keep you company?

10:54PM: DANI

You don't have to do that, I know you're probably tired. I assume training gets pretty intense when you have people at the gym getting ready for fights.

10:59PM: AIDEN

You remember that?

11:04PM: DANI

Of course

11:05PM: DANI

Max seemed excited

11:08PM: AIDEN

Ah. Yeah he is. His is a rematch against a guy he lost a controversial decision to, so he's pretty fired up.

11:10PM: DANI

Sounds like a good matchup

11:36PM: DANI

Thanks for keeping me company while I close up

11:37PM: AIDEN

Of course. You know I live to entertain.

11:43PM: AIDEN

Can I ask you to text me when you get home? Or will you give me a feminist speech if I do that?

11:48PM: DANI

Careful. You're starting to sound like a concerned boyfriend.

11:50PM: AIDEN

Just a concerned friend

11:56PM: DANI

Are we friends, Aiden?

11:59PM: AIDEN

I'd like to be

12:03AM: DANI

Ok. Friends then.

12:05AM: AIDEN

Good. Great.

12:24AM: DANI

I'm home

12:25AM: AIDEN

Good. Night, Dani.

12:27AM: DANI

Night, Aiden

CHAPTER 11
Aiden

I'm WARMING UP for my workout when I hear Coach bark my name. I turn to see him walking out of the office with his usual hardass expression.

"What's up?" I ask, nerves already simmering below the surface.

Because that's an *I have a fight for you* look.

"I have a fight for you," he confirms.

He stops in front of me and looks at me with an expression that can only be described as pleased, smug, and leashed, all in one. And with the next words out of his mouth, I know why.

"Ready to go pro?"

My first response is shock. Yeah, going pro has been a dream ever since I got involved in this sport in high school, but I thought I was still a few fights away from that happening. I still have so much to learn. Typically Coach's mentality is to leave your losses for the amateur fights—that's where you want to learn, and losses are the best way to do that. That way when you go pro, you've got a rock-solid base and can really take things to the next level.

I'm knocked out of my open-mouthed stupor when Tristan grins and claps me on the back. "Fuck yes," he says. "It's about time you stepped into the big leagues."

"You think I'm ready?" I ask Coach, still shell-shocked. "I mean, who am I fighting?"

He cocks an eyebrow, which I immediately interpret as, *How many times have I told you that it doesn't matter who you're fighting? You run your game plan, not theirs.*

"Only reason you're allowed to ask that question now is because we will actually start training for pro opponents now," he answers, the unspoken ending to it clearly being *but you know better.* "You're fighting Tyler Hastings in six weeks."

I swallow nervously, my cocky façade cracking for the first time in a long time. Fighting is the only thing that ever threatens it, though I'm still pretty good at keeping it in place—usually.

Leave it to the thought of my first pro fight to be the thing that reduces me to a nervous mess.

"Aiden," Coach murmurs, giving me a knowing look. Because he can read his fighters better than anyone else can. "You're ready. Do you trust me? Do you trust your team?"

I nod without hesitation. Of course I trust him. And the team he's created. Not only are he and Tristan the ideal leaders—because of their experience but also because of their patience and way of teaching—but my teammates are the best, too. Because even though fighting is an individual sport, it's the people you surround yourself with that really make the difference. Without them, fighters wouldn't even make it into the ring.

"You'll do great," Tristan tells me, squeezing my shoulder in the most encouraging gesture I've ever seen from him. I nod numbly.

"You good?" Coach asks. It's his way of asking if I want the fight—if I'm ready to take my career to the next level.

"I'm good," I murmur, already coming to terms with the fact that *of course* I want this fight, I'm just a little nervous about how huge of a step this is. I straighten up and clench my jaw as I look directly at Coach. "I want it."

"Attaboy," Tristan says with a grin and another slap on the back. Coach just gives me a nod of approval.

"Take him through some sparring rounds," he instructs Tristan. "I want him working on landing from the outside and avoiding takedowns."

Tristan nods. "Yes, sir."

I wait for Coach to walk back into the office before I let myself mutter a quiet *fuck*.

"You're fine, you're just in your head," Tristan says in an effort to appease me. "You'll feel better when you start moving around and you realize you're actually good at this shit."

My eyes widen and my lips part in surprise as I swivel to face my friend and coach. "Was that... encouragement and *praise?*"

He rolls his eyes and shoves me in the direction of the locker rooms. "Don't get used to it, asshole. Go get ready. I'll grab Max."

But before I can turn and do as he says, we hear shouting coming from the other end of the gym.

"What the fuck is he doing..." I hear Tristan murmur from

next to me. My eyes follow the commotion until they land on the pair that's sparring in the cage.

Or, they *were* sparring. Now they're in each other's faces and shoving at each other's chests.

Kane, the new guy, and… Jax?

"What the *fuck* is wrong with you?" Jax is yelling, emphasizing his question with another shove to Kane's chest. "This isn't a fight, you asshole, I'm your *teammate!*"

"Get the fuck off me," Kane growls, pushing Jax away. "This ain't ballet, man. If you didn't wanna get punched in the face, you shouldn't be stepping in the cage."

"You *broke* my *nose!*" Jax yells. And now that he mentions it, I can see the blood on his face. "Since when does 'drilling' translate to 'throw the first punch as hard as you can' in your brain?!" He steps forward to get in Kane's face again.

"Fuck you," Kane snaps, not backing down an inch. In fact, he does the opposite. He meets Jax in the middle, their noses almost pressed together. "If you suck at fighting, just say that."

Jax's eyes flash with fury, and an actual growl sounds from his throat. He looks like he's about to cock back and smash his fist into Kane's face, which is saying something because Jax is the chillest, nicest guy in here. This whole situation is insane.

Tristan intervenes before it can escalate any further. "Alright, *enough!*" he bellows. He puts himself between the two men and holds them both at arm's length. "Both of you, take a fucking walk. *Now.*"

Jax shoves his best friend's hand off of his chest and scoffs once more at Kane. Then he rips his gloves off and walks out of the gym without another word.

I focus back on Kane as he throws his gloves as hard as he can against the cage. *"Fuck!"* he bellows. It's a sound of pure rage, an emotion that he clearly isn't capable of containing.

Before he can start punching the padded corners of the cage, Tristan demands his attention.

"Hey," he snaps. "I know you're new to this sport, and new to this place, but this isn't where you go to brawl, man. We're not street fighting in here. This is a *sport*. We act like *athletes* on the mat. Which means we use technique, and discipline, and good sportsmanship. We're not in here just to measure who has the biggest dick, you hear me?" Kane still hasn't looked at him or acknowledged anything, he's just glaring at nothing in particular and shifting his weight from foot to foot.

"Hey," Tristan snaps again, this time putting his face in front of Kane's and forcing the bigger man to meet his gaze. He does, and I can see the flames of anger licking at his pupils. His jaw clenches, and he looks like he's physically stopping himself from shoving Tristan away from him. "I said *do you hear me?*"

And either Kane is calming down, or he's realized that taking a shot at the second-in-command isn't a bright idea, because he nods once, stiffly.

"I want 150 burpees from you, right now," Tristan barks. "If I have to tire you out to burn that anger away then so be it. I have no problem making you start every session with a burnout."

Kane's jaw clenches again but then he launches into the exercise, jumping up before landing and dropping into a push-up position. Down for a push-up, then he's right back to jumping high. Over and over again, he keeps going.

"Emotional motherfucker," Tristan mutters under his

breath as he steps out of the cage and passes by me. "I swear to God, I don't even have this problem with the girls when they're trying to cut weight on their periods."

I glance back at the cage where Kane is still going through the motions, looking like he's barely even breaking a sweat. "You think he'll be alright?"

Tristan lets out a heavy exhale as he follows my gaze. "I really fucking hope so," he mutters. He studies Kane from where we're standing on the other end of the mat, his stare thoughtful. "Sometimes I forget that not everyone thinks of this sport as a privilege," he says quietly. "Sometimes people are so used to fighting for their lives that they automatically come out swinging when they feel trapped." He nods in Kane's direction. "I have no idea what made that boy so angry, but I really hope he figures it out before he hurts someone. Or himself."

We've barely finished training when I'm grabbing my phone.

AIDEN

DANI

AIDEN

What're you doing right now?

DANI

Fighting the urge to throw my computer out the window

AIDEN

Editing not going well?

DANI

Something like that

DANI

Boss gave me some changes to make and they're next to impossible. I'd need magic software to make this happen.

DANI

Why the heated texts? What happened?

AIDEN

I want to celebrate. Come over later?

DANI

I don't know, celebrating doesn't sound nearly as enticing as banging my head against my desk

AIDEN

Can I entice you with a different kind of banging?

DANI

You've convinced me.

DANI

What time are you home?

AIDEN

Leaving the gym now. I'll be ready for you in an hour.

DANI

I like the sound of that. I'll meet you there.

An hour later, I've eaten, showered, and am waiting like an excited puppy by my front door. I hear a knock at exactly the hour mark.

"Damn, you really do have good news," Dani says with a laugh when I swing the door open with a big flourish. "What the hell happened today?"

I usher her inside with an excited pat on the butt. "Come inside and I'll tell you. And then I want to hear all about your trip to DC."

She turns around with a look of surprise. "You remembered my assignment? I barely mentioned it to you last time."

Now I'm the one that's confused. "Of course. I remember everything you tell me."

That seems to make her uncomfortable.

"I mean, *you* seemed excited about it," I blurt, trying to backtrack. "That's what I remember."

She seems to settle at that. And when I nudge her toward the couch, she relaxes even more. "Oh. That makes sense. I guess I do get slightly obnoxious before a good assignment."

I let out a snort. "A little?"

Her eyes narrow and she shoves me playfully in response. "Ass," she mutters. "What's *your* good news? After that, it better be spectacular."

A grin stretches across my face, and I place my hands on my hips as I stand confidently in front of where she's sitting. "I'm going pro," I announce proudly.

"You got offered a fight?" she asks, her eyebrows rising in surprise.

I nod. "Six weeks. My first pro fight."

There's silence, and then...

"Holy *shit*, Aiden, that's *incredible!*" she yells, launching off the couch and into my arms. "Congratulations!"

I chuckle and tighten my arms around her. "Thanks. I'm excited too."

She unwraps her arms from around my neck and puts space between us, as if realizing that her reaction was slightly over-eager. A small blush lights her cheeks as she steps back. "Seriously, that's incredible. You should be proud."

I let a genuine smile warm my face as I chuck her chin playfully. "I am proud. I've been working toward this for years. It's a huge accomplishment."

Genuine joy lights her eyes—she's practically vibrating with excitement. "So how are we celebrating, then? What can we do?" She looks around the apartment with a skeptical look, as if she's just now seeing it for the first time. "I'm assuming no partying, no drinking. Healthy stuff only for the next six weeks, right? Are you allowed to do anything but train?"

Fuck, she's adorable. "Yeah, I can do other stuff. Just nothing that takes away from rest or a healthy diet. But I don't necessarily have to turn into a hermit." I look over her with a heated once-over. "Why, what did you have in mind?"

She matches my vibe in an instant. "Well, that's not exactly the direction my brain went in, but now that you mention it… can you… you know?"

A sly grin slides across my face. "Yeah, baby, I can… you know."

Her eyes widen at my words, since it's the first time I've called her by that endearment. I half expect her to put some distance between us—it's definitely too comfortable of a comment—but to my surprise, her only reaction is to smile as her cheeks pinken in pleasure.

I decide to push my luck a little further. "At least for the next five weeks," I continue, wrapping an arm around her waist and pulling her tight against my body. Her smile only grows at my gesture.

"Feel like celebrating from your knees for a little bit?" I murmur, dropping a light kiss to her neck. Kissing down the length of it.

I relish the shiver that runs through her at my touch. "I think I can do that," she whispers.

Then she's pulling me down the hallway to my bedroom.

When she yanks me inside and shuts the door behind me, she catches the wince on my face at the last second.

"What was that?" she asks, a frown marring her perfect face. "Did you get hurt?"

I roll my shoulder with another wince. "Nah, I'm just sore. Coach worked me into the ground today after we agreed to take the fight."

A thoughtful look settles on Dani's face, and then she's pulling me toward the bed and pushing me facedown on the mattress.

"Uh, this isn't exactly what I had in mind," I mutter. "I know we joke about you being Daddy but..."

When she lets out a delighted giggle, I have the insane thought that I'd give this girl anything she wanted.

"Don't worry, besides riding you, I doubt I'd be into owning you," she says with another giggle. "But I'll keep your open-mindedness in mind." She lifts my legs and arranges them on the bed so she can straddle the backs of my thighs. When her hands settle on my shoulders, I immediately melt into the mattress. Then they start to dig into my shoulders, and a long groan sounds from me as she finds a knot with her thumb.

"Fuck, that hurts," I hiss, forcing myself not to tense up.

"Just give it a minute," she scolds. And sure enough, after a painful minute of her digging her thumb into my shoulder, I feel the knot start to loosen and my muscles start to relax.

"God, why are you so good at this," I moan, enjoying the bliss of her hands on me. My eyes flutter closed at the sensation of her hands running over my body.

"My mom was briefly interested in massage when she was in medical school," she explains absentmindedly, her thumbs working over my muscles. "She always jokes that if she ever needed to go back to work, she would be a masseuse." A bite of bitterness hardens her words. "From the best regional neurologist to a masseuse. What a backwards life plan."

I don't exactly want to engage with Dani on a topic that I already know I won't win, but I can't help myself from saying quietly, "I mean, if she could make people feel half as relaxed and happy as your hands are making me, I could definitely appreciate the career change."

A pause. "I'll be sure to pass the message on."

Her comment reminds me of something, and I hesitate a moment before asking, "Does she know about me?"

I can *feel* her stiffen with the question.

"No, of course not," she hurries to say. "Why would she need to know who I'm fucking?"

And even though it's exactly the answer I expected, it still drives a shard of something into my gut.

But I ignore it and roll onto my back, Dani still straddling my legs. I reach for her waist and bump up with my hips so she's higher up on my body. And, wanting to put her more at ease, I make a joke to try to lighten the mood.

"She doesn't. I'm just wondering if I have a chance with the older Mrs. Monroe. Cougars love me, you know."

It works. The tension ebbs immediately from her shoulders. "You're disgusting," she says with another laugh. And I breathe a sigh of relief that she's not pulling away from me, that she's still here, still running her hands over my chest.

"So what do we think about that celebration from your knees?" I murmur, eyeing her from where she's still settled on top of me.

"I think I can make that happen," she whispers, letting her hands run down to my belt buckle. "Still feel like you want to be worshipped?"

"Always," I say, unable to keep the breathlessness from my voice.

She needs no further urging. She undoes my buttons and tugs my pants over my hips, unveiling the proof of my attraction, glancing up at me with an appreciative look.

I expect her to give me a rough and dirty blowjob—the kind she loves to give when I can stay off my knees long enough to let her—so I'm surprised when she leans down to slowly drag her tongue along my length, her gaze glued to mine as she does it. When she reaches the tip, she swirls her tongue around it before sucking it into her mouth.

My head drops back and a deep groan leaves my lips at the sensation. "*Fuck*, Dani."

She drops down again, taking me deeper into her mouth this time. Again she slides up, just as slowly, still with her eyes on me. Between the torturous pace and the way she's staring at me, it doesn't take long until I'm completely lost to the feeling of *her*.

I sink my fingers into her hair and watch with slack-jawed wonder as she worships me with her mouth. As she drives my cock deep enough to make her lips kiss my abs, and then as she pulls away so only a strand of saliva connects her to my length.

"Goddamn, that's a pretty sight," I mutter, guiding her head with my hand on the back of her head. My hips want to pump myself deeper, but I hold myself back, content with watching myself disappear between her lips.

My lust-filled comment takes a second to register, but when it does, an idea starts to take root. I watch myself disappear between her lips once, twice, three times, before forcing myself to look away and reach for the object that is suddenly the focus of my attention.

Thankfully, Dani had thrown her backpack on my bed when we walked into the room. So it's easy to reach for it and pull her camera out.

I see her eyes open and look up at me when she feels me moving around, though her mouth never stops what it's doing. She's singularly focused on slowly driving me out of my mind. It's the whole reason I reached for the camera in the first place, because the sight of her this obsessed with my pleasure is too addicting not to document.

"Can I?" I ask her quietly, taking the lens cover off and holding the camera up in question.

She continues her lazy movements for a few seconds, her eyes never leaving mine. There's an air of seriousness surrounding my question, because even though it's Dani's camera, and I'd have no access to the pictures unless she gives them to me, I'm still *taking pictures of her*. I'm still solidifying this moment between us and creating a way for us to remember it long after the pleasure has subsided and the sweat has cooled on our bodies.

So I find myself holding my breath as I wait for her answer. Even the urge for release dies down, as if *my* body senses the importance of the question and shoves the lust down for a few moments.

But then she pulls her mouth off of my length and says quietly, "Yes." And the breath immediately rushes from my lungs.

When she doesn't go back to what she was doing, just extends her tongue and swirls it around the tip, I scramble to turn the camera on so I can quickly snap a picture.

"Fuck, Dani," I growl. "I want a copy of this. This is the hottest thing I've ever seen."

She doesn't answer, just huffs a laugh and sucks me between her lips again.

I think I snap another picture but I can't be sure—I'm too busy groaning through the pleasure and fighting my hips from driving up into her mouth.

It only takes me three more pictures to lose that fight. Eventually, I drop the camera to the bed and weave my fingers into Dani's hair so I can hold her in place as I thrust my hips up. She moans at the show of control and takes me as deep as she can.

"You're going to make me come," I say tightly, unable to stop my hips from pumping. I'm *thisclose* to letting her finish this, even though I don't want it to be over. I never want these moments with her to be over. But *she* seems to want to do it this way, and I'm finding myself more and more helpless to give this girl what she wants.

She pops her lips off of me and straightens, letting her hands take over the job. I somehow manage to reach for the camera again when I see the look of unabashed hunger on her face. Her head snaps up when she hears the click of the camera.

"Take your clothes off," I say in a voice more breathless than I intend. But I'm dying here and I can't take this for much longer.

Then again, it doesn't help matters when Dani whips her shirt off and I see that she's braless. And turned on enough to make her nipples tighten into perfect little points that immediately make me desperate to suck on them. Or when she wiggles out of her leggings and I realize that she's once again not wearing any underwear.

"Ride me, baby, please," I beg mindlessly. "I don't want to come anywhere but inside you. Get up here and put me out of my misery."

She hesitates, the fist that's been pumping me slowing to an easy pace. I think her original intention was just to give me a blowjob, but I can see the desire light in her eyes and I watch as the temptation to take her own pleasure becomes too much to fight. Her resolve to tease crumbles before my eyes.

The second after I see her make the decision, she reaches over me to open my nightstand and retrieve a condom. She slides it over my length just as I snap a picture, this time wanting to capture her desperation for me. But when she settles over me and takes every inch of me inside her in one smooth glide, the only thing I'm conscious enough to do is groan and let the hand holding the camera fall to the bed.

"*God*, that's never going to stop feeling incredible," she breathes, her eyes drifting closed. She shifts her hips slightly, taking her time getting used to how I feel.

I think I'm holding my breath as she does it. While I stare at her as she does it.

Then she lifts up and slowly drops back down.

A groan rips out of my chest at the sensation.

Slowly, almost lazily, she starts to move. Up and down, rocking her hips and grinding down on me every time she drops her weight into my lap. With her hands braced on my chest and her head thrown back, eyes still closed, she's a fucking *vision*.

And I'm the lucky bastard that gets to witness it.

I'm too mesmerized by the sight to do anything more than clutch the camera in my hand and stare at her. But when she hits a rhythm that makes a whimper slips from her lips, I can't stop myself from lifting it and snapping a picture. Suddenly wanting, more than anything else, to capture this new feeling between us.

The click of the camera causes her eyes to open. I watch as awareness returns to her gaze—as she slips out of the haze she fell into and finally senses the weight of this moment.

I see a flash of panic in her eyes, which is the absolute last thing I want her to be feeling. So I drop the camera beside me and grip her hips instead, joking tightly, "This is starting to feel more like a reward for you than a celebration for me."

The tension immediately disappears from her shoulders. Her eyelids droop, and a small smile appears on her lips. Then she leans forward so her hands are braced beside my head instead of my chest, which brings her weight over me and her face closer to mine.

"Are you saying you're not enjoying this?" she purrs, her hips never stopping their slow and sexy rolls.

My grip tightens on her waist. "I'd like it better if you came so *I* could come," I admit.

She lets her gaze travel over my face for a moment, before the full smile blooms across her face. A second before she picks up the pace of her hips.

"Oh *fuck*, Dani," I groan. She's not using slow and lazy movements anymore, she's riding me for broke and forcing me to hold back my own orgasm while she works for hers. I grit my teeth and let one hand travel between us so I can press my thumb to her clit and start rolling circles.

"What about now?" she asks, though her voice is breathless

this time. "Do you feel celebrated yet?"

"Getting there," I say in a tight voice. My thumb circles faster.

When her breath hitches, my gaze flies to her face. She's staring at me in a way she's never done before, looking so open and vulnerable that my own breath catches. I have no idea what she's feeling, but she seems to want to say something.

I don't push. I just let her look and wait.

After a moment, she lowers her head the last few inches and whispers against my lips, "I'm proud of you, Aiden."

And that's it. I can't handle any more.

I can't handle this gorgeous, perfect girl admitting that she's proud of me, all while pleasuring me and looking breathtaking while she does it. I can't do it anymore.

I flip Dani onto her back in one quick move and push as deep inside her as I can. Then I capture her gasp in my mouth with a searing kiss.

"You can't tell me that and not expect me to come immediately," I growl against her lips. My hips never stop moving, my thrusts getting deeper, *harder*, with every stroke. "Sexy as fuck *and* proud of me? I can't take it, baby. If you don't come in the next thirty seconds I'm going to embarrass myself, so you better come on my cock right fucking now."

"I—oh my God, I'm—" she doesn't get another word out before she's coming so hard, she starts to shake in my arms. I grit my teeth and continue driving into her, determined to make her orgasm last as long as possible before I give into my own pleasure.

When her muscles go limp and a content sigh sounds from

her lips, I let go. I drop my face to Dani's shoulder and let out a groan, pumping my hips once, twice, three times, before finishing in a condom that I suddenly wish wasn't there.

And in that moment, I realize things between Dani and I are changing.

It doesn't hit me until the next morning that this is the first time Dani has slept over.

After last night, we both were tired enough that it felt completely natural to fall asleep right where we were. I think I wanted to offer her a ride home, but by the time I opened my mouth to ask, I looked over to find Dani softly snoring on my chest. At the sight of her sleeping, completely unguarded and without her usual sass, there wasn't a chance of me waking her up and asking if she wanted to leave.

And when I wake up to her body pressed against mine, it hits me that this is the first time we've done this. After more than three months, of countless quickies and hours of time spent together, this is the first time we've slept together.

And... I like it. I like having her here.

I can't help the smile that ticks up the corners of my lips at the sight of almost her entire body sprawled across my chest and legs. Calling her a cuddler would be an understatement, because there isn't an inch of her front that isn't plastered against some part of me. And with her arm wrapped around my waist and her nose pressed into my chest, dark hair fanning out everywhere, she's wrapped around me in a way that lets me know it's going to be hard, if not impossible, to extricate myself.

Not that I want to. Even though my bladder is screaming at me to get up, there isn't a part of me that wants to move.

I brush her hair away from her face, my movements gentle because I don't want to wake her up. I'm not quite ready to shatter this moment. And I'm slightly desperate to see her sleep-face again, the one I got a glimpse of when she fell asleep on me last night. The one with no mask on, with no playful smiles hiding her vulnerable thoughts.

I can only see part of her face, that's how much of it she's got pressed against my chest. So I brush her hair back, lingering on the wisps surrounding her face, and then absentmindedly start to run my fingers over the gorgeous ink that runs the length of her arm. But when I can finally see her face, when I watch her lashes flutter in her sleep and feel her sleepy breaths puff against my skin, I see enough. I see *her*.

I'm still memorizing her face when she starts to wake. Slowly, her eyes blink open, and when they focus on the body she's sprawled across, she lifts her head to look up at me.

And just for a moment, I see relief. I see contentment. The same emotion I felt waking up to her, I now see on her face. It's in the way her gaze relaxes when she looks at me, the way a small smile appears on her lips.

I could get used to this.

That's the thought that spikes through my brain. And if the way Dani freezes is any indication, she sees it happen.

Slowly, seemingly trying not to draw attention to what we both just experienced, she pulls away from me and straightens to a sitting position.

"Sorry, I guess I fell asleep," she murmurs, reaching for her shirt at the end of the bed.

Wanting to lighten the mood—and not wanting to acknowledge the fact that we very obviously just overstepped our clearly-defined friends-with-benefits boundaries—I force a grin onto my face. "There's that ego-boost again. Did I fuck you into a dick coma?"

She rolls her eyes, relaxing slightly, but still not entirely. I can read her thoughts from a mile away, and I know she's worried this is becoming too affectionate.

It takes me a second to figure out how to put her mind at ease, but when I do, it feels like the right thing to do. I could probably benefit from some distance, too.

"I'm going to be busier now with the fight coming up, so I probably won't see you as much," I tell her, standing and starting to pull on my own clothes.

At that, she really does relax. Like I've finally appeased her that last night didn't magically make me catch feelings. That we can keep going on as we have.

"You going to be okay without 24/7 access to Little Aiden?" I tease with a grin.

She shakes her head, a smile tugging at her lips. "I've never met a guy who felt comfortable calling his dick 'little.' Leave it to you to be arrogant enough to pull it off."

"I'd be happy to show you again just how ironic that nickname is," I murmur, reaching forward to fist my hand in the front of her shirt and pull her against my chest. When I start to run my lips along her neck, I feel a happy shiver run through her before she braces her hands on my hips.

"So cocky," she says, but she sounds breathless.

But then she pushes away and reaches for her pants on the floor. "I have to get going. I'm hoping I've got another assignment coming in tomorrow, so I have some editing I need to finish before that happens. I might be traveling this week, so the timing works out well for your fight camp." She shoots me a hesitant look before saying, "I'll just… see you when I see you, I guess."

I give her a stiff nod. I really want to kiss her goodbye, but something tells me that's not the kind of period I want to put on the end of this interaction.

So instead, I lean forward and quickly nip at her neck.

"Sounds good to me. I'll walk you out." Then I spin her toward the door and smack her ass.

And as I follow her out, reveling in the sound of her laugh, I let out a breath of relief that we're back on solid ground.

Not because I didn't enjoy waking up with her in my arms, but because I finally feel like I'm in a comfortable friends stage with Dani, and the last thing I want to do is put any distance between us.

I want to keep her around for a little longer.

CHAPTER 12
Aiden

As it seems to be happening lately, it only takes me two days to start missing her enough to want to call her. And then another two days before I give into the urge and actually do it.

But when I call her, she declines it on the first ring. Which tells me she's working. And if I wasn't so stressed about the last time I saw her—and second-guessing the distance I think she was trying to put between us—it would be easy to fight the urge to call her again. I'd tell myself that I don't do double texts, or double calls, because I don't like pushing anyone to give me their attention. Except, I'm finding it harder and harder to care about how desperate I might seem.

Which means twenty minutes later, I'm walking into the dive bar and hoping Dani is ignoring my calls because she's busy beating off drunk college students with a bat. Yet it only takes me a second to realize she's not here.

Part of me wants to wish that's because the bar is empty and I could see it, but the truth is, the bar is packed. I know she's not here because I can *feel* it.

But I'm not ready to analyze what that means, so even

though I already have my answer, I still spend a minute stretching my neck and looking behind the bar and toward the entrance to the kitchen.

I sigh and start to leave the way I came in, but then the older woman behind the bar catches my eye, and I realize she's been watching me look around. And when she jerks her head toward the back, indicating I should meet her over there, I'm moving before I can even question it.

I give her a quick look-over as she steps through the Employees Only door ahead of me. She's a beautiful woman, with a no-nonsense air about her that tells me she's probably the owner—or at least the one that handles rowdy bar patrons around here. She's clearly older in age but only because I can see the deep smile lines around her eyes and mouth; right away I can tell she's been living a good—and likely exciting—life.

I can tell she's exactly the kind of woman my Dani would be drawn to.

"You Aiden?" she asks without preamble, leaning against the wall and crossing her arms over her chest.

I nod mutely. *She knows who I am?*

"Dani's not here," she tells me. And as the words settle, and realization sinks in, a slow grin spreads across my face.

"She talks about me?"

The woman's lip twitches with an amused smile. "I'd tell you you're the first one she's ever told me about, but I'm afraid the knowledge might make your head explode with that smile you've got going on."

"You're not wrong," I admit without shame, that smile growing another inch wider.

She smirks at me for another moment, but then her expression sobers. "She's not here. She's working a job tonight. Otherwise I would've had her in here to help me with this shit show."

I glance through the window in the door to the masses packed out front like sardines. "No kidding. I don't think I've ever seen this place so busy."

"Normally I'd tell you not to bother her at work, but I know what you two did on my pool table, so I'm considering this payback. She's down at City Hall."

I feel the blush burn my cheeks, which is enough to make her chuckle. She flaps a hand in the air. "Don't worry about it. I was young once, too. Go get her."

"Thanks," I murmur awkwardly. I turn to leave the room, but then something occurs to me and I face her again. "Are you hiring bartenders?"

"I just need the occasional one that I can call when I know there are events in the city that will keep me busy. Tonight it's the margarita crawl that has this area teeming with drunk college kids." She straightens from her spot on the wall. "Why, you know someone?"

"Maybe," I answer thoughtfully, the wheels turning in my head. I give her another hard look. "Are you single?"

At that, she raises an eyebrow. "Are you hitting on me two minutes after I implied my girl is into you?"

I chuckle, liking this woman more and more. Knowing someone *else* would like her even more than I do. "Not me— someone just like me, but about twenty years older. He used to bartend when he was in college. Sometimes he says he misses the excitement of it."

She looks intrigued despite herself. After a moment, she nods. "Okay. Send him in. We'll see if he can keep up."

I grin, unable to help myself as I say, "I'm sure he's not too old to keep it up."

She lets out a bark of laughter at that, then turns to gently push me through the doors. "I can see why Dani likes you. Get out of here, kid. Your girl is waiting."

I spot Dani as soon as I step into the crowd gathered around City Hall. It's just like at the bar, where I subconsciously knew she wasn't there, except this time my gaze is immediately drawn to her. Something inside me just knows to look to the right of the spectators that are currently crowded around the podium where the mayor is standing.

And there she is. Camera up, so focused on the shot she's taking that the world could probably collapse around her and she wouldn't notice.

And yet, she pauses and drops the camera. Slowly, her eyes travel over the crowd until her eyes land on me, and pleasure lights up her eyes. She gives me a smile and holds up her finger with the universal signal of *give me a minute.*

I don't mind. I like watching her work.

And *fuck*, is she gorgeous doing it. Just as breathtaking as she was the first day I saw her. Only now, there's an air of seriousness about her as she does it, a sense of *this is what I'm meant to do.*

So I don't mind letting her finish getting the shots she wants. I don't even know how long I stand there, with my hands in my pockets and my gaze glued to the dark-haired siren slowly making her way around the space, teeth sunk into her bottom lip in concentration. I just know I could watch her do this all day.

These kinds of thoughts have been happening a lot more lately. For weeks it was enough to just have the best sex of my life, but then we spent more and more non-sex time together and we became friends. I got to talk to her, get to know her, make her laugh. Talk about her work and see her light up when she did. I got to know way more of Dani than I anticipated, and the more I knew, the more I *wanted* to know.

It's become a borderline addiction. Definitely an infatuation, as is evidenced by the fact that I'm content to stand in the cold February air and watch her work.

Eventually, she puts the camera back in the padded bag hanging off her shoulder and starts walking toward me. It vaguely registers that the mayor is still talking up on the podium, but my entire focus is zeroed in on Dani coming closer, her smile growing bigger with every step she takes toward me.

"Hi," she chirps. "What're you doing here? And how did you know where I was?"

"Your bar manager may or may not have outed you," I admit wryly. "And then she said it's payback for what we did on her pool table."

Dani lets out a loud laugh. "That bitch. She's fucked on that thing more than she has at her own apartment."

I wince at that news. "Noted. No more pool table sex."

Dani cocks an eyebrow. "No? You think you could hold out long enough to get me home instead?"

A cocky grin stretches across my face. I lean forward slowly and get close enough to her that my quietly spoken words brush air across her ear and make her shiver. "Not a chance. I'd just lift you into my arms and bounce you on my cock instead."

I can practically feel the shiver run through her. "You're evil," she hisses. "I still have to take some pictures of City Hall itself before I'm done today, and now I have to do it while I'm distracted by the promise of an orgasm later." Her eyes narrow at me. "That better be a promise of an orgasm later."

I let out a laugh. "I might be evil enough to send you back to work with drenched panties, but I'm not evil enough to deprive you of an eventual orgasm."

She seems satisfied with my answer because she nods and asks, "So then what are you doing here then? I'm assuming you texted and I didn't answer."

I shrug. "I know. But I also know you never eat when you're working—or even after you finish, since you get excited and go straight to editing—so I figured I'd bring you some food." I can't help smirking as I add, "And not even because I need you to have energy later. This is strictly the selfless act of a friend."

"Selfless, huh?" Dani says in a disbelieving tone. "Not because it takes all of my energy and concentration to not choke to death when your gigantic dick is in my mouth?"

I can only blink at that. "That… is not how I thought this conversation was going to go."

She lets out a happy laugh, the sound ringing through the air and making my heart squeeze.

I don't realize I'm just standing there in silence until she cocks an eyebrow and gestures with her hand. When I can only look at her in confusion, she says, "Well? What'd you bring me?"

That snaps me to attention. I bring my backpack around so I can unzip it and pull the cheesesteak out. Before I can even hand it to her, Dani's grabbing it and asking in a breathless voice, "You got me Dalessandro's?"

I can't help chuckling at her excitement. "I did. Had some time before I head to the gym. Whiz wit, right?"

Her eyes widen in surprise that I know how she likes her cheesesteaks.

I don't tell her I remember every detail she's ever shared with me about herself. That I eat it up like the starved fighter I am.

But she's not watching me to see that secret flit across my face. She's too busy opening the wrapping and taking a massive bite of the sandwich, letting out a huge moan when the flavor hits her tongue. A few people even turn around when they hear it, but, in true Philadelphian fashion, when they see the cheesesteak in her hand, understanding dawns on their faces and they turn back toward the mayor.

She goes to take another bite but pauses when she sees my rough swallow. Her eyes narrow in suspicion. "What? Don't tell me this is turning you on. I refuse to add cheesesteaks to our sex life. Most I'll allow is whipped cream. Or strawberries. *Oooh*, I've always wanted to try chocolate syrup, too."

I quirk an eyebrow at her rambling. "When was the last time you ate? You just had an orgasm over fruit. Who are you and what have you done with my Dani?"

And then suck in a breath at my slip.

But she obviously didn't hear me because she's too busy taking another big bite of the cheesesteak and waving me off with a hand. "It's always like this when I have to shoot. It helps me focus when I'm hungry, like the ache makes me a little sharper."

When she takes another bite, and when I once again swallow visibly, she frowns at me. "Seriously, what's wrong with you?"

I shuffle uncomfortably where I stand. "I, uh… I'm a little hungry," I admit. "The smell is kind of killing me."

"Oh my God!" she exclaims, quickly wrapping up the cheesesteak.

I stop her with a hand on hers. "No, don't. It's fine. I want you to eat."

She doesn't resume eating, but she does pause what she's doing and give me a skeptical look. "I totally forgot you're cutting weight now. Why did you even bring me one then?"

I put my hands back in the pockets of my joggers and shrug. "I knew it was your favorite and that you probably needed to eat," I answer simply.

For a moment, she only stares at me. Then she shakes her head and continues wrapping the sandwich. "You're such an idiot. Now I have to give you the blowjob of all blowjobs tonight to say thank you."

A grin slowly stretches across my face. "This selfless act is turning out better and better for me."

She pins me with a suspicious look. "It's meeting the

definition less and less, pretty boy." When my smile doesn't dim a single watt, she sighs and gently shoves my shoulder. "Get out of here. I'll see you later tonight."

The smile doesn't leave my face the entire walk to the gym.

I somehow manage to turn my focus back on when I walk into the gym an hour later. Maybe it's the look Tristan gives me the first time he spots me grinning at nothing in particular. Either way, I force all thoughts of Dani out of my head and throw myself into fight training.

I'm in the process of dying under Tristan's weight when suddenly there's a gasp from the doorway at the entrance to the gym. Tristan and I both stop our movements and look questioningly at the girl standing a few feet away from us, a shocked look on her face as she stares at us rolling around on the mat.

I feel Tristan's leader and businessman personality snap into place as he pushes off of me and stands up. "Hi, can I help you?" he asks her.

"Uh, I doubt it," she responds bluntly. Her eyes dart around the gym again before snapping down to the phone in her hand. "I'm looking for a dance studio, but clearly this is the wrong spot."

And now that she's mentioned it, I realize this girl looks like the definition of a ballerina. She's tiny, tinier even than Hailey, and everything about her screams *graceful*. Even the way she turns her head is effortless, like not a single motion of her body is unintentional. Plus, her dark hair is slicked back into that perfect bun that ballerinas always wear.

I don't miss the smug look Tristan sends Remy, or the exasperated eye roll he gets from his girlfriend in return.

"You're close to the right spot," Tristan tells the girl. "Unfortunately some websites still have the wrong address listed for the studio. It's in the building at the other end of the block."

She blinks at Tristan. "Oh. That's weird. Okay, thanks, I guess."

But she doesn't quite move to leave yet because Kane chooses that moment to walk into the mat room. He's shirtless and fresh off another Tristan-ordered burnout, which means he's drenched in sweat and breathing heavily. I know he's covered in tattoos but I always seem to forget *how* covered he is—and how fucking terrifying he looks when they're sweat-drenched and on display.

I don't blame the girl when her eyes go wide, because God knows if I was ninety pounds soaking wet and used to beauty and grace, Kane would scare the shit out of me, too.

Kane seems to notice her at the same time. His strides slow when he sees her, and he doesn't hide his perusal of her. But in typical Kane fashion, there is no room for any emotion besides anger on his face, which makes it impossible to tell what he's thinking. And which definitely makes him terrifying. I'm sure Tristan is about two seconds away from trying to save this tiny ballet dancer from Kane's hateful glare.

Except… she's not scared of him. Because she glares right back.

Her gaze hardens, her spine straightens, and she returns every bit of the energy that he's currently aiming at her.

It's enough to make Kane pause. His strides slow, and he gives the girl a second glance, as if he's trying to get a second read on her. But she's not giving anything up beyond the hard stare she's giving him, so after a moment, his gait becomes determined again. He walks toward the heavy bags on the other side of the room, tosses a dummy out onto the mat so he can straddle it, and begins raining punches down on the padded face.

The weird crackle of energy between them evaporates when Hailey walks out of the office and asks, "Did I hear someone asking about the dance studio?"

The girl's gaze snaps over to Hailey, as if she'd forgotten why she's even here. "Yeah, that's me. It had this as the address but that's obviously wrong."

Hailey smiles warmly at her. "Yeah, some websites still have the wrong one listed. I can walk you over there, though. I'm not taking class tonight, but I can at least show you around."

The girl raises an eyebrow. "You go there? *And* you do this?"

Hailey chuckles. "Nah, punching things isn't really my thing. I'm only here because my boyfriend and sister train here."

Right on cue, Jax exits the office to stand behind his girlfriend, wrapping an arm around her shoulders, forever unable to stand any distance between them.

"Hey," he greets with a big smile. "I'm Jax. I'm the boyfriend."

"And I'm Hailey," Hailey tacks on.

The girl stares at them both for a second before answering.

"Nice to meet you both. I'm Isabella."

It registers in the back of my mind that the gym has quieted, that the sound of fists against leather has stopped. But I'm too curious about this girl that's captured the entire gym's attention to really notice.

"That's such a pretty name," Hailey gushes. "And so perfect for a ballet dancer." She smiles knowingly. "That's your main dance style, right?"

Finally, Isabella cracks a smile. "I guess it's pretty obvious, huh?"

Hailey returns the smile. "It's okay, there are worse things to be obvious about. Come on, I'll walk you over to the studio."

Isabella takes another look around the gym before turning to follow Hailey outside. I watch as her eyes lock with Kane's again, both of them freezing in place when it happens.

I don't know what passes between them in that split-second glance, but it causes a shiver to run through Isabella before she turns to follow Hailey.

You could hear a pin drop in the gym once the door closes behind the girls. Even Jax is staring after them, looking equal parts confused about what just happened, happy that Hailey could help, and miserable that he can't follow her.

Tristan sees the look, too, and immediately rolls his eyes before calling, "Alright, boys and girls, rest time is over. Back to work."

In a split second, the gym fills with the sounds of heavy breathing and leather hitting leather.

"Well that was interesting," I mumble to Max as we square up to start another round. "Who knew anyone could even catch angry boy's attention?"

"I wasn't even aware he had attention to attract," Max returns.

We've only just shaken off the weird encounter and engaged for body control when I hear my name called again.

"Aiden, you've got company."

"Good lord, this place is like social city today," I comment, disengaging from Max. "This is the most rest I've ever had during a training session."

"Enjoy it while it lasts," Tristan says. "As soon as your dad leaves, I'm putting you through hell just to balance it out."

I turn toward the gym entrance in surprise. Sure enough, my dad is standing by the check-in desk.

"Dad? What're you doing here?"

He holds up the box in his hand. "I bought those gloves you wanted for padwork, so I wanted to bring them by since I was working in the area. Figured with the fight coming up you could use them."

I take the box from my dad in a daze. "You bought me Winning lace-up gloves?"

He only shrugs in answer.

And like a kid on Christmas morning, I tear into the box and pull out the gloves inside. "Holy shit, Dad," I breathe. "These are incredible." I think I hear a whistle of appreciation in the background.

"Damn, Mr. Reeves," Tristan comments, lifting one of the gloves from the box. "Any chance you want to adopt another kid? Because I would definitely be interested."

I chuckle, even though I know a part of Tristan is being

serious. Unfortunately, not every parent of fighters is as supportive of the sport as mine is.

"Dad, you didn't have to do this," I mumble. "The gloves I have work just fine."

He shrugs again, clearly uncomfortable with being the center of attention. Because he is—everyone that just watched the Isabella interaction is now staring at my dad.

"I figured with you going pro and all, you could use the quality gear," he says gruffly. "Just take it."

I look down at the gloves in awe. They're easily the most expensive ones on the market, and definitely the best. This is a huge gift. One that I know my father can't quite afford, but that he made work because he supports my choice of sport.

Swallowing roughly, I eventually choke out, "Thanks, Dad. These are amazing."

Not one for affection beyond a *thank you*, he merely nods his acceptance.

"Do you want to grab food later?" I blurt out. "I have to finish training, but I can meet you for an early dinner after if you have time."

He's shaking his head before I've even finished my sentence. "I'm working late on the site today and then I have to prep the new designs for the engineer tomorrow. So today doesn't work. But maybe this weekend?" He spares a glance at Tristan. "If you have time for a salad somewhere."

I let out a bark of laughter. "Sure, Dad, a salad sounds great. I'll call you."

He nods his approval, looking pleased with himself.

But then he winces and rubs a hand over his chest.

"Dad?" I ask. "You okay?"

"I'm fine," he says in an almost-wheeze. "Must be the Mexican I ate last night—my heartburn has been unbearable today. I swear I've eaten half a box of Tums already."

I can only shake my head in disbelief. "I will never understand why you keep trying to force your body to accept spicy foods. Just admit it, Mexican food doesn't sit well with you."

He straightens with a determined look. "You shut your mouth. I was *born* to eat enchiladas."

Laughter erupts from all around me. It lightens the mood instantly, and I clap a hand to my dad's shoulder.

"Go back to work, Dad. I'll call you this weekend for some food. And for the love of God, stay away from Mexican food."

"I make no promises," he huffs. But there's a pleased smile pulling at the corner of his lips, and I know he's happy with the way his gift was received.

"Alright, let's break those gloves in, shall we?" Tristan interjects. He nods at the bag room at the other end of the gym. "Burnouts on the bag. Ten rounds."

At the same time that I groan, my dad lets out a chuckle. "I guess that's my cue. Enjoy the gloves." He claps Tristan on the shoulder as he passes him on the way out the door. "Put him through hell, kid."

An excited—and slightly insane-looking—grin stretches across Tristan's face.

"Yes, sir."

CHAPTER 13
Dani

I'M EMAILING MY agent to accept a new job when my phone buzzes with a text message.

DRUNK WEDDING MISTAKE GUY

Hey stranger :)

DRUNK WEDDING MISTAKE GUY

What're you doing tonight?

DRUNK WEDDING MISTAKE GUY

Wanna come out with me? I promise I'll show you a good time ;)

Scoffing, I slide my phone across the table. Yeah, that's never happening again. I turn back to my computer and hit *Send*.

Another buzz.

I almost don't look at it again, but I haven't heard from a certain someone in over a week and I'm slightly, *definitely* hoping that it's him. Even as I hate myself for wishing for something like that at all.

We're not getting attached. We just enjoy his humor. And his company. And his dick.

Even though there was a super weird, super heavy moment last time that made me wonder if this is getting too serious for Aiden.

I fight the urge to check my phone, but it only lasts for a moment before I'm muttering a curse and sliding it back.

Sure enough…

AIDEN

What do you call a line of men waiting to get haircuts?

DANI

What?

AIDEN

A barberqueue

I can't help it: I laugh. Loudly. It even takes me a minute to compose myself enough to type out a response.

DANI

That was one of the worst jokes I've ever heard

DANI

And that's saying something because my dad is the king of dad jokes

For a moment, I see the bubbles that he's typing. But nothing comes through, and then the bubbles disappear, and I realize that's the first time I've ever implied Aiden and my dad might share some similarities. That they might get along.

I'm chewing nervously on my lip when the bubbles appear again. *Fuck, is he going to make a comment about meeting him? That's the opposite of casual. Fuck.*

Thankfully, that's not the response that comes through.

AIDEN

> He sounds like a delightfully smart man

AIDEN

> But now that I have your undivided attention, I'd like to ask you to crash a party with me

DANI

> A party? What kind of party?

AIDEN

> A networking party full of the most boring business people you've ever met in your life. Please save me from the torment.

DANI

> So I would be crashing, but you're actually supposed to attend

AIDEN

> Unfortunately. It was "highly recommended" by my senior seminar professor. You're the only one that would make it bearable.

Chewing on my lip again, I think over what this might mean to Aiden. It's definitely not a *date*, but it's closer to one than we've ever been. So far, I've stayed away from anything formal with Aiden—basically, anything that's more than a beer at a sports bar. A networking event where formal attire is required would definitely be far past anything I've allowed so far.

But... Aiden is fun to hang out with. He's the only one I know that might make an event like this fun, and I like the idea of *how* he might make it fun.

I'm imagining all the different ways he might do that when my phone buzzes again.

AIDEN

I know it might seem like a date, but I promise it's not. It'll be fun. And if we find a secluded hallway somewhere, I'll even fuck you in your dress.

AIDEN

...God, now I'm thinking about what you look like in a cocktail dress. Please wear a dress with nothing under it.

DANI

Down, boy. No one tells me what to wear.

AIDEN

I did not. If you'll notice, I asked nicely and said please.

I let out a heavy sigh, my head dropping back as I mull it over in my head. And it only takes a moment to make the decision.

DANI

Fine. I'm in. When and where?

AIDEN

I suppose you don't want me to pick you up?

DANI

Nope. When and where?

AIDEN

Saturday at 8pm. Loews Philadelphia Hotel, next to the convention center.

DANI

Perfect, I come back from DC the day before. And I'll need a little entertainment to get over the trip.

DANI

I'll meet you there.

DANI

Now go away so I can get some work done.

AIDEN

Yes ma'am. Text me if anything comes up.

I'm shaking my head again as I slide my phone across the table, but this time there's a small smile on my face that I can't for the life of me get rid of.

As the Uber pulls up to the building, I bunch my dress in my left hand and step out of the car, making sure to keep my heels under me so I don't face plant. It's no secret I prefer Converse and combat boots, but a girl has to know how to wear heels, too. I can look presentable when I need to.

A fact that is immediately confirmed when Aiden walks out of the building.

"Holy fuck," he breathes from the top of the stairs. He's dressed in a dark blue suit and a crisp white button-up, looking stunningly good-looking with his dirty blonde locks styled and his hands casually resting in his pockets. I'm momentarily distracted by just how good he looks like this.

Except, when I finish my shameless once-over and track my gaze back to his face, I realize his eyes are wide and his mouth has dropped open. Because I'm not the only one shamelessly checking the other out.

"Damn, pretty boy, you clean up nice," I say with a quirked eyebrow and an appreciative look. "Looks like that name is well-deserved."

"Me?" he chokes out, then starts down the stairs toward me. "I'm not the one that's about to turn this event on its head when we walk through those doors."

I let a cocky smile slide across my face. Then I'm dropping the dress that's still bunched in my hand and spinning in a circle to show off the full effect.

If I was going to do this, I was going to do this right. And while I could have chosen a pantsuit to play with Aiden's emotions, I decided to go all out instead.

The dress I chose is a full-length, gold, silk dress with a

slit up the right leg. It's somewhat conservative—with the slit being at an appropriate height and the top only showing off a hint of décolletage—but it fits me so well that every curve is accentuated by the light color and skintight fit. It's conservative but also… not.

Combined with my full sleeve on display and my eyes painted with smokey makeup, I'm basically a walking contradiction in this environment.

"*God*, you're so fucking hot," I hear Aiden breathe when I complete my twirl. His hands are no longer in his pockets, but squeezing into fists at his side. He looks like he just wants to grab me and throw me over his shoulder.

I take a small step closer to him, until we're practically chest to chest and I can tease in a whisper, "And I'm not wearing any underwear, as requested." I pull back enough to catch the shocked—and pained—look on his face.

"You're going to be the death of me, woman," he groans, dragging his hand down his face. Then he's holding his arm out for me to weave mine through and saying, "Let's get this over with so I can get you home and into my bed as quickly as humanly possible."

I tuck my arm through his with a smile. "Yes, sir," I purr.

To be met with another groan and an agitated tug as he steps forward.

We mingle for the first twenty minutes. Aiden grabs two flutes of champagne for us when we walk in, and we both quietly sip on them as we walk around to see the exhibits. I have a feeling Aiden is trying to give me the real feel of this event before we do anything else.

"So this is what your world looks like," I comment, taking another sip of my champagne as my eyes travel around the now-overfull room. "It's not that bad. How many people should you be talking to tonight?"

He shrugs before throwing back the last of his drink. "There's no right or wrong answer. I get out of it what I put into it, but since my internship offered me a paid position at the end of my semester, this is just bonus networking."

My gaze jerks to him in surprise. "They offered you the job? You didn't tell me that!"

He shrugs again, this time looking slightly bashful as his cheeks pinken. "Didn't know if you were interested in that kind of information."

And I think I'm offended by that, a fact I reinforce when I give him a decidedly unladylike shove.

It only makes him grin.

"I want to tell you congratulations, but now I also kind of want to give you the cold shoulder," I grumble.

And yet, a moment later...

"Congratulations, Aiden." The soft-spoken words flow unbidden and honest between us.

"Thanks, Dani," he responds, equally quiet, but pleased smile firmly in place. A matching one creeps onto my face, as well.

His gaze moves over me for the thirteenth time tonight as he finally says, "I was going to introduce you to some people, but now I think I want to keep you all to myself."

I can't stop myself from grinning at his possessive side, or from taking pity on him and patting his chest in understanding.

"Let's compromise," I suggest. "Why don't you tell me about the people you know in this room instead."

And when his eyes begin to twinkle with mischief, I'm immediately reminded that *this* version of Aiden was the reason I came tonight.

"I've got a better idea," he says in that quiet, deep voice of his. "Why don't we make up our own theories about the people in this room?"

"Oh," I breathe. "I like that idea way more." My gaze moves around the room, looking for the best targets. I gesture in front of us and ask, "Would you like to do the honors? Since it was your idea."

Taking a deep breath, he looks around the room, his furrowed brow and over exaggerated look of concentration making me have to swallow a laugh.

"Okay, I'm going to have to pick someone I don't know so I'm not going into this game with an unfair advantage. A lot of them are classmates and professors." He shoots me a playful wink. "Some of these people's real lives are a Spanish soap opera you wouldn't believe."

At that, I really do let out a laugh.

He looks delighted, as he always does, at the sound. It even takes him a moment to turn back to the crowd, and another few seconds to decide on his target.

"Okay, how about that guy?" He sneakily gestures at a lanky young man who's currently trying to force his way into a circle of middle-aged businessmen that are clearly here representing a company. None of them are giving him even the time of day.

"Alright, I got him," I say. "Make it good, pretty boy. If

you tell me he looks like a nerd who would rather be home playing video games, I'm going to be extremely disappointed in you."

Aiden lets out a mock-gasp of outrage. "How dare you underestimate me. I'm the king of this game."

I gesture at him to go ahead, swallowing another laugh. "Fire away, then."

He clears his throat and straightens, as if he's about to give a monologue. "Alright then. His name is Art, and he's a business student at Temple. But he's only studying business because his father forced him to. It was the only 'acceptable' and 'honorable' career."

I roll my eyes. "Too easy. Anyone could tell that."

"Please don't interrupt me, Miss Monroe, I wasn't finished with my analysis." He turns his attention back to Art. "He's forced to be here, and forced to make an effort, because someone in this room has some kind of relationship with his father and will be reporting back to him. But in reality..." Aiden pauses for dramatic effect, his eyes sliding to me. "...he'd much rather be home with his cat and his homemade pottery set."

"Pottery? Like in the movie *Ghost*?"

"No, more like the overexcited kid at the art store—get it? He loves that his name matches his favorite place—he has zero artistic talent, but for some reason gets a lot of enjoyment out of arts and crafts." He pauses, almost thoughtfully. "Also, it allows him to finger something because he's still a virgin and that's the closest he can get to the real deal."

I laugh so hard, I'm pretty sure champagne comes out of my nose.

"Okay, I see why you're the king of this game," I eventually choke out.

"Thank you," he says, bowing at the waist. Then he looks around the room as he says, "Alright, your turn. Make your pick."

My chuckles fade as I look around the room, trying to decide on someone equally interesting. It takes me a minute, but eventually I find my target.

"Her," I say, aiming a subtle nod at the woman walking into the room. She's beautiful, middle-aged, and walking around like she owns the place.

Aiden's lip twitches briefly. "Alright, go ahead. What's her story?"

"Well, she's here as one of the 'contacts' that the business students should be meeting. She represents a successful company, but she hasn't quite reached the level of success that she's vying for. It's why she's here. Even though she's representing a company already, this event is also an opportunity for *her* to network. Because she's still looking for that last little boost." I cock my head thoughtfully. "And yet, she thrives on being the alpha. And it bothers her that she's not yet in that position in her career. So she finds it elsewhere."

"I'm dying to hear," Aiden murmurs.

"She's married, and yet... she picks up young men at these events. It's why you'll see her at every one of these. She's a cougar."

"So she's a cheating cougar?"

"That's where the fun part comes in," I say with a grin. "She's not cheating. She brings the young guys home and makes her husband watch." I turn toward Aiden, mischief sparking in my eyes. "Her husband is a cuckhold. *That's* where she gets her power from."

After a mesmerizing moment where I can tell he's only a breath away from losing control, he barks a laugh, popping the lid off the sound and letting out the raucous laughter that he's clearly been holding back.

"I think I might have some competition in this game," he says when he finally gets himself under control.

"Thank you," I respond, mimicking his bow from earlier.

"It's too bad you're way off base," he says, a final chuckle slipping out. "In reality, she's the youngest professor at the school and *also* the most successful. She's started and sold technology companies for millions of dollars—teaching is just her way of taking a break and giving back. And her husband? The most alpha guy you'll ever meet, which becomes apparent if anyone even looks at his wife the wrong way. They're blissfully married with three kids." His gaze shifts to me, his eyes twinkling. "No cuckholding involved."

When I groan and drop my face into my hands, Aiden erupts into laughter all over again.

"It was a valiant effort," he says, patting my shoulder.

"Don't make me go over to Art and ask how much of *your* theory is real," I bite back.

"Be my guest. I guarantee you I got closer than you did."

But despite the fact that I really am two seconds away from approaching Art, we never get the chance, because two older men choose that moment to step in front of us.

They're looking at Aiden, but they're trying—and failing—

to hide their sidelong glances at me.

"Aiden, so glad you could make it," one of them says as he reaches to shake Aiden's hand. He's the older of the two by a lot, likely in his seventies, and he's definitely got the whole professor vibe going on. His hair is grey, his jacket has elbow pads, and he looks like he's been teaching since the dawn of time.

He's also looking at me with that gaze that old people think they can get away with because it should be adorable but in reality is very creepy and unsettling.

"And who is this?" he asks, gleefully turning his attention toward me. "I didn't know you were going to bring a guest. Especially one that is so exceptionally stunning." He reaches for my hand without waiting for my reaction, and brings it to his lips so he can press a dry kiss to the back of it. "What's your name, sweetheart?"

Just the fact that he touched me within ten seconds of seeing me makes me have to stop myself from cringing. But instead, I step into the role he wants me to play and decide to beat him at his own game.

"My name's Danielle," I say with a warm smile, subtly shaking my head at a frowning Aiden beside me—who looks two seconds away from stepping in.

"That's a beautiful name," Old Professor says, still not letting go of my hand. He shoots Aiden a quizzical look before asking, "And are you… Mrs. Reeves? Or may I steal you away from Aiden for a moment?"

At that, I pull my hand away from him and instead weave it through Aiden's arm, dropping my head onto his shoulder with a happy sigh. "Nope, not married, I'm just his girlfriend. But that's still probably not appropriate." When I feel Aiden stiffen against me, I quickly add, "I left my husband at home tonight," and exhale a relieved breath when I hear him cover a laugh with a cough.

Now, Old Professor looks *really* confused. He glances between Aiden and I, opening his mouth like he's about to say something, then snapping it shut when nothing comes out. I almost laugh at the shock on his face.

"What kind of a man lets his wife go out with another man?"

Everyone's attention snaps to the other guy standing behind the professor, a much younger man who looks more like a sleazy sales guy than a college professor. He's got that business daddy look going on, with perfectly styled hair and an obnoxiously nice, custom suit, and he looks like the kind of guy that is used to getting what he wants.

My favorite kind of guy to shut down.

"The kind of guy that's secure in his masculinity," I answer with a charming smile, my hand starting to stroke Aiden's arm in a comforting pattern.

His gaze morphs from sleazy to aggressive in an instant. Enough so that I feel Aiden shift automatically into a fighter's stance.

"David, maybe we should—" Old Professor tries to cut in, clearly uncomfortable at this point.

David ignores him entirely when he lets out a bark of condescending laughter. "Trust me, that's not why he's doing it. He probably can't satisfy you himself, so he sends you off to let some other guy try it. Although, I'm not sure how much luck you'd have with this kid, either." He looks down the length of my body, leering so openly that the hair on the back of my neck stands up. "How about trying out a *real* man?"

And the moment he insults Aiden is the moment that the game dies and true anger flames in my veins.

I let an insane, mocking smile slide across my face. I don't respond for a moment, I just let him sit with the silence and watch as uncertainty and discomfort start to take the place of arrogance on his expression.

Eventually, my voice is sickly sweet as I tell him, "Sweetheart, you look like you would tap out before I even finished taking my clothes off. I'd eat you alive."

His expression becomes instantly enraged.

Before he can respond with some kind of stereotypical *yeah, well you're not that hot, bitch*, and before Aiden steps in to fight the guy, I let my mask drop and give Sleazy Salesman a disgusted once-over.

"Don't ever insult my date again."

In that moment, Old Professor finally decides to step in and tug his buddy away, his discomfort obvious on his face. He's not embarrassed about *his* behavior, he's embarrassed about his friend's. Which just riles me up all over again.

But when I turn to face Aiden again, to apologize for how that just escalated, he doesn't look at all angry. He looks... amused.

I pluck another glass of champagne from a passing waiter, somehow knowing that Aiden is done at one. I take a cooling sip before saying, "I feel like I should apologize just in case that was a contact you needed to make, but then I remember you invited me for this reason and had to know what that meant."

He chuckles as he puts his hands in his pockets, and the sight of him so comfortable, so *happy,* immediately knocks any other guy out of my brain. There's only this one in front of me.

"Are you kidding me? That guy was my TA freshman year and I wanted to punch him in the face every day I sat in his class. You just did what we've all wanted to do for years. I can't *wait* to tell my other friends that had him how he just got turned down and destroyed by a woman."

For the second time tonight, I execute a mocking bow. "Glad I could help."

Aiden watches me down the rest of the champagne, then plucks the flute from my hand and passes it to a nearby waiter. "Alright, I think I've had about enough of tonight. Feel like grabbing some food?"

"*God*, yes, please," I groan. "I'm starving. Where are we going?"

"There's a diner around the corner that we always eat at. Best waffles in the entire city."

I pick up my dress with one hand. "Waffles? Say no more."

CHAPTER 14
Dani

TEN MINUTES LATER, we're sitting in a booth, both of us decked out in formalwear and not giving a fuck about how out of place we look. Others in the diner look drunk, or tired enough to be coming off the night shift, but we're the only ones that are clearly out of place in the crowd.

"Are you a pancakes or waffles kind of girl?" Aiden asks, not even looking up at me from where he's hunched over his menu.

I can't help marveling over the sight of him in a suit again. He's taken his jacket off, so he's left in only a white button-up shirt that he's rolled up to the elbows.

It's easily the hottest he's ever looked.

"Waffles," I answer easily. "And that's even if you hadn't introduced this place as having the best waffles."

"I'm more of a French Toast person myself," Aiden admits, looking lost in the menu options.

I can only gawk at him for a moment. "You did not just pick French Toast over waffles."

He finally looks up from the menu with a raised eyebrow.

"You got something against French Toast, Dani?"

"Not unless it's keeping me from a good waffle."

He lets out an exaggerated sigh as he looks up at the ceiling. "It's things like this that make me wonder how we got as far as we did in this friendship." He waves the tired waitress down to quickly order for us: French Toast for him and a strawberry waffle for me.

"I thought you couldn't eat carbs during fight camp," I ask, handing the menus back to the waitress.

"I got eggs on the side and I'll only eat a few bites. Don't you dare snitch on me to Coach." He pauses to glare at me. "Or Tristan."

I hide my smile in my coffee. "I wouldn't dream of it."

"You think this is bad, just wait until fight week," he grumbles.

My brow furrows in confusion. "What happens during fight week?"

"I turn to food porn."

For a moment, I can only blink at him in answer. "I think I'm scared to ask what that means in a fighter's world."

"It means my entire social media page becomes filled with restaurant and cooking accounts. Donuts, pizza, cheesesteaks, you name the carb, I salivate over it. When it gets *really* bad, the algorithm even makes it to Taco Bell ads."

I'm now as confused as ever. "But you hate fast food *and* Mexican food."

He lets out a lofty sigh. "I know. That's how bad it gets."

I try to tamp down on my laugh and fail miserably. But Aiden seems pleased by the sound, a smile lifting his lips at my reaction.

The waitress chooses that moment to appear with our food. She slides the plates in front of us, too tired to even ask which of us gets which one. I end up with the plate of French Toast in front of me, a smaller side of scrambled eggs slid to the side. Aiden gets the waffles placed in front of him.

I go to switch everything but before I get a chance, Aiden is sliding into the booth next to me. I let out a grunt of annoyance at the crowding but when he drapes an arm along the top of the booth behind me and gently hip-checks me with a playful smile, I'm suddenly not as irritated. And when he excitedly digs his fork into my waffle, every emotion is replaced with fondness.

"Still think French Toast is better?" I ask, amusement ringing in my tone.

His expression is thoughtful, even as he chews the bite. Then he lifts some of the strawberry topping to my lips, leaning in to take the piece of fruit from me before I can swallow it.

My eyes automatically flutter closed at the feeling of Aiden's lips against mine. He sucks the fruit into his mouth, but before he pulls away I feel his tongue swipe across my bottom lip, gathering the last of the juice. It's enough to make me whimper and press forward for more, even though he's already straightening with a grin.

"I may have just been converted," he says.

"Asshole," I grumble, forcing myself to lean back in my seat.

The sound of his laugh is one I'll never get tired of.

Aiden quickly swaps our plates. I dive into my waffles,

trying to ignore the sudden fluttering in my stomach. I tell myself it's because I drank on an empty stomach, and not because the boy sitting next to me is giving me the most fun night of my life—a night made up of a stuffy networking event and diner food.

I stuff bite after bite in my mouth, the silence between us a comfortable one. I shoot hesitant glances at Aiden as he hums happily and eats more and more egg off his plate.

"Good?" I find myself asking after a few minutes.

He nods and turns to me with the brightest smile I've ever seen. And the sight of it is enough to remind me just how pure Aiden really is—how pleased he is with the simple things in life, nothing complicated about it. Just give him some good food and a partner he can have fun with and he's the happiest person in the room.

It's enough to make my heart ache for more of him. To want to be closer to him.

Because of that, I find myself sliding my leg over his, pulling us even tighter together than we already are. I feel his curious glance, but I'm already distracted and digging into my waffle for another bite. I stab into a piece with my fork and lift it to his lips. When he cocks his eyebrow and gives me a curious look, I whisper, "I won't tell your coach, I promise."

That seems to placate him because he leans forward and slowly tugs the bite off of my fork with his teeth, his eyes never leaving mine.

"Delicious," he murmurs.

And at the sound of that word leaving his lips, at the look in his eyes, it feels like the most natural thing in the world to lean in and press my lips to his. He lets out a quiet hum and kisses me back, his mouth laying a claim to my own in a way that only Aiden could do. In a way that makes me sigh happily and throw myself further into the kiss.

Eventually, he pulls away, looking like he's forcing himself to do so. He presses a quick peck, then another, to my lips before he's able to fully straighten in his seat. But even then, his face is only inches from mine.

"Finish your waffle so I can take you home," he murmurs.

"What about your French Toast?"

His pupils darken as lust flares in his gaze. "I'm suddenly much more interested in a different kind of dessert," he says in that deep voice, his eyes trained on my lips.

A shiver runs through me and I do nothing to hide it. I let him see how much he turns me on, how close I feel to him after tonight.

It doesn't even occur to me that not going out to restaurants was one of my first rules for Aiden. It's been the easiest way to distance myself from guys I've been with in the past, since dinner dates were the most obvious way to expedite a relationship. But whether it's not the same thing tonight or because I *want* to further my relationship with Aiden, something has me fully embracing this date and reveling in the pleasure of it.

Aiden must also realize the severity of the situation because he doesn't make a joke or ask if I want to split the bill. He just throws his card down and pays the waitress without a single glance at me.

"Let's get out of here," he murmurs, then takes my hand and pulls me from the booth.

I follow him without any comment, letting him tug me through the diner and out the front door. And when we get out onto the sidewalk, I find myself stepping closer to him, and weaving my way under his arm so he has to throw it around my shoulders. Which he does without question. Actually, he does it with a pleased smile on his face.

And whether it's the culmination of tonight or the warmth I enjoy pulling from him, I bite down on my lip to smother my smile and curl in tighter to his body.

Unfortunately, the second we turn the corner toward Broad Street, all of the warm feelings in me immediately evaporate.

"Dani?"

When I come face to face with my ex-boyfriend, everything in me freezes. My spine straightens where I stand and I automatically take a step away from Aiden, putting as much distance between us as I can.

"Matt," I say in a breathless voice. "What are you doing here?"

He glances at the diner we just left. "Late night at the office, I was just—"

"No, I mean what are you doing *here*," I correct bluntly. "In Philly."

He gives me a startled look, blinking in confusion. "I moved back here six months ago. After I graduated."

"Oh," is all I manage to say. "Okay."

"Um, how are you doing?" he asks me in return.

"Good," I answer stiffly. Awkwardly.

"Where are you working nowadays?"

And it's that question that throws me back into a memory

I've tried so hard to forget, the one that started me on my road to being forever single and that made me never want to get close to anyone, even friends, ever again.

But instead of shrinking away from the memory—of raised voices, of my ripped-up acceptance letter to a prestigious photography program, of his subsequent and pitying *it's not you, it's me* breakup speech—I straighten my spine and look him directly in the eye.

"I'm a photojournalist," I tell him proudly.

And it's there, in the barely-perceptible flash of disappointment, that I see he still thinks of me the same way he did on the night of our high school graduation. That I should've gone to college for a real degree, and not pursued my hobby as if it was a sustainable career.

Not for the thousandth time, I regret passing on the program that eighteen-year-old Dani was accepted to. And I hate her a little bit for even *thinking* about following Matt to his out-of-state college like an obedient little puppy.

Thank God he broke up with me.

"That's amazing, Dani," he says, the lie freezing his lips into a tight line.

"Yeah," I say quietly, never looking away from him. "It is."

I snap back to reality when I feel Aiden looking between Matt and I. There's a frown on his face as he studies the interaction, as he tries to read between the lines of our reactions to each other. But something about it tells him not to insert himself into the conversation.

After a few tense seconds, Matt aims an awkward glance at Aiden, then down to the space between us that wasn't there a minute ago. He swallows roughly then mumbles, "Well… it was good to see you. Have a good night."

He pushes past us on the street, and in a flash, Aiden and I are alone again.

For a moment, I can only stand frozen on the sidewalk.

"I'm going to assume that was the ex that turned you off of relationships," Aiden says. And when I hear how stiff his tone is, I turn to him in surprise.

Sure enough, his mouth is a tight line on his face. I don't think I've ever seen a version of Aiden that wasn't smiling—or at least playfully unhappy—so this one throws me off a bit.

"Yes," I say slowly. "We dated in high school."

"So, years ago," he confirms. His studies me for a moment, seeming to weigh his next words. "Do you still love him?"

"What?" I ask in surprise. "Of course not. We were kids when we broke up."

His stare remains thoughtful, though controlled. I have no idea what he's thinking.

I don't like it. I want the Aiden back from ten minutes ago, the one that I was wrapped around and joking with in the diner.

Stepping closer to him, I offer a shaky smile and reach for his hand that I was holding not long ago.

And I'm shocked when Aiden takes a step back and pulls his hand away from mine.

"So then why was him seeing us holding hands so disgusting for you?" he asks, and now, I can definitely hear the tone.

"That's not what—" I sputter.

"Is it really that bad being seen with me?"

I grimace and look away. "You know it's not you. I just don't need that in my life."

"Yeah, that would be the *worst*," he says, his words coming out with a slight bite.

My head whips to face him. "Come on, Aiden, that's not fair. I've never been anything but honest with you about how I feel." Swallowing roughly, I force myself to take a step back, sensing I need to back up my words with some distance. I've already broken two of my rules tonight—first with a dinner date and then with being way too affectionate with him—so the last thing I need is to give Aiden more mixed signals. "I'm sorry I hurt you when I pulled away just now. That wasn't a reflection on you. But I shouldn't have been holding your hand in the first place. We're friends, and that's a line I shouldn't have crossed—"

His gaze flares with anger at those words. So I decide to try a different tactic.

Lowering my eyelashes and plastering a sensual smile on my face, I give him a look that clearly reads like sex. "Why don't you take me home and we can forget all about this? I believe I was promised a different kind of dessert."

He lets out a harsh bark of laughter, the sound ringing with anger and disbelief. "Right, because I'm good enough to fuck. But God forbid there be any affection in between rounds of it."

My eyes widen with shock. "No, that's not—"

"You know what, Dani, I don't think I feel like being the hired dick for tonight. I'm going home. Maybe you can find another guy to ride." He then turns to wave down a taxi coming down the street. When it pulls up in front of him, he opens the door and steps back, his posture rigid as he stuffs his hands in his pockets.

And when he finds me still standing there, frozen with my mouth agape, he waves a mocking hand at the car.

"Good night, Dani."

His words, and the tone they're spoken in, are enough to snap me out of my frozen state. I'm too stunned and hurt by his cold dismissal to recognize the hurt in *his* voice, which makes a bite appear in my own.

"You know what? You're right. We should definitely call it a night, you're being an ass. Call me when the Aiden I like makes an appearance again."

I'm too busy gathering my dress in my hands to notice my own blurted confession. And if I wasn't already sliding across the back seat, I may have seen the look of surprise—followed by a flash of regret—on his face before I slammed the car door behind me.

CHAPTER 15
Aiden

DANI

Hey

AIDEN

Hey

DANI

You busy?

AIDEN

No, just cleaning my apartment

DANI

Can I come over?

AIDEN

Sure

DANI

I'm sorry about last night. I didn't react very well.

AIDEN

It's ok. I shouldn't hold ex run-ins against anyone.

AIDEN

I'm sorry too. I didn't react very well either.

DANI

Truce?

AIDEN

Truce. Come over.

Two hours later, I'm stress-cleaning my kitchen for the third time today, needing something to do with my hands while I wait for Dani. I'm seriously hoping I didn't fuck everything up last night, and that I'll somehow be able to convince her that I was just hurt and reacting without thinking—that I wasn't pushing for more. That I don't *want* more.

Even though I can't figure out if that's the truth or not. Because as much as I don't want to let a woman into my life or give her any power over me, there's still a part of me that's wondering what it would be like with her. If Dani would be worth taking a chance on.

If taking that chance would be harder than dealing with this new idea of being without her.

My stomach drops at the thought, but thankfully a knock sounds on the front door before I can dwell too much on it.

I open it and find a smiling Dani. And even though the smile is slightly more tentative than every other one I've seen on her face, a breath still stutters out of me at the sight.

Fuck, I'm so gone for her.

"Hey," I greet in as normal a voice as I can muster.

"Hey," she responds in a relieved breath.

I gesture inside the apartment. "Come in."

Her smile grows in comfort at that, and she steps past me into the entryway. But the moment she gets close to the kitchen, her eyes widen and her nostrils flare.

"What is that smell?" she asks.

Rubbing the back of my neck, I admit, "Uh… I was kind of going to apologize with a Santucci's tomato pie. I had actually called it in right before you texted me."

And then I watch as surprise, awe, and finally a full-blown smile blooms across her face.

"You did not," she says on a breath.

I close the door with a relieved chuckle. "Would I lie about Santucci's?"

"I really hope not," she says, grabbing a paper plate from beside the pizza box. She pulls a square out with a pleased hum and immediately takes a massive bite. Her eyes close on a groan.

"Note to self: Santucci's gives you an orgasm."

Her eyes open at that and she watches me for a moment as she chews.

"You give better orgasms," she says bluntly. When I let out a bark of surprised laughter, she quirks an eyebrow, a smile twitching at the corner of her lips. "What?"

I only shake my head and reach into the fridge for a bottle of water. "Nothing."

She glances at the water and then down to her plate. "I feel guilty eating when you can't eat. You really didn't have to do this."

I merely shrug and tell her, "I'm fairly certain good food is your love language, so I figured it was the best way to apologize."

Fuck. Her eyes go wide at the L-word, and I instantly panic that I ruined this all over again.

"I-I didn't—I just know you like good food. That's all I meant. I was still wrong about last night, I shouldn't have gotten angry at you after what happened. I ruined our night and I never—"

"Aiden," she cuts me off. "It's okay, I promise. I appreciate the gesture, really. You've gotten me food plenty of times before; this doesn't have to be a big deal." She puts her slice back on her plate, then takes a second to wipe her face with a napkin so she can give me her undivided attention. "You were right to be upset last night. And I'm sorry I hurt you with what I did—I never should have reacted that way. *I'm* the one that ruined the night."

She swallows and glances away, and suddenly the look of nervousness appears on her face again.

"But this won't work if you want more, Aiden," she says quietly. Her gaze shifts back to mine, and it's tired—almost sad. "I like hanging out with you. A lot. You make me laugh, and you're fun, and exciting, and you fuck like a dream. I *love* hanging out with you. But I still can't do a relationship. I won't. So if this is becoming more than just sex and fun for you… we need to cut it off before one of us gets hurt."

I swallow nervously, hoping she doesn't notice it as my tell. My answer is rushed—desperate to convince her. "It's not," I blurt out. "I promise. I just… I reacted the wrong way. That's all. I want things to stay as they are."

The words taste like acid the second they touch my tongue. I know as soon as I say them that I'm lying—though there's nothing I can do to take them back. If I do, I have no doubt Dani will walk out that door and never return my calls again.

I pause, letting her study me for a moment. Hoping she can't see the lie on my face. Hoping she'll let me sweep this under the rug and go back to how things were before last night.

"You're sure?" she asks hesitantly.

I nod quickly. "I'm sure." I'm hurrying to convince her, so I try to settle back into my cocky, joking self. "If you'd like me to convince you that this is just sex, I could prove it to you in the bedroom."

The tension leaves her shoulders at that. She huffs out a quiet laugh as she picks her food back up. "Three orgasms and you're forgiven," she says.

I let out a relieved breath that we're back on even ground. Maybe not where I want to be, but at least she's still here. With me.

"Any preferences on my methods?" I ask with a grin, reaching for my water again. "Maybe I'll be generous enough to take requests."

She quirks an eyebrow, a delighted expression on her face. "Oh yeah? You'll be *generous* enough to—"

Her words are cut off when a distinct ringtone sounds from the other end of the counter. Frowning, I reach for my phone.

"It's my dad," I tell Dani. "Sorry, I always try to answer his calls." I swipe the green button on my screen. "Hey, Dad, what's up? I thought I was going to see you tomorrow—"

"Is this Aiden Reeves?" a sharp voice interrupts in my ear.

I frown. "It is, who is this? Why do you have my dad's phone?"

"I'm sorry to inform you, Mr. Reeves, but your father's had a heart attack. He's currently at Jefferson Hospital receiving care. You're listed in his phone and on his insurance as his emergency contact so we wanted to give you a call to inform you. Is there anyone else he would want us to call?"

In an instant, all the blood drains from my head and my mouth goes dry. *A heart attack? How? When? He's the healthiest 50-year-old I know, how could—*

"Mr. Reeves? Is there anyone else you'd like us to call?"

"N-no, there's no one else," I stammer, feeling frozen. "I mean, it's just us. It's always been just us." Somehow, a little bit of clarity seeps into my brain. "Wait, you said he's receiving treatment? So he's okay?"

"It would be better if you came into the hospital to discuss with his doctor. We can explain everything then."

"And I can see him?" I ask in a desperate rush.

"Yes. Although he might be resting when you get here. The attack hit him pretty hard."

That's the sentence that drops my stomach through the fucking floor.

"Okay, I'll be right there," I murmur in a daze. "Thank you for calling."

I press *end* on the call and put my phone down. For a

moment, I can only stare at the counter in front of me. I can't wrap my head around anything right now, how did this even…?

A quiet voice sounds from beside me. "Aiden? Is everything okay?" I feel a gentle touch on my arm. "What's wrong?"

I turn to see Dani standing beside me with a worried look on her face.

"It's my dad," I say in a monotone voice. "He had a heart attack."

She sucks in a startled breath. "What? When? Is he okay?"

Swallowing roughly, I nod in answer. "Yeah," I croak out. "He's at Jefferson."

"We have to go then," she says immediately, tugging on my arm. "Come on, I'll call the Uber."

Something about that strikes me as odd. With a frown, I ask her, "You're coming with me?"

"Of course I'm coming with you," she says in a rush. "I'm not letting you go by yourself. Come on, we should go."

The next twenty minutes are a blur. I let Dani take the lead, calling an Uber and shuffling me into it when it arrives. She figures out where we need to get dropped off, and asks people for directions inside the hospital. Finally, they give us a room number for my dad.

It isn't until I'm standing in front of it that it hits me what I'm about to walk into. I clutch at Dani's hand and ask in a rushed whisper, "Can you come in with me? Please? I—I don't know what I'm about to walk into."

She wraps her other hand around mine where I'm probably squeezing her hand way too hard. "Of course. If you want me to." Nodding quickly, I keep her close to me as I force myself to walk into the hospital room with my sick dad.

As soon as I'm through the door, it hits me how serious this situation is. My dad had a *heart attack*. I could've lost him. I almost did.

And the thought of that—of being truly alone in the world—is enough to make me freeze in place. In shock. In pain.

"It's okay," I hear Dani murmur beside me. She's pressed tight to my side, squeezing my hand in encouragement and letting me know I'm not alone. "He's okay, Aiden. He's just sleeping. Look."

Sure enough, when I force myself to look at my dad, I see his chest rising and falling in its normal pattern. Physically he looks fine—minus the machines that he's currently hooked up to. But if I block all of that out, and focus instead on the small snores I can hear him letting out, then it really does just seem like he's just sleeping.

"Oh thank God," I find myself breathing, rushing to his side and collapsing in the chair beside his bed. I reach blindly for his hand and squeeze it, more desperate for the feel of his warm skin than anything else.

"He's okay," Dani whispers. I feel her take a stand behind my chair, resting her hands on my shoulders and squeezing reassuringly. That simple touch is enough to bring me down from my panic and settle me into a slightly more controlled state.

"Thank you," I whisper. I don't take my eyes off my dad, but she knows I'm talking to her. She squeezes my shoulders again, not needing to say anything else.

I lose track of how much time passes. It feels like forever. I sit in the chair beside my dad's bed, holding his hand and waiting for him to wake up at the same time that I will him to rest. At some point the doctor comes in to explain what happened and what his body went through, but I'm still too out of it to fully comprehend the details. Thankfully Dani is there to ask questions, and when I finally shake out of my haze later that night, she calmly answers my panicked concerns.

"You should go home," I eventually croak out when I realize what time it is. She's been here for hours, despite the fact that she's never even met my dad.

"I'm okay," she says with a yawn. She's laying on the uncomfortable bench on the other side of the hospital room, the same place she's been for the past four hours since the doctor last left us.

"You don't need to stay, Dani," I try to tell her, but even I can hear the lie in my voice.

She levels a look at me, seeing right through me. "I'll stay until he wakes up and you realize he's okay," she says in a firm voice. In a voice that says she means what she's saying and nothing but an act of God will pull her away before she's ready.

"Okay," I whisper miserably. Helplessly.

I must fall asleep at some point, because I'm bent over his bed with a crick in my neck when I eventually feel a hand smooth over my head. I jerk upright with a gasp.

"Calm down, kiddo, it's just me," he says. And just hearing that voice is enough to bring tears to my eyes.

"Dad," I choke out.

"I'm here," he croaks. "Can you get me some water? My

throat's drier than a nun's cunt."

My laugh is wet and infinitely grateful. I force myself to my feet so I can grab a cup from the table beside him and fill it with water from the bathroom sink, then I'm bringing it over to him and handing it over.

"What happened?" he says after taking a big drink.

"You had a heart attack," I say tightly.

He gives me a look that almost seems guilty. "Guess I'm not as healthy as I thought I was, huh?"

I collapse in the chair beside his bed again. "*Fuck,* Dad, I thought I was going to lose you. Don't ever do that to me again. You're all I have."

At that, Dad's gaze darts over to the sleeping Dani curled up on the hard bench.

I swallow roughly. "She was with me when we got the call. She just didn't want to leave me alone when I panicked."

Dad's eyes track back to me. "You sure about that?"

No. I'm not. But I'm not ready to examine the other possibilities.

Instead of starting that conversation, I launch into questioning him about every detail of his diet and exercise routine, and add in my own comments about the doctor's suggestions.

An hour later, he's long since drifted back to sleep when Dani's eyes open.

"Hey there, sleeping beauty," I say with a tired smile.

She blinks herself awake, looking confused as she watches me. "You seem better. Did he wake up?"

I swallow again and nod. "He did. We talked for a while but he fell back asleep."

When her eyes dart to my dad, she seems nervous for the first time since I got the phone call.

"I'm glad," she says, although her tone is stiff. "Did the doctor say when he'll be discharged?"

"Probably a day or so. Physically he's fine now, just tired. I'm going to take him home and stay at his house for a few days. Just to make sure he's okay and taking it easy."

"That's a good idea," she says, straightening from the couch and getting to her feet. I can't for the life of me figure out why she seems uncomfortable *now*, versus when she first came to the hospital.

She cuts off my internal confusion when she says, "I'm going to head home then. I have to reschedule my trip to Virginia, so I should probably get that sorted."

The reminder of her trip is enough to make me startle. "Shit, you were supposed to leave today. Why didn't you say something?"

She flaps her hand at me as if that's a non-issue. She doesn't answer with anything, which makes me think she doesn't know what to say. But then she grabs her bag from the couch and throws it over her shoulder, suddenly avoiding eye contact.

"I guess… call me later," she mumbles. "Maybe… let me know when you get home okay?" And when she meets my eyes, it feels like she's saying *let me know when he's home and* you're *okay.*

"I will," I choke out. I stand from my chair, feeling suddenly awkward about how to express the sheer amount of gratitude I'm feeling. Everything in me is screaming to sweep her into my arms, to tell her thank you for staying with me during the absolute worst day of my life. But her posture is telling me that's not what she wants. She's pulling back, and I think it's killing me.

"I will," I force myself to say. "Thank you for staying with me. It… I mean, you were a huge help, so… thank you."

She gives me a stiff nod. Then she's walking toward the door, looking like she's desperate to get out of here. And then she's gone, like she didn't just spend twelve hours with me when I needed her the most.

Dad gets released from the hospital a day later. I take him back home, listening to him bicker about babysitters the entire way but knowing there isn't a chance in hell I'm leaving him alone anytime soon. I'm still vibrating with the fear I felt when that phone call came through. Thankfully, when he's finally back in his recliner watching the Flyers win their Sunday afternoon game, he becomes a little more amenable. He doesn't even protest much when I make him a dinner with chicken and vegetables.

I stay with him for five days before he finally kicks me out. Five days of skipping class, of leaving for only training and my internship, of fawning over him like a nurse caretaker. It takes three days for him to start complaining that I'm an overbearing mama bear, but it isn't until I stop feeling the panicked ache in my chest that I can bring myself to leave him.

It's been the two of us for as long as I can remember, which means every time I think of what I would've done if he hadn't made it…

I shake my head clear of the toxic thoughts, resisting the urge to rub my chest again. The last thing I need is Dad worrying about how badly this freaked me out, and he's already noticed the motion a few times.

"Alright, *call me* if anything happens," I tell him in only a slightly-frantic voice. "If you feel dizzy, if you feel weak, if you feel *anything*—"

"Yeah, yeah, I'll call you. Right as the heart attack starts, I'll call you."

I want to scold him for joking about that, but he's got a teasing lilt in his voice and I think I can see his lip twitching with a smile. And I'm so damn grateful for the sight of it that I can't bring myself to do it. I just sigh and give him a look.

"I'll stop by tomorrow after class to make you lunch and dinner. *No more steak*. At least for a while. I swear you're incapable of making it without a gallon of butter."

At that, he's rolling his eyes and pushing me toward the door. "Jesus, kid, you're worse than a nursemaid. I can feed myself, you don't need to cook for me. Go do your thing. You've got enough shit going on without organizing your day around your old man."

"Yeah, that's not up for debate," I mumble under my breath, doing a quick check over his shoulder to make sure I left him everything he needs.

He finally deflates with a sigh in front of me. "Aiden," he says softly, and for the first time in who knows how long, his voice sounds serious. Tender. "I'm fine, I promise."

I swallow roughly, forcing myself to look at him. I open

my mouth to say something but I'm suddenly choked up, and I have to swallow again to get past the lump. Eventually, all I get out is a croaked, "Fuck, Dad."

"I know," he murmurs. And despite the fact that it's been years since he's done it, he grabs my jacket and pulls me in for a rough hug.

I force the tears back as I squeeze my arms around him. It only lasts for a second, but just that contact is enough to convince my subconscious that he's okay, to calm me down from the constant near-panic I've been in.

When he hears my grateful exhale of breath, he lets me go and steps back.

"Go," he says gruffly. "You've got the gym to get to and your girl to go see. Go."

"She's not—" I start, but then stop, not knowing what I want to follow it up with. Or maybe I just don't want to voice the denial. "I'll call you tomorrow. Bye, Dad."

And then I begrudgingly move back to my little college apartment. It takes me a few days to get caught up on school and work, but it ends up acting as a welcome distraction from everything else. By the time things feel normal again, it's been a week since Dad's been discharged from the hospital.

I'm spread out in the living room working on a report for work when I hear a knock at the front door. I look toward it in confusion.

"Who's there?" I ask, standing to walk over to the door.

"It's Dani."

Bolts of joy and nervousness hit me simultaneously. Joy because her comfort was monumentally helpful last week, but nervousness because I still have no idea where we stand with each other, and I'm terrified I'm going to make a wrong move.

When I open the door, I come face to face with a Dani I'm becoming familiar with lately and don't like one bit. Her nerves are evident on her face and immediately my brain starts flying through ideas of how to make them disappear right the fuck off.

It takes me a second to notice the multiple grocery bags hanging off her one arm.

"You came over to cook for me?" I blurt out.

I see a flash of discomfort—possibly even a blush—on her face. She even shrugs her shoulders as much as she can with the weight of everything in her arms.

"I just figured food would be a good way to get you to let me in."

"You think I need a reason to let you in?" I ask in utter confusion.

Another, self-conscious shrug.

With a curse, I dart forward to grab the bags from her hands. She mutters a quiet *thank you* and then follows me inside.

With both of us standing quietly in the kitchen, I'm now feeling a little self-conscious myself. I feel like the past two interactions we've had have put us into this weird limbo, where all of a sudden our usual fun, sexy times together have somehow morphed into nerves and uncertainty.

I hate it.

I glance at her from beneath my eyelashes, trying to study her without her noticing. She's obviously here to cook for me, but that's so out of character for her that I don't know how to act. I've cooked for her plenty of times—mostly because I'm used to cooking for myself—but Dani is typically a bigger fan of trying new restaurants on food delivery apps.

Her cooking for me now is almost… caretaking.

Fuck, this is so different from anything we've ever done.

I'm knocked out of my introspection when Dani slides a water bottle across the counter to me. Without meeting my eyes, she says, "I'll throw the chicken on. Should only take me about twenty minutes to make everything."

I nod mutely. "Sounds good."

She hesitates before opening up her own water. As I watch her out of the corner of my eye, she finally turns to me and asks, "How's your dad doing?"

That's what she had to work up the courage for? To ask how my dad is?

And that's the moment I realize just how much Dani distances herself from others. How hard it is for her to open up.

I mean, I obviously knew before this, just based on all the conversations we've had about not getting close to people, but watching her now and seeing how hard it was for her to ask a simple question, it fully hits me in the chest.

I can't meet her eyes as I fidget with my water bottle on the counter. "He's good," I admit woodenly. For some reason my throat tightens and I can't get anything else out.

"Yeah?" Dani asks, her voice so full of hope that I can't help but lift my gaze to hers.

It makes me smile. My first genuine smile since everything happened. "Yeah, he's good. He's been home for a week, resting on doctor's orders, and we've talked about cutting out anything that may have contributed to the heart attack. So we feel confident we can reduce the risk of it happening again."

"That's great," she breathes out. Like she's relieved, like she's been worrying about this since we last talked.

Fuck, has she? Should I have given her more of an update?

The thought seriously fucks with my head. I don't know how to deal with an overly thoughtful and caring Dani, because I've never seen her before.

So I take a big gulp of my water before forcing out, "Thank you for this. You didn't have to."

She's already started unpacking the groceries, not looking my way when she shrugs and says, "It's no big deal. It was too much to cook for myself, so I figured you wouldn't mind helping me eat it all. You know, growing boy and all."

I let out a breathless chuckle. "Yeah, I can definitely help with eating. Can I help with anything else?"

We spend the next twenty minutes quietly moving around each other in the kitchen, Dani making the chicken while I set the counter and throw a salad together. I put some fights on in the background to combat the silence, because after a few minutes it becomes apparent that neither of us really knows what to say. She seems slightly uncomfortable, like she's out of her element here, and I still can't figure out how to act.

Because I *like* her here like this. I like that it doesn't always have to be playful or sex-filled. I never would've wished a heart attack upon my dad to create this kind of serious environment, but I'm realizing now that I want more heartfelt conversations with her. I *want* to know her through more than just the fun stuff.

But I can't tell if she wants the same, so I'm just... left in limbo.

When we finally sit down and start to eat, the act seems to settle Dani enough that the tension goes out of her shoulders. With food between us, the sounds of men yelling and punches flying in the air, it feels a little more casual than it did ten minutes ago.

She's cutting up the chicken breast on her plate as she asks, "So did you keep the fight? Or did you pass it up because of... everything?"

I finish the last of my salad before diving into the chicken on my own plate. "I kept it," I answer simply. "Coach and I talked about it, and since Dad is okay and my internship isn't overly time-consuming, I still felt like I could keep it. There's never going to be a perfect fight camp where no wrenches get thrown in, so it didn't make sense to drop out of this one."

Dani nods in understanding. "That's pretty admirable. I imagine a lot of people would've dropped out for less." I only shrug in answer, not knowing how to respond without slipping back into my usual playful façade.

"So are you excited?" she asks, and I let out a grateful exhale that she's steered us back to the easy questions.

"As excited as anyone can be when they're prepping to get locked in a cage with a man that wants to kill them," I joke with a weak half-grin. Her chuckle further comforts me. "Yeah, I guess I'm excited. I've wanted to go pro for a while now, so I'm excited to test myself against a new level of competition."

She smiles at me, a soft, genuine smile. "I'm sure you'll do great."

"Are you going to come?" I ask her. She's been supportive of my training, and has made plenty of mentions of wanting to see me fight, so it hardly feels like an off-base question.

But when her expression becomes tense, I wonder if I've misjudged something.

"Are people going to think I'm your girlfriend?" she asks tightly. "Are you going to pull me into the cage for a celebration kiss after you win?"

My heart drops into my stomach.

"Only if I lose and need you to kick his ass for me," I joke, my skin turning to ice at the lie. *Of course I want you by my side when I win. I want you.*

And in that moment, I realize just how true that is.

Despite her rules, despite everything we set out to do—or in this case, *not* to do—at some point between the sex, the laughs, the time spent with my friends… I began wanting Dani for more than just her body, or even her friendship. I began wanting *her.* Every piece of her, in every way possible.

But she doesn't want the same.

A fact that she emphasizes when she says, "I'll come if I can buy my own ticket and cheer from the sidelines. But I can't be your plus one ticket or anything."

I push my plate away from me, my appetite gone. "Come if you want to, but obviously there's no obligation. It would just be nice to have the support."

She nods eagerly and pushes her own plate away. "I want to come. I want to watch you fight. I'll be there."

I only nod in answer.

Standing from the counter, she asks quietly, "Want to watch a movie or something? I… don't really want to leave yet."

I nod in agreement, even though things still feel a little tense. But even still, I'll take as much time with her as I can get.

"I'll put something on," I agree with a small smile.

We take a seat on the couch, and I choose some weird Netflix movie that I'm not even aware of as I hit play. I couldn't care less what we watch, and when Dani doesn't say a word, I think she doesn't either. We simply settle into the cushions, side by side, and start to watch the movie.

Nothing happens for about fifteen minutes. We're not quite on opposite ends of the couch, but we're far enough away from each other that we're not touching. Because as much as I'd love to put my arm around her and pull her against my side, that's always felt like a too-much move. So I sit where I am, not touching her, with my hands in my lap.

It isn't until she scoots closer to me and drops her head on my shoulder that I even notice something is different.

My breath catches at the contact.

I think she hears it, and takes it as permission to move closer, because she shifts farther until her entire side is pressed against mine.

And then she boldly reaches over to grab my hand.

"Dani…" I murmur, unsure. This is unlike anything we've ever done before, and I have no idea how far to push this. I'm solely moving by her lead.

"It's okay," she whispers. "I want this, if you do."

I straighten up at that. *If I want this? How could I not want this?*

The second I turn to face her, wearing an expression of disbelief, she wastes no time bringing her lips to mine.

The kiss feels almost… tentative. Like she's waiting for me to kiss her back, to let her know I want this, too.

"Dani…" I whisper again, trailing off as I sink a hand into her hair. My unspoken message is *of course I want you. I'll always want you like this.*

She lets out a relieved breath, and I capture it with another kiss. I'm angling her face and kissing her deeper, suddenly wanting as much of her as I can get. I want her now, as much as I can have, and I want to capitalize on whatever it is she's giving me.

I bear down on her until she's laying underneath me on the couch, until I'm settled between her legs and aligning every part of me with every part of her. When she lets out a whimper at the contact, I groan and slide my tongue between her lips to deepen our contact.

"Take me to bed," she gasps against my kiss. Her hands begin to slide eagerly under my shirt, over my skin, trying to reach as much of me as she can. Like she's desperate to touch me. "Not here. Take me to bed. Please, Aiden."

I let out another groan and drop my forehead to hers. *Like I'll ever not be completely powerless against that request.*

I climb off the couch and reach down to pull her up with me. Without a word, I tug her down the hallway to my bedroom, pull her inside and shut the door behind her. All I want is for her to be in my arms.

The second I shut the door, she's flattened against me, her

lips pressed to mine, kissing me as if she'll never get a chance to kiss me again.

"Aiden, please," she breathes.

It's all the encouragement I need.

I scoop her into my arms and take her straight to my bed, until I can lay her down in the center of it and crawl over top of her like I'm dying to be. I just want to be close to her. My lips travel along her jaw, down her throat, until I'm kissing along the edge of her shirt and silently begging for her to let me make her mine.

She doesn't respond with words, she just reaches down to the edge of her shirt and pulls it off in one swift motion. Then she's cupping my face and pulling me back to her like she can't stand a second of being without me.

It drives me into a frenzy. Without taking my lips from hers, I reach down to her jeans and begin to undo them so I can tug them over her hips. Eventually I have to pull away, just long enough to slide down her body, but it's worth it when I straighten up and realize she's almost completely naked beneath me. Other than a pair of lace panties, she's completely bare and desperate for me.

I don't get a chance to fawn over her because almost immediately, she's tugging at my shirt and whispering, "Off, off. I want to see you." And because I couldn't deny this woman anything ever, I give her what she wants. I pull my shirt off over my head, then immediately lean down to undo my pants and tug those off, as well.

It's still not enough, though. For me or for her. When she begins to impatiently tug at my boxer-briefs, I realize I can't go another second without seeing, smelling, *tasting* her, and immediately turn to ripping the lace off of her. I'm moving down her body and burying my mouth between her legs before she can make any other requests.

Not that she tries to. The second my tongue splits her in half, she lets out a surprised cry of pleasure. Her fingers dig into my hair, her legs squeeze around my head, and she gives herself over to my touch. She lets me taste her the way I'm dying to do.

"Aiden, *Aiden*, I'm going to—" she gasps.

I can't even pull away long enough to answer her, that's how frantic I am for her pleasure on my tongue. I merely growl my approval at her reaction and double down on my efforts.

I want her mindless for what I can give her.

It doesn't take long to make her that way. A minute later, she's already tugging on my hair, squeezing my head between her legs, until the pain and suffocation is almost enough to pull me away from her incredible taste.

I drive my tongue inside her and look up the length of her body, watching as she explodes in ecstasy. Ecstasy that *I* gave her.

"Aiden," she gasps as she comes down from her high. "I need you."

I straighten immediately, feeling just as eager for her as she is for me. Everything about this moment is different than before—this isn't just lust, it's... need. Her expression is *desperate*. Like she needs me more than she needs her next breath.

I'm so distracted by this vision of a Dani I've never seen

before that it isn't until I kick off my boxer-briefs that it hits me.

"Fuck," I hiss, dropping my head to hang between my shoulders. "Dani…"

"What?" she whispers, frantically pulling my hips against hers. "What is it?"

"I don't have a condom," I mumble. I totally forgot to buy more after the last time. I start to pull away from her, forcing myself to come to terms with the fact that I fucked up and won't be getting mine tonight.

That thought is shot to shit when she grabs my hips and pulls me even closer.

"I don't care," she gasps. "I need you, Aiden, right now. I don't care."

My head pops up, and I stare at her in shock. "What? Dani, I don't have a condom, are you sure—?"

"I'm sure." She reaches down to wrap her hand around my cock, aiming it right against her entrance as she wraps her legs around my waist. "I need you. I trust you."

And *fuck* what hearing that does to me.

I can only stare at her for a moment. She holds my gaze, letting me see everything. Letting me see her hunger, her affection, her need. For *me*.

She drives the nail in the coffin with another whispered *please*.

"Dani," I groan, dropping my lips to hers at the same time that I push into her with one, hard thrust.

We both moan at the feeling of completeness. And I know I'll never get tired of this.

"God, you always feel so perfect," I groan, starting to drive into her. I couldn't stop myself from fucking her even if the world was collapsing around us.

"More," she moans. "More, fuck me harder. I want to feel you."

"Goddamnit, Dani," I hiss, picking up my pace. Shifting my hips all the way back and then driving as deep as I can, over and over again. Harder and harder, until we're both panting and delirious with pleasure.

"I want to feel you come," she gasps, her nails scratching down my back. "Oh my *God*, Aiden, I'm so close, I want to feel you come. *Please.*"

I let out a long groan, my forehead dropping to her shoulder, already helpless in the face of my lust to do anything but obey her. I'm too lost in the moment, too lost in *her* to even have a hope of trying.

"I'm going to come inside you," I grit out, moving in short, hard thrusts. Driving against that perfect spot with each one. I can feel her body start to tremble, can sense the orgasm bearing down on her the same way it's about to overtake me. "I'm going to come inside you and I want you to come at the same time. Right now, Dani. Come with me."

I lift my head at exactly the moment her body freezes and her mouth opens in surprise. It seems to last forever, and then… she fucking *shudders* as the orgasm explodes through her. It's enough to immediately set off my own.

My groan comes from the pit of my stomach. It vibrates through my chest, my forehead dropping to hers, until we're face to face and shaking through the last of the sensations.

I can't take my eyes off her. She can't look away from me.

"Dani…" I whisper when my mind no longer feels like it's splintering apart. When I can breathe enough to say it.

"I…" she looks shell-shocked after her come-down, like she can't believe what just happened. So instead of giving her the space to think about it, I press a kiss to her lips before dropping beside her and pulling her against me. I tuck her head under my chin and wrap my arms around her body. And when I pull the comforter over us, she seems to accept it and settle in.

At least for tonight.

CHAPTER 16
Dani

I WAKE UP to the feeling of warmth and safety.

And for the first time in my life, I don't question it.

Oddly enough, I remember everything that happened last night. And what's even more odd is that none of it feels wrong. It feels... right, sharing that with Aiden.

As if hearing my thoughts, his arm tightens around my waist, and his nose buries deeper into my hair where he's plastered against my back. Even in his sleep, he lets out a content hum at our closeness, and I find myself wiggling farther into his embrace.

"Morning," he mumbles into my ear in a sleep-heavy voice.

"Hi," I respond quietly. Despite the comfort that I feel, I'm still unsure about how to deal with this intimacy between us.

"Are you hungry? I can whip up some waffles if you're interested."

I let out a sleep-drunk giggle and turn in his arms, reveling in his lazy smile and tousled bedhead. "How much do you hate that you can't eat carbs?"

"Worst part of fighting," he says without even a second's

hesitation.

I raise an eyebrow in disbelief. "Worse than not having sex the week of the fight?"

He shrugs and pulls me closer. "I'm not really in a sexy kind of mood the week that I'm cutting weight anyway," he admits, making another giggle slip from my lips.

A thoughtful look crosses his face, and then he says, "I dated a girl once who got mad at me for that. She said I made her feel unattractive when I didn't want to sleep with her for a whole week." A frown mars his face. "She also felt guilty for eating carbs when I couldn't, and blamed *me* for the carb-less diet she said I put her on when she decided to match what I was eating. That might have been the last time I ever dated during a fight camp."

I wince. "Ouch. That sounds painful."

"It was," he says with a chuckle. "Looking back, it wasn't even worth it. She wasn't into any of the stuff I—"

I clap a hand over his mouth, stopping the flow of words even as his eyes twinkle at me.

"You're teasing me," I accuse with an involuntary pout.

"Maybe," comes his muffled response from behind my hand.

Before I can pull my hand away, he licks my palm. When I scowl and pull it back with a shake, he takes advantage of the opportunity and leans in to press a kiss to my lips. "I liked last night," he admits in a raw whisper.

I squirm with discomfort at the direction this conversation is heading. "I—I got a little carried away," I stammer, pushing against his chest. "I'm on birth control, but I probably shouldn't have been so eager to… do that."

A frown creases his forehead. He looks slightly confused and very lost, which becomes apparent when he says, "After everything we've been through, I don't think going without a condom should be that big of a risk, Dani."

At his words, everything in me freezes.

Because the last time someone tried to convince me to start having sex without condoms, the topic was all wrapped up in an even larger argument. One that was solely focused on getting me to make huge changes in my life for a man that I loved.

By a man that I thought loved *me*.

And just like that, all the warmth and happiness from last night—from the past few weeks—pops like an overinflated balloon.

Because I realize in this moment that I'm heading down the exact same path I swore I would never, *ever* go down again.

I'm immediately so lost in the memory, so panicked about making the same mistake I've worked for years never to repeat, that it doesn't even occur to me that I was the one who begged to have sex without a condom last night. Fear is suddenly filling my chest, choking me too much to be rational, and instead, all I hear is Aiden making the same *it's not a big deal* comment that Matt did five years ago.

"We haven't been through anything," I snap, sitting up and jerking the sheets away from my body. "We're not even exclusive. I don't even know if you're fucking other women. The last thing we should be doing is going without condoms when this entire relationship is based on sex."

Aiden's eyes widen and his head rears back in surprise. For a moment he only stares at me, as if in disbelief over the words that are coming out of my mouth. Then he seems to compose himself, and snap back with matching energy.

"Don't give me that bullshit," he barks, sitting up and jerking the covers off himself. "Don't downplay our connection like that. This hasn't been just sex in weeks, Dani, and you know it."

Now it's my eyes that widen, and my body that's going stiff.

I knew he was lying about keeping this casual. I've been blatantly ignoring the fact that Aiden is getting too invested in this relationship between us. I've been waving off the little comments, convincing myself that he's that charming with everyone, that it doesn't mean anything with me. But based on the look in his eyes this morning, the sheer affection radiating from his expression, there's no mistaking how he feels about me.

I hated the idea of ending this thing with Aiden so much that I ignored all the warning signs and let this get too deep.

Fuck.

"Don't you dare talk down to me," I snap back. "You don't get to tell me how I feel, or how I feel about *this*."

"And what is *this*?" Aiden questions, straightening up until we're both standing on opposite sides of the bed and glaring at each other. "What lie are you telling yourself this time, Dani?"

My temper flares at that. I don't even care that I'm naked, I just prop my hands on my hips and glare at Aiden.

"We have never *once* had a conversation about this

potentially turning into anything more. You can't just *declare* something and expect me to go along with it."

He throws his hands up in the air in aggravation, completely uncaring about the fact that he's also naked. "We've never had a conversation because you're *impossible* to talk to about it! You balk at the first sign of emotion!"

Tearing my gaze from him, I start to look for my clothes. I spy my shirt and underwear and angrily throw them both on. "We started this whole thing with the understanding that there weren't going to *be* emotions," I remind him. "I never once made this to be anything other than what we said it would be. You don't get to change the narrative now that you... now that you've—"

"Now that I've what?" he accuses, grabbing his boxer-briefs off the floor and angrily pulling them on. "Now that I've caught feelings? Go ahead and say it, Dani, admitting it out loud is the first step to making this work."

My eyes widen at that. "There is nothing to make work! There is no *it!*"

At that, he rounds the bed in a flash, crowding me until I'm plastered against his body and staring up into his increasingly frustrated gaze. He doesn't actually touch me, but with how close he is, he might as well be. I feel his presence in every atom of my body.

"Stop lying to yourself. Just stop it. You're not changing anything, and you're only hurting us when you do it."

He must see something in my eyes—the fear, the panic, *something*—because his expression softens slightly. He hesitates before wrapping an arm around my waist and pulling me tight against his body, his tone gentle when he asks, "Would it be so bad if there was an us? Would you hate it that much?"

And I'm not sure if it's the question or the vulnerability—the *want*—in his eyes, but something makes the panic inside me peak. Something makes me push away from him and put distance between us, just enough that I can pull in a hasty breath and attempt to scramble my thoughts into order.

"Yes," I choke out. "Yes, it would be bad. Aiden, I've *done* the boyfriend thing, and it *sucks*. It almost ended with me throwing away the most important thing in my life, and I absolutely refuse to do that again." I hurriedly grab my pants and pull them on. "I told you I wasn't looking for a boyfriend, so *stop* pushing. Stop making me out to be the bad guy, when I've only ever been clear with you about what I want. Why are you making this so complicated?! Why would you try to make this more than it is? It's been months, and we've been fine!"

"Why?" he asks in a shell-shocked voice. When I turn to look at him he's just standing there, half-naked and looking as gorgeous as ever. "Why am I trying to make this more than it is? Are you *kidding* me?"

I tear my gaze away from his, unable to make eye contact. A part of me knows what he's about to say, but the other part of me is hoping he's not about to take it there.

"You want me to say it?" he asks quietly. Desperately. "You want me to admit, out loud, that you're the most incredible woman I've ever met, and the only one I can think of anymore? That every time I even *see* another woman, you're the one I compare her to? That I can't imagine anyone more amazing, or more perfect, than you?"

"Stop," I whisper, squeezing my eyes shut. "Just stop talking."

"I don't want to just be a fuck buddy anymore, Dani," he says bluntly, closing the gap between us again. "Even being your friend isn't enough for me anymore. I want your mind, and your passion, and your emotions, and anything else you're willing to give me. I want all of you."

"Please stop," I choke out in a whisper. I need him to stop talking, to stop making this worse, but—

"Dani, I—"

"Don't," I bark suddenly, flashing him a look that is equal parts angry and panicked. "*Don't* say it."

At that, his expression becomes one of sadness. His shoulders droop, his eyes fill with pain, and his hand comes up to stroke my cheek with the gentlest touch he's ever shown me. I realize in that moment what he's about to do.

"I have to, baby," he whispers, voice rough and filled with heartache. As if he already knows how this is going to end.

I plead with my eyes, plead with him not to do this, not to force this thing to end between us like this.

But his decision has already been made.

"I love you," he admits quietly. His thumb strokes my cheek where he's cupping my face, his gaze boring into mine as he admits the thing that is about to break us. "I fell in love with you the first time you ever spent the night in my arms, and I've loved you more fiercely in every moment after that." His eyes search my expression, search for something that might tell him he's not baring his soul for nothing. But all I can give him is a blank stare.

He sees that and swallows roughly. Nervously. "I know this scares you. I know you have this vision of love that is going to take away the things you care about, but I promise that's not—"

His words snap me out of my trance. I place both hands on his chest and shove him away from me, eager to put some distance between us so I can *think* for a damn second.

"You don't know that," I manage to spit. "You have no reason to think this would end any differently than any other relationship. You might get bored, or maybe I will, or God forbid the *opposite* happens and we end up sacrificing everything else we want out of life in order to be together. How would that make any of this worth it? How could you think that this is anything special, that we might be—?"

"Because *you're* special, damnit!" he roars. "Because *this connection* is special. How can you not see that?"

My eyes round with shock at his outburst. Aiden has never once yelled, and yet he truly seems to be at his wit's end right now.

He takes a deep breath before continuing. "I know this freaks you out. I know why you feel the way you do about relationships, and believe me, I get it, but… at some point you have to believe it's possible to make it work. That it's worth it. You *have* to."

Whether it's the word choice or the fear that's still choking me, I feel the words come out of my mouth that part of me has known all along I would one day end up saying to Aiden.

"I don't have to do anything. You don't get to tell me how to feel, Aiden, or what to do. You just have to accept the rejection for what it is."

It freezes both of us to the spot. We blink in surprise, looking at each other in disbelief that those words just came out of my mouth.

"That's not—" I stammer, immediately wanting to take the words back. Because hearing them out loud—hearing *those words* used in a sentence with Aiden—didn't feel the way I thought they would. They feel wrong, *taste* wrong, and suddenly, I'm terrified.

Because I think I may have been wrong all along.

Aiden lets out a humorless laugh. "You meant every word," he says, shaking his head. "You're so terrified of this being something that you're pushing me away. I should've known you wouldn't stick around."

"No, wait, I didn't—"

"Save it, Dani," he says, turning away from me to look for the rest of his clothes. He pulls them on with determined jerks, suddenly looking like he wants nothing more than to get away from me. "I don't want any more excuses. You're right, you've made your feelings perfectly clear since the beginning. Stupid me for thinking that might have changed. That you might actually want *me*."

And his voice sounds so bitter, so broken, that I find myself pressing forward to grab his arm and spinning him to face me. "Aiden, I didn't mean that. Don't go, let's just talk about this—"

He lets out a bitter laugh as he shakes my grip off. "Why? So you can push me away some more? I can only take so much, Dani." He pulls his shirt on with a quick tug, looking immediately more guarded when he has the last layer of clothing between us. "I'm not going to fight for someone who doesn't want me. That's not the kind of relationship I'm interested in."

Then he's turning away and moving toward the door, yanking it open and pushing into the hallway.

"Wait, that's it?" I ask, panic making my voice higher than normal. But I really am panicking, suddenly realizing that I pushed him too far, that I did too much damage and won't be able to pull him back.

That I may have just lost him.

"That's it," he says in a tight voice, turning to give me one last look. A look that's equal parts determined and pained. "It's been fun, Dani—" He spits my name, and for the first time it doesn't contain any of the usual teasing that I'm used to— "but I think I'm done. Enjoy the rest of your lonely life."

And with that, he walks off, leaving me to stare at his retreating form in shock, and flinch when he slams the front door behind him.

And I immediately feel more alone than I ever have in my life.

CHAPTER 17
Dani

I'M A MESS at work for the next few days. Thank God I only work bartending shifts—and that Bobby has known me long enough to cut me some slack and not comment on it—because the amount of mistakes I make behind the bar would surely get me fired from a permanent job. I fuck up orders, I drop glasses, and I definitely snap at one too many drunk customers. By the end of the week, everyone is giving me a wide berth, despite the fact that the bar is packed and clearly understaffed.

I can't get a handle on the emotional turmoil swirling inside of me.

For days, I alternate between regret that I hurt Aiden, anger that he pushed us to a point that he knew would break us, confusion that I hate where we ended up but I don't hate *him*, and just plain… hurt.

It's that last emotion that fills my chest the most.

I thought I knew what heartache felt like in high school. I thought losing a friend and boyfriend all wrapped in one was the last time I would feel it—it was the reason I first vowed to never get close to anyone again. And yet… that felt like a papercut compared to the gutting that is losing Aiden.

But every time I think about calling him to apologize, to talk through what happened, confusion makes an appearance, and then anger, when I'm reminded of the reasons I didn't want more than a friends-with-benefits relationship in the first place. Because in reality, nothing has changed. I still don't want a boyfriend, because I'm still scared shitless that a relationship will take my life in a direction I don't want to take it. Nothing that happened did anything to weaken that conviction. In a way, things may have actually strengthened it. The fact that I've developed feelings for Aiden *despite* my reasoning is only fueling the fear that this could blow up in my face if I try to talk to him.

So instead of calling him, I distract myself with the bar, with walking around the city taking pictures of random things, and eventually fumbling through a single photography assignment. Through it all, I hope that the confusing swirl of emotions eventually dwindles and goes away.

It doesn't. Two weeks later I'm still just as confused, just as hurt as I was that morning.

I decide to visit my parents, feeling unnaturally tense as I walk into the kitchen. My mom gives me a big smile by way of a greeting.

"Hi, honey. I didn't think we'd see you before Sunday dinner. Everything okay?"

Because of course she can tell something's wrong. Mother's intuition has never failed anyone. "I'm fine," I answer tightly, grabbing a water bottle from the fridge and taking a seat next to her at the breakfast bar. "I'm just... restless. So I thought I'd come by."

Her forehead creases with a frown. "Work?" she asks simply.

My first instinct is to lie and nod, to bury everything I'm feeling even deeper down so I don't have to deal with it, but it only takes one look at Mom's face to decide against that.

"No," I answer instead, my voice cracking on the word.

"Oh, Dani," she says soothingly. She doesn't hug me or offer any affection, knowing I'd just reject it, but her expression softens knowingly. "Do you want to talk about it?"

Again, my instinct is to lie and shake it off, but I'm exhausted trying to shake off these feelings. All it's done is send me into a deeper spiral.

So I give her a stiff nod instead.

Closing the book she was reading, she settles into the cushions and focuses her attention on me. Without saying a word, she encourages me to unload everything.

"It's this guy I was seeing," I blurt out. "Well, not seeing, necessarily. But, we were sleeping together. Regularly. And we became friends."

With no judgment at all, my mother nods for me to continue.

"It was going so well," I rush out, suddenly desperate to defend my reasons for doing what I did. "It was casual, and fun, and nobody had any expectations, so we could just enjoy each other and not think it was anything more than it was. It was exactly what we said it would be when we first started hanging out."

"But you started to care for him?" she asks softly.

And despite the fact that I'm past the point of lying to myself about that answer, I'm still not ready to vocalize it. I can only give my mother a wounded look that hopefully shows her exactly what I'm feeling.

She gives me a sad smile, immediately reading the emotions on my face. Understanding that I *did* start to care for Aiden, but also seeing that I wouldn't be sitting in front of her with heartache in my eyes if things had gone well.

"Okay, so he pushed for more. What did he want? Was he too needy?"

I frown at that, immediately thrown off by the question. "No, he's not needy. He's been super supportive of my crazy schedule. Most guys would get clingy if I didn't jump at every chance to see them, but Aiden is never like that."

"So then what's the problem?" she asks. "Are you not into him? If he's the same guy I caught whiff of a few months ago, then you two have been seeing each other for quite a while. Usually you get bored after a couple of weeks. I assumed that was a good sign."

"No, it's not that. I *do* like him," I admit gruffly. "It's just that we agreed we wouldn't turn it into anything more. He's ruining a good thing for no reason."

At that, her eyes widen. "No reason? Really?"

"Well… yeah. I've been telling him since day one I'm not looking for a relationship, so he knew exactly what was going to happen when he brought it up. I can't keep seeing him knowing he's… that he's…"

The surprise on her face softens into tenderness. "Oh, honey. You can't even say the word? Why are you so against the idea of falling in love?"

"I-I'm not," I say defensively. "I just... don't want that."

She studies me for a moment. Then, with only curiosity in her voice, she asks, "Why not?"

And I gawk at her. Not because I'm shocked she doesn't understand, but because I'm realizing that I never admitted to my own mother why I feel the way I do about relationships.

My mom's look isn't one of pity, but one of sadness. Like she's just now realizing how scared her daughter has been of love.

"I know Matt broke your heart in high school, but Dani, that was years ago. He was a stupid kid, and you were a love-struck teenage girl. That's not a reason to sign off of love forever." She pauses, seeming to contemplate something for a moment. "Did your father and I do something to make you think relationships can't work?"

I hesitate. Of course I hesitate. I've never talked to my parents about how I feel about this, and the last thing I want is my mother to think I love her any less. Or my father.

I *do* love them, I just don't understand their relationship.

"It's not that I'm worried. It's just... I have... *theories* about love, and yes, they started because of Matt, but it makes me not want anything even resembling a relationship. Is that so wrong? I'm young, I should be allowed to want—"

"Dani, stop dancing around whatever you're trying not to say and just spit it out."

I meet my mother's eyes and swallow roughly.

"Well... typically when someone doesn't want a relationship, it's because they're scared of getting hurt," I start tentatively. When she nods to urge me on, I take another deep breath. "Which I get, but it's still kind of an odd deterrent. You can't live life without bumps and bruises. But what *I* don't get—" I cast another nervous glance her way— "is when it *does* work out and it *still* comes with sacrifices. How is that supposed to make me want to find a partner?"

At this point, my mom just looks confused. "Sacrifices? What do you think your father and I sacrificed because of our marriage?"

I throw my hands up and lean back into my seat with a huff. "Are you serious? Mom, you were the *best neurologist* the Tri-state area has ever seen. And you *loved* your work! What else would you call becoming a stay-at-home mom?"

Now she's the one leaning back in her chair. "You think that was a sacrifice?"

It's my turn to be shocked. "Of course it is! Tell me it didn't kill you to give up your work."

Her eyes are wide, a stunned expression on her face. "Is that what you think?" she breathes. "You think I *hated* giving up my work for you kids?"

"How could you not?" I ask, looking equally stunned.

She stares at me for another moment, as if she's seeing me in a whole new light. Then she shakes her head, clearing her brain of its fog, and leans forward to brace her hands on the table. "Okay yes, if it weren't for you kids, your father and I would have absolutely kept on track with our individual careers. We *loved* doing what we did, and we were damn good at it. So you're right that we hold a special kind of pride at being the best in our fields. But... at some point you realize that sometimes there are things that are more important. Like kids, or a hobby, or a relationship. Even a friendship."

She doesn't drop my gaze, doesn't let me pull away from her. She knows I want to scoff at that, knows I want to immediately separate myself from anything that might try to put itself above the love I have for the life I live.

"What would you do if something felt *more* important to you?" she continues, unrelenting. "What if something came along that made you more proud than the art that you create with your photos?"

My jaw drops at her question. "*More* proud? I make you more proud than being the best in a medical profession? How is that possible?"

Her eyes widen at my question. "How can you even ask me that?" she asks in a breathless voice.

I'm too stunned to answer. I can only wait for hers, feeling even more confused as I was when I walked in here.

So I just stare at her. I'm trying desperately to understand what she's saying, but I've spent a decade convincing myself of the opposite—that she gave up on her career because of her marriage and kids—and I'm struggling to rework my perceptions about it.

"Wait... what about dad?" I ask in a clueless burst. "You can't tell me he feels the same way."

She looks equally floored by that. "Why not? Because he's a man?"

I feel a slight tingle of shame at that, my mouth snapping shut.

"Is this what you've thought this whole time?" she asks in

a disbelieving tone. "That I had to sacrifice the things I love to be with your father? To be with you?"

I can't keep the confusion out of my voice. "I... well *yeah*."

"Becoming a stay-at-home mom was the greatest life decision I ever made," she says. "Giving up ten, twelve, *eighteen* hour days so I could be with you and your brother? How could I ever call that a sacrifice? Whether you can understand it or not, I *wanted* to be with you kids. Giving up my practice was never a sacrifice. It was a *reward*."

I'm... speechless.

She's right, I never once stopped to consider that it might be a good thing. I was so caught up in putting their careers on a pedestal, in the idea that she and my dad were giving up their lives for love, that I never once stopped to think about whether they were happy about it. Whether they *preferred* it.

"So you've never regretted giving up your career?" I ask in a small voice.

"Not for a single second," she answers immediately.

"And Dad?"

She shakes her head. "Him either. We've never once looked back at our decisions and wished we did anything differently." She leans forward to cup my face in her hands, giving me a loving smile as she says, "We've only ever cherished the moments that have given us more of *you*."

I can't bring myself to pull away, or to acknowledge that what she's saying makes sense. My head is whirling, confused about what I heard and what I'm thinking—

"This whole time I thought you gave up on your work because you felt obligated to be a stay-at-home mom." I turn my startled gaze toward her when something occurs to me. "Do you even miss work?"

She shrugs, and the look in her eyes comforts me that she's going to be brutally honest with me.

"Sometimes," she admits. "I loved my career, and I was damn proud of it. I loved the science of it, and being able to save lives. So yes, sometimes I miss it. In a perfect world, I would clone myself so I could do the job without ever missing out on a second of your and your brother's life. That's the truth. But I never, not once, ever second guessed my decision to leave."

I shake my head, trying to clear it of the fog of confusion. I'm reeling, trying to understand, *trying* to understand how I could have gotten it so wrong and been so blind—

"I have to go talk to him," I blurt out, grabbing the armrest in order to steady myself. "I don't understand how we got this far. I just... I need to talk to him." Then something occurs to me and my gaze jerks down to my phone. "What's the date? Is it Saturday?"

"Yes, it's the fourteenth," my mom answers calmly. Completely oblivious to the new turmoil bubbling inside me.

"Fuck. His fight is tonight." I burst out of my chair at the reminder. "I have to go. I told him I'd be there."

"He's a fighter?" my mom asks in confusion. "Like... a boxer?"

I'm tossing my bag over my shoulder as I wave off her concern. "Trust me, he's not what you're picturing. He's charming and handsome and so, *so* funny. He's amazing. You'll love him." My own words make me pause in my haste, and my voice loses its natural conviction when I say, "If... if he forgives me."

Now it's my mom that's waving me off. "Just talk to him. If he's as amazing as you say, you two will figure it out."

And despite the confusion over everything I just learned still mixing in my gut with the feelings I *know* I have for Aiden, those words are the ones that give me hope on my way out the door.

By the time I get to the arena, I'm practically vibrating with nerves. I'm pretty sure my Uber driver wanted to chuck me from the car for how many times I suggested a different route.

I hurry to the ticket counter, and even though the event started over an hour ago, there's still a lengthy line of people buying last-minute tickets. I can't keep my feet from shuffling anxiously as I mentally will the line to move quicker.

Glancing down at the phone in my hand, I debate for the millionth time whether I should text Aiden. Not necessarily to put all my buzzing thoughts in writing, but at the very least to say I'm sorry and that I'm here to support him. But I'm pretty sure the day of a fight is the worst possible time to bother a fighter with anything that isn't thoughts of victory, so I lower the phone.

And then pick it up again twenty seconds later.

"Fuck, fuck, fuck," I chant under my breath. I have no idea what the right option is here.

I start to type out a message. Delete it. Type another one.

"Goddamnit, Aiden," I whisper under my breath.

Thankfully, my indecision has distracted me from the pain of waiting, something I'm startled to realize when I'm poked in the back and not-so-nicely told to hurry up and buy my ticket already.

"Sorry," I say in a breathless voice as I step up to the ticket counter. "I just need a ticket to get in. Any ticket."

"Which fighter are you supporting?" the lady working asks in a bored voice. "We'll give him the credit for the ticket sale."

At the reminder, my heart jumps into my throat. I have to swallow twice to be able to talk around it.

"Aiden Reeves," I answer quietly. "I'm here for Aiden Reeves."

The second I have the ticket in my hand, I'm rushing through the crowd and hoping like hell I haven't missed his fight. I'm so busy looking at the fighters in the cage, and trying to figure out which fight number they're on, that I don't see Aiden's dad until I collide with his chest.

"Whoa, easy there," he says, gripping my arms to steady me. "Where's the fire?"

"Oh my gosh, I didn't see you there, I'm so sorry," I babble, wringing my hands. Nervously shooting glances at Mr. Reeves because I have no idea how much he knows about Aiden and I.

When he doesn't tell me to go to hell for breaking his son's heart—he merely gives me a small smile and steps back—I risk the question. "Do you know what fight they're on? I got the fight card at the ticket counter so I know Aiden's number eight but—"

"They're on six right now," he answers. Shooting a quick

look over my shoulder to the cage, he adds, "Looks like it's just ending. So your timing is perfect."

"Well, not perfect," I mumble before I realize what I'm saying. Once I do, my eyes widen and I stare helplessly at Mr. Reeves.

He sighs when I acknowledge the elephant in the room. "Look, Dani, I know things between you and Aiden are... rocky, but—"

"I never meant to hurt him," I blurt out. "I know I did, and I am so, *so* sorry I did. Believe me, you can't imagine how much." Once the apology starts, I can't seem to stop it from continuing. The words tumble out of me.

"He's the most incredible man I've ever met. He didn't deserve what I said to him, and I hate myself for ever making him believe he isn't worthy of love. It kills me that I hurt him. I just... I got scared when he... when he—"

"Dani," Mr. Reeves interrupts softly. "You don't have to explain yourself to me. I get it. Relationships are scary. Especially since you're the kind of woman who doesn't want to be tied down. I have a little experience with that, so trust me when I say I understand." I see a flash of pain in his eyes, a memory loosened by his words, but his gaze shutters and he continues on. "But what you don't understand is that there weren't any shackles to begin with. They're all in your head."

His words make me pause, a frown appearing on my face.

"It's not that I don't think *he's* worth it, I've just never thought the changes that come with relationships *in general* are worth it. I'm not ready to give up who I am."

Mr. Reeves gives me a sad smile. "What would make you

think my son would want to change even a hair on your head?"

At that, the true insanity of my internal conflict reaches the light, all in one fell swoop.

I've been so worried about never being ready for the changes that settling down comes with, that it never once occurred to me that settling with *Aiden* might not come with any changes at all. Or at least not any bad ones.

"I'm an idiot," I breathe.

Mr. Reeves coughs awkwardly into his fist, barely hiding his smile. "A little."

I let out a loud laugh at that. And, feeling suddenly relieved, I throw my arms around his neck and give him a grateful hug. "Thank you," I whisper.

It takes him a second but eventually he squeezes me back. When he pulls away, there's genuine happiness on his face as he says, "Let's go find some seats, yeah?"

Nodding quickly, I look past him to the cage where the next fight is just starting.

And then I make a split second decision to pull my phone out so I can type a message and hit *Send*.

CHAPTER 18
Aiden

It's been two weeks since I've taken a real breath. Two weeks since I've felt like I've had my head on straight, like I've had my shit together enough to do what I need to do tonight.

And it's fucking up my focus.

After I left Dani in my apartment, I went to the gym and did the same thing that every fighter does after a breakup: I trained. I pushed myself so hard that Max basically had to drag me into the showers once I was done, and still, it wasn't enough to forget the fact that I can't accurately call what happened a breakup.

You have to be together to break up.

For two weeks, I threw myself into training for this fight. There was no way I was going to pull out of it, no way I was going to call my dad up and tell him another woman leaving was going to affect my life decisions.

She made her choice, and I made mine.

I don't blame Dani for it ending the way it did. I knew what she was scared of while we were dating; I *knew* what my comment would make her do. There's no part of me that's surprised at her reaction.

I'm just… fucking hurt.

Despite my constant inner reminders, I realized there was a part of me that thought she might change her mind. That she might fight against her fears and decide I'm worth taking a chance on.

I should've known I don't have that kind of hold on women.

By the time fight day approaches, I'm a shell of my usual person. I'm not doing anything besides going through the motions, cutting weight on autopilot and feeling thankful for the pain that twenty-four hours without food and water comes with. The physical pain temporarily outdoes the emotional pain, allowing me to sink even further into a state of numbness.

I feel no relief from that first sip of water after weigh-ins, and instead of the usual team dinner that is customary the night before a fight, I beg Tristan and Jax to let me go home so I can go to sleep.

I somehow end up at Dad's place instead of my own. There's still a lingering scent of Dani in my apartment, and I haven't been able to sleep in my own bed since everything went down.

Dad knows something's up with me but knows enough not to ask about it before a fight. Although with the amount of concerned glances I get from him, I'm thinking he might break his usual *we don't talk about emotions* persona and ask me what the fuck is wrong with me.

I take that as my cue to go to bed, and I fall asleep with the memory of a black-haired girl that broke my heart and the hope that fight day nerves are enough to wash it away.

The nerves hit hard the next day. I exhale a breath of relief when I wake up with them, thankful to have something else to preoccupy my mind, at least for a day.

I don't think of her all day. Not through breakfast, or the ride to the arena, or as I'm warming up with Jax and waiting for my name to be called. Fight day stress is so bad that it overshadows every thought that isn't *kill or be killed*.

That chant rings in my head the entire walk down to the cage. I no longer feel numb, but I do still feel frozen—or at the very least, not like my usual arrogant, energetic self. I smack my gloves and force the internal chant to be louder, trying to *will* myself into my usual fighting headspace.

And yet the second the bell rings, instead of the sound lighting a fire under my ass the way it usually does, I still just feel... flat.

And despite Coach yelling *touch and then go right away* from his place in my corner, I'm still not quick enough to spot the gleam in my opponent's eye.

He taps my glove with his and before I can react, he's on me.

Fuck, fuck fuck is all I can think as I cover up against his onslaught. His punches glance off my gloves and forearms, but he's throwing quick enough that he's not giving me a chance to catch my breath or retaliate. I'm left to shell up and start moving backwards.

"*Move*, Aiden, get off the fence!"

I hear Jax yelling but it's like my brain is moving in slow

motion. I can't seem to make my legs work.

Especially when Red suddenly drops down and takes them out from under me.

"Come on, Aiden, don't let him bully you! Get back to your feet, we have to take this round back."

I manage to wrap my legs around his waist and secure him in my guard but it doesn't stop him from continuing to rain down punches. I try to grab a hold of his neck and arms to pull him down so he doesn't have as much room, but he's already too slippery to get a good grip on him. When he lands a big right hand to my jaw, it only makes me double down on my efforts. I blink away the ringing in my head and yank him closer to me with my legs around his waist.

I have no idea how long this back-and-forth goes. A few times I find a controlling position, sometimes even landing a few punches of my own, but then he overwhelms me again and puts me flat on my back, unleashing more ground and pound on me.

The sounds of our corners yelling that there's thirty seconds left in the round somehow injects Red with an even bigger burst of energy. In an act of desperation, I open my legs and throw them up around his head, trying to catch him in a triangle choke.

But it's sloppy and clearly a desperate move, because my opponent shrugs out of it easily and ends up in an even better position at my side. Now, not only do I not have my legs controlling him, but he also managed to get a grip on my arm during the transition.

"Watch the arm, Aiden, *he's going for the armbar!*"

With a muttered curse, I try to snatch my arm back before he can fall back and torque it. But I'm too slow, still moving through mud, and he's too good at being one step ahead of me. In a flash, he swings his legs around and falls back with my arm, raising his hips to put pressure on my elbow in an armbar submission.

"*TIME!*"

Now Red is the one cursing, begrudgingly letting go of my arm when the bell signals the end of the round. But by the time he stands up, he has a grin on his face and his hands in the air in a sign of clear victory.

Fuck, that was a bad round.

I climb to my feet and make my way to my corner. Coach and Jax are already there, shoving me onto the stool and putting ice on the back of my neck in an effort to cool me down.

"Give me three deep breaths, Aiden," Coach barks.

I do as he says, forcing my heart rate to slow down and trying like hell to get my brain to wake the fuck up.

"Forget that round," Coach says as he pours water over my head. "We still have two left. I need you to stay off your heels, Aiden. Do you understand me? I need you to be the aggressor this round. Get your jab in his face and *keep* it there because he's going to give you the opening for an uppercut the next time he shoots for a takedown. But *I need you to stay on him.*"

"Okay," I say in a rush. Nodding quickly. "Stay on him. Lots of jabs. Got it."

"You got this, man, come on," Jax encourages. "Get your head in the game."

Get your head in the game.

Because of course Jax can see I'm not here mentally. *Of course* he knows why I was fucked up even coming into this fight.

"Seconds out!" The ten second clap sounds, telling cornermen to get out of the cage. I stand up off the stool and watch as everyone hustles back to their seats.

"Let's go, Aiden, *let's go, Aiden!*" I can make out Remy's voice clearly over the crowd. Normally I'm able to respond to it with a smirk and a wink, but for some reason I can't seem to recapture any of my normal swagger.

It's been two weeks since I've had any swagger.

I shake that thought from my head as the bell rings and I stride toward my opponent. But then the thought is knocked from my head for a whole other reason, because it takes all of two seconds for Red to land a huge right hand to my jaw.

The crowd *roars* in delight.

I stumble backwards, ears ringing and my sight blinking out. I vaguely hear Coach and Jax screaming at me to let my hands go, to hit back, to do *something*, but it's like I can't get any of my limbs to work. That mud I was wading through last round has turned into quicksand and it's dragging me down so far and so quickly that I can't make sense of it.

So when Red shoots for another takedown and slams me down to the mat, I can't make a single move to stop it.

And all of a sudden, I'm in a shit position with a fighter on top of me that has an endless gas tank, and I can't seem to do anything about it because my brain is functioning at half speed. Less now, because of the punch.

Less still when Red starts raining down punches from his

position on top of me.

I feel wetness on my cheek when he splits me open with one.

My ribs crack when he hits me with another.

"Aiden, you have to *move*, you can't stay here. Let's get to the cage and stand up."

I grit my teeth and try to roll onto my side so I can scoot away, or at least get closer to the cage. I eat a few more punches in the process but when my back hits the cold wires of the cage, I exhale a breath of relief. I manage to create enough space between Red and I that I can get my feet under me, and then I'm standing.

But only for a moment, because as hard as I had to try to get to my feet, it's equally that easy for my opponent to get me back to the ground. And this time he's in a better position.

Which he immediately capitalizes on by aiming several quick punches to my face. I feel my eye start to swell.

And as his weight settles on top of me, with it settles such an overwhelming sense of dejection that for a moment, I can't breathe.

It's not just that I'm losing this fight, it's that I'm losing *this badly*. It's the second round and I couldn't make it twenty seconds before being beat with the same thing that he hit me with in the first round; even after being told how to fight against his strategy, I *still* ended up on the ground. It doesn't help that my mental health was trash going into this fight, because it makes the desire to push through this and fight back that much harder. And all I want to do is take this ass-kicking and accept the fact that nothing in my life is going right. That I can't fight, can't do this thing that I invest so much of my life in and am so proud of, this sport that I thought I was good at. That I can't hold on to the things that make me happy, including Dani. *God*, I didn't fight for her either. I just walked out and left her there at the first sign of trouble. No wonder she didn't want to be with me.

At that thought, all the fight goes out of me. I don't deserve Dani. I don't deserve to win this match. I'm just… *losing*.

"Aiden. *Aiden*. Come on, man, don't give up on me. *Wake up!*"

Jax's voice somehow filters into my subconscious. It's not enough to ignite a fire in me but I do bite down on my mouthpiece and grab hold of my opponent to stem the flow of punches. Thankfully, the ten second bell sounds and I only have to hold on for a few more seconds.

When the round finally ends my cheek is already swelling up and I can feel the blood coaching my face and neck from where his punches have split me open. I somehow manage to stagger to my feet and force myself toward my corner.

Coach pushes me onto the stool and immediately dumps water on my head. I'm vaguely aware of a towel wiping away the blood, of the cutman pressing cold metal to my swelling cheek.

"I know you're hurt," Coach says in the most calming tone he can muster. "I know this is a hard fight. But Aiden, *this* is the difference between amateur and pro. *This* is where you show me you're a fucking champion. I know you have it in you, I wouldn't believe in you if you didn't. *Show me* you deserve to be here."

On a normal day, a speech like that would be more than enough to light a fire. The fact that it doesn't now is a testament to how mentally fucked up I am.

"Come on, man, you can do this. You can win this fight, I know you can." Jax gives me encouragement from where he's standing on the outside of the cage. Even Remy is shouting something from the crowd. Neither does anything to help.

"Aiden. I need you to wake up," Coach commands, slapping my cheeks a few times. "You have one round, and I need you to leave everything in the cage. Throw everything you've got at him." He must see a blank stare in my eyes that usually means a fighter isn't present or really absorbing instructions because he barks, "What did I just say? Repeat it back to me."

"You said to leave everything in the cage," I repeat in a monotone voice.

I think I hear Jax mutter a *fuck*. But I'm not sure because the ten second bell sounds that tells the coaches to wrap it up and get out.

As I stand from the stool, Coach gives me another encouraging nod before grabbing it and leaving the cage. I'm watching his path in such a daze that I almost miss Jax's words through the cage.

"Alright *look*, you asshole. I wasn't going to say anything, but you're seriously blowing this fight, so I'm hoping it can't get any worse."

I turn around in confusion. He's leaning against the cage and all but glaring at me, but he keeps talking in a rushed voice.

"I know the past two weeks have been hard. I know everything with Dani was shit timing. And normally I wouldn't say anything because I think you should pull your head out of your ass all on your own. But I know what it feels like to lose your girl, and maybe I'm being too soft, but fuck it." He takes a deep breath before jerking his head over his left shoulder. I try to see what he's nodding at but I can't make anything out over the chaos of the crowd.

"Dani's in the crowd," he says quietly.

My eyes widen and my head jerks around to look for her. And it's as if my eyes are already trained to find her, because I pick her out instantly in the crowd. She's not sitting in the gym section, but that's okay, because she's sitting with my dad instead.

God, she's even more beautiful than I remember. She's wearing that leather jacket that paints her bad bitch energy like nothing else can, and the long black hair that I love so much is falling in waves over her shoulders. The only thing that seems different about her is her facial expression.

In the place of her usual self-assured smirk, there's only… emptiness. Nervousness. Maybe some desperation. But none of it is happy, and the lack of joy on my girl's face is enough to gut me.

My girl.

Because she's still my girl, isn't she? Even after everything? All the bullshit that's happened over the past two weeks only emphasized how far gone I am for her. How hard I fell for this brilliant, sexy, incredible girl.

And she's *here*.

Does that mean she cares about me after all? There's no other reason she would seek me out again, is there? Did she change her mind?

"She's been cheering the loudest," Jax says as I continue to stare at Dani in wide-eyed shock. Then he lets out a chuckle. "I didn't think it was possible, but she's even louder than Remy."

"Fighters, are you ready?"

In any other moment, the ref's shout would've shocked the ice back into my veins and gotten me back into fight mode. But Dani chooses that moment to mouth something at me and my heart stops for another reason. I can't make out what she says but the look she gives me when she says it is enough to convey the message.

She wants me. She came back to me.

"*Fighter*, are you ready?"

The ref's words pierce through the bubble—of happiness, of relief, of *something*—in my chest. I tear my gaze away from Dani and turn back to the cage, now remembering that I'm in the middle of a fight. A fight that I'm losing.

But with this new cocktail of emotions growing in my chest, comes a new feeling. *Determination.*

"Come on, Aiden, let's *take* this round from him! This is *our* fight!" Coach's voice filters into my brain and finally—fucking *finally*—fills me with adrenaline. Adrenaline that I need to perform the way I need to, the way I know I can.

"There we go, Aiden, *there we go!*" screams Jax, clapping enthusiastically as the arena roars around him.

"*Fight!*"

The second the word is out of the ref's mouth, I bite down on my mouthpiece and stride forward.

Red must sense something has changed because he's not

as in-my-face at the start of this round as he was the last two. He still comes right at me, but it's not with the same intensity as before.

We exchange a few punches. I throw out my jab, just like Coach called for, and Red throws a combo of his own. We both land. I pop out a double jab and follow it up with a right cross that just barely grazes his temple. Suddenly, Red is eyeing me up and down, respect blazing in his eyes for the first time since the fight started.

But tangled with that respect is the same determination I've seen on plenty of other fighters, the expression that takes over when you find a worthy opponent and double down on your desire to win because of it. So it shouldn't surprise me when he unleashes a barrage of punches, each one thrown hard enough to hurt me if they landed. And despite the fact that he outstruck me and knocked me down in previous rounds, it isn't until I hear his corner make a call that I realize his striking might be better than I'm giving it credit for.

"Three count! Throw the three count!"

The first punch lands flush on my chin and snaps my head back. The second comes with so much extra power that my vision starts to blink in and out. And it's as I'm staggering backward, watching in slow motion as that third punch comes for my temple, that the realization crystallizes in my mind: this is the shot that's going to put me down. If this punch lands, I'm going to lose this fight.

And that thought is so… abhorrent, so *unacceptable*, that my resolve strengthens instantly. Determination tightens my muscles, and fire flames in my blood.

Fuck giving up, that's not who I am. In the cage, in life, anywhere. I'm a goddamn fighter.

So as I watch that third punch move toward my temple, time slowing to a crawl, I make the decision to fucking fight. And to *win*.

I duck under the punch at the last second. I feel my opponent's glove skim the top of my hair, but it doesn't matter because I'm already driving a hard shot into his liver with the same motion.

I hear the breath *whoosh* out of him, the oxygen driven from his lungs with a single shot. He doubles over and backs away, desperately trying to put some space between us.

Because he knows what's coming. He knows that posture in front of another fighter is like waving a red flag in front of a bull.

I'm on him before he even gets his breath back. I'm throwing punch after punch, alternating between his head and his body, never giving him a chance to cover up entirely or guess where I'm going to strike next. And when his back hits the metal chainlink fence and my fist connects with his liver once more, a sense of victory settles over me. Not because the fight is over, but because I'm finally able to put him in the same position he's had me in for two thirds of the fight.

He drops to the mat and in seconds I'm on top of him, raining down punches the same way he did to me. He tries to hold on to me to keep me from having enough space to attack, but all that does is make me switch to the shorter range elbows. One of them splits his eyebrow open and the sight of blood on his face makes me immediately feral. I increase the power of my shots tenfold.

"Fighter, protect yourself! Fighter, you need to protect yourself!"

The ref's words fuel me even more than the sight of blood does. I throw faster, and harder, and I don't stop until I see the ref leaning in out of the corner of my eye, getting ready to stop the fight.

It only takes a few more punches, and one more elbow, for the ref to throw himself between us, his arms waving off the fight.

"It's over! The fight is over! Aiden Reeves is the winner by knockout!"

I push off of my opponent, standing up with my arms in the air and a massive grin on my face as the arena *explodes* around me.

"Fuck yes!" Jax screams, pushing his way into the cage. His grin might even be wider than mine, the excitement visibly rippling through his body as he wraps his arms around my waist and lifts me straight up in the air with a gleeful whoop. "That's champ shit, baby! Fucking beautiful!"

My head drops back and a victory-drenched scream explodes from my chest.

I did it. *I fucking did it.*

When I open my eyes, my gaze clashes with Dani's. She's wearing a look of such joy, of such *pride,* that seeing it immediately knocks the breath out of me. I'm more winded by the sight of a girl than I am after three rounds with a pro fighter.

Suddenly, I want nothing more than to rush toward the

girl and away from this fight.

Jax finally drops me back to the mat, just in time for Coach to appear next to us with a proud smile. "Nice work, kid," he says, clapping me on the back. "That was a hell of a comeback. You should be proud."

More warmth blossoms in my chest at the praise. He rarely dishes it out, so I eat it up like the rarity it is.

We fly through the announcement and interview, Jax tugging a shirt with my sponsor over my head before I even realize what's happening. I'm not sure what I say to the announcer; I just know I'm desperate to get out of this cage and into the crowd to see Dani.

But that doesn't happen either—I'm hustled out of the cage and into the tunnel to the back, moved by the tidal wave of people so I can't even make eye contact with her before I'm swept along.

"Fuck *yes*, that was amazing!" Jax says, clapping me on the back when we finally make it to the locker room. He's hopped up on the adrenaline of the victory and too happy to realize I'm anxiously looking at the door. The most he manages to do is notice that I'm looking around for a pair of scissors to cut the tape off my hands. He does that, then goes right back to excitedly recapping the comeback.

When the door to the locker room opens, my gaze jerks to the entrance, but just as quickly my excitement plummets because I realize it's just Tristan.

"Fucking congrats, dude, that was incredible," he says with a big grin. Bigger than he's ever given me before. "*That* is exactly the kind of fight you go pro with. You're going to be a hot commodity after this.”

“Thanks, man,” I force myself to say. Despite being restless to get out of here, I can’t bring myself to ignore the compliments of my teammates and coaches when this was clearly a huge victory. I just wish it wasn’t happening when I was desperate to get back to my girl.

“The doctor has to come check you out, and you might have to go to the hospital to stitch up that cut, but we’ll get you out of here soon,” Coach comments, being the first to notice that I’m not all here. I only nod my acknowledgement.

With that confirming that it’ll be a little while before I can get out of here and go find my girl, I grab my phone instead. At the very least I’ll send her a text to wait for me.

But before I can do that, I see a text from her.

Dani: You were right, it’s not just sex. I’m so sorry about everything I said. And if you pull me into the ring after you win and give me a celebratory kiss, I promise to be every bit the supportive partner you deserve.

And as hope blossoms in my chest, as love fills every bit of my broken-down body, Dani chooses that moment to slink into the locker room. The guys look at her in surprise as she shuts the door behind her, clearly confused about how she managed to get into the fighter locker room without a VIP pass.

“Uh, we’ll leave you to it for a minute,” Tristan says, awkwardly ushering Coach and Jax out of the locker room. “I’ll fend off the media so you have some privacy.” Then he shoots me a wink and shoves Jax out of the room. “Good luck, pretty boy.”

Stepping farther into the room, but still several feet from

where I'm sitting on the massage table, Dani asks, "Pretty boy, huh? I thought I was the only one that called you that."

Her nervousness is palpable. After seeing her in the crowd, seeing her text, I know why she's here. But she doesn't know how *I* feel yet.

So I crack a joke, trying to lighten the mood and put her at ease. "You would be, except sometimes it slips out from Tristan and Remy. I think they're secretly infatuated with me and trying to coax me into joining their little love nest. I forgot to tell you you're third in line."

The teasing look drops from Dani's face as she takes another tentative step closer, her uneasiness growing. "Third, huh? I would've expected the list to be much longer."

I hesitate, fairly certain I understand the direction of this conversation but not wanting to fuck it up or make her any more uncomfortable than she already is. Eventually, I manage to ask, "Yeah? Why's that?"

She reaches the massage table then, almost close enough to touch my legs, and she looks up to meet my gaze. Her eyes are filled with pain and she wraps her arms awkwardly around her stomach. She looks torn up in a way I never thought I'd see her. In a way confident, self-assured Dani has likely never looked before.

She swallows roughly before answering my question. It's almost like she's actively trying to keep her walls down, forcing herself to answer honestly so I can see into her mind.

It makes me fall in love with her all over again.

"Because you're the most incredible man I've ever met," she admits on a whisper, shuffling in place. She ignores the way my eyes widen at her honesty, ignores the way my hands twitch with the urge to reach out and touch her. She just forces herself to continue. "Because you're charming, and hilarious, and you care about your friends in a way that should make anyone love you on the spot. You make me laugh more than anyone else, and you make me feel adored without it ever being stifling. You're… everything a person could want in a friend." Her gaze shutters, looking uncertain again. "And a partner," she finishes quietly.

My heart beats faster at that admission than it did during the fight itself. "Yeah?" I ask in a breathless whisper. "Not just a fuck buddy?"

That finally makes her suck in a startled breath, but she answers immediately. "Not just as a fuck buddy." A small smile lift her lips. "Although you're still the best fuck I've ever had."

I bark out a laugh at that. Then, taking a chance, I reach for Dani's hips so I can pull her between my legs where I'm sitting on the massage table. She lets me move her, which gives me the courage to nudge her shirt out of the way and rub gentle circles on her hips.

I take in a shaky breath before letting my own shields drop. No teasing, no playful comments to lighten the mood, I just let my pain from the past two weeks bubble to the surface and expose every fear that I'm feeling. I let her see my vulnerability.

"If you're not ready for a full-blown relationship, I don't think I can do this, Dani," I admit hoarsely, tightening my hands on her hips in a subconscious effort to ground her to me. Even if it's just for a little bit longer. "I can't meet you halfway anymore. I could before, kind of, but I'm so in love with you now that I don't even think I could handle being friends with you without a piece of me dying every time I see you but can't tell you just how fucking gone for you I am. When you… said what you did—"

"Aiden," she chokes out on a sob. She steps further into my embrace, our bodies so close to each other now that her hand barely has room to slide up my chest and settle over my heart. "I didn't mean any of that, I swear. I realized it the second you walked out. And I am so, *so* sorry I ever let you hear it."

And even though the apology soothes the jagged pieces of my heart, I force myself to push her further. To see just how she feels, and how ready she might be for this.

"What about everything you were scared of?" I ask, my gaze boring into hers. Wanting to catch every emotion, every piece of honesty she might give me. "What about your family?"

She pulls in a shaky breath. "I don't care about anyone else. I don't care about divorce rates, I don't care about success rates, I don't care about anything that isn't you and me. I'm done comparing, and I'm done thinking I know why other people's relationships are the way they are. I just… want you."

My breath leaves me in a rush. For the past few weeks—months, if I'm being honest with myself—I've been fantasizing about these words coming out of Dani's mouth. About her admitting that she actually wants me and isn't just using me for a good time.

Even still, I push her a little more. I ask the question that I always sensed was the real fear her past caused.

"And work?"

"I don't care about work," she tries to assure me immediately, but at my raised eyebrow, a blush lights her cheeks. "Okay, that's not true. But I realized it might not be all there is to life. And I don't want it to stop me from finding other kinds of happiness." She swallows thickly, a silver sheen in her eyes as she says, "I would hope I would never have to make a decision between you and photography, but if it comes down to it, I would—"

"Dani," I interrupt sharply. A heavy exhale leaves my lips, even as I wrap an arm around her lower back and sink my other hand into her hair. "I will *never* ask you to make that choice. I'll never ask you to make *any* sacrifice if it wasn't what you wanted. It's what I've been trying to tell you this whole time. I want you *because* of who you are, and the idea of you changing even a single hair on your head for me kind of makes me want to vomit."

Some of the tension ebbs from my body when my words win me her trembling smile. With the hand holding her neck, I start to stroke my thumb over her jaw. Lightly. Lovingly.

"That's exactly what your dad said," she says thoughtfully.

"Smart man," I murmur.

"He also said I was an idiot."

"Maybe a little."

A laugh bursts out of her, and a smile lifts my lips for the first time. Distantly, I wonder if the sound of her laughing will ever not be my favorite sound in the world.

But when it dies down, the air between us settles. I keep us grounded by pressing my forehead to hers, my thumb continuing to stroke her skin.

"Be with me," I say quietly. "I know it's scary, but I just need you to trust me enough to know we'll figure out anything that happens. Together. I just… I don't want to be without you, Dani."

"I don't want to be without you either," she whispers, pressing her body closer to mine. She hesitates, then adds, "I can't promise I won't have some days in the beginning when old fears pop up, but I'll never take them out on you again. I don't ever want to panic like that again. I hate myself for hurting you."

I smile, then inch forward just enough that my lips brush against hers. I'm not kissing her, I just want to stamp a promise of my own on her lips.

"Tell you what," I say quietly. "If you promise to come to me with those fears, I promise to talk you down every time and remind you just how much I love you and how good we are together. Deal?"

Her nod is immediate, as is the smile that stretches across her face. "Deal," she whispers. I love the sight of her happiness so much that I can't help reaching for more of it.

"Maybe I'll even issue that reminder with a few orgasms."

Sure enough, a laugh bursts out of her before she throws her arms around my neck, burying her face in my neck and hugging me tight. It's all I can do to tighten my own grip around her waist and brush my other hand down her hair.

"So are we really doing this?" I finally ask, wanting her to say it out loud. Between the past two weeks, the adrenaline of the fight, the emotions of this conversation, it suddenly feels like those words might be the only thing to ground me.

She pulls back to look at me, just far enough that I can see her face as she says, "We're doing this. I love you, Aiden. I'm already so in love with you that even waiting for you in the arena felt like more than I could handle. I was this close to rushing the cage so I could get to you just a little bit sooner—"

I kiss her then. Because I can't *not* kiss her when she just said those words, just gave me everything that I've wanted but was too scared to hope for. I weave a hand into her dark hair and pull her lips to mine, unable to spend another second without the taste of her in my mouth.

And it's everything I remember it being. The way she feels, the way she smells… it's just as intoxicating as it was the first time I had her in my arms.

"I love you," I mumble against her lips. "I'm so in love with you it's insane. And I'm so proud of you for taking a chance."

She pulls back and gives me a small smile, keeping close enough that she can continue touching me. "I figured if you could survive that combo in the ring, we could make it past a 3 count of our own."

I let out a chuckle, even though the memory of our two arguments before this—and the reminder that this conversation could've been our last one if it had gone differently—sobers me at the same time.

Her expression becomes thoughtful. "I'm proud of you too, you know. That fight was incredible. Not just because you pushed past everything with your dad, and with… us, but because you looked like a true professional in that cage tonight. I couldn't take my eyes off you."

"Yeah? Even though I'm all cut up and broken?"

She grins. "Even then. Also, let's please make sure we introduce you to my parents while you've still got the black eye that I'm sure is coming tomorrow." When I only wince at the thought, she laughs.

After a moment, an errant thought makes me frown and pull farther away from her. "On another note—and speaking of rushing the cage—how did you even get in here? This is a fighters and coaches only area and they have it locked down tighter than a bank. How'd you get in?"

She throws her head back and laughs, and the sound is so beautiful that I fall in love with her all over again.

"Don't you know? I'm really good at evading security."

EPILOGUE

IT TAKES APPROXIMATELY two seconds for Aiden to grab me once I walk into the gym—much to Tristan's annoyance.

My boyfriend grins and wraps an arm around my waist so he can pull me against his body and press his face into my neck. "Hey," he murmurs. "How's my girl doing?"

I try to keep the smile from my face but it's next to impossible nowadays.

Goddamn charmer.

"Good, but if Tristan kicks your ass for leaving the mat and you end up too tired to fuck me later, I'm going to be upset."

When he pulls away from my neck, if possible, his grin is even bigger. Even happier.

"He would have to do a lot more than kick my ass for that to happen, don't you worry."

I only scoff and shove him toward the mat. "Go. I'll wait until you're done, then we'll go eat."

With perfect timing, Tristan chooses that moment to let out a very angry growl of Aiden's name.

Aiden has the good grace to wince when he turns back to his coach. "Sorry. You know how it is, right? *Women*."

Remy and my growls reach his ears at the same time.

Tristan sighs and shakes his head. "You've got a lot to learn about women, kid. Get back on the mat."

There's still another forty-five minutes left of their training session—most of which Aiden spends getting mauled by a pissed-off Remy—but I don't mind waiting, computer perched in my lap as I get some editing done. I *like* watching him work out. Ever since he won his pro debut four months ago, he's had a whole new hunger for training. He's been at the gym more, he's worked harder when he's here, and he seems *excited* to fight again. To push his new pro career as far as it can go. We don't know how far that will be, but for the first time in my life, I'm excited to stand by someone while they pursue something that makes them feel alive.

As alive as Aiden makes me feel every day.

"Thanks for waiting, babe," he says, smacking a kiss to my cheek. But when he goes to do it again, this time reaching to wrap an arm around my waist, I smack his hands away.

"Not until you go shower. I swear, I've never met anyone that sweats as much as you do."

"You love it," he says with a grin, kissing me again. But he backs away anyway and reaches down to grab his gym bag. "Wait here, it'll only take me a few minutes." He pauses, a smug look appearing on his face. "Unless you'd like to join me?"

"*Aiden,*" Tristan growls as he passes us.

"Okay, maybe not at the gym," Aiden grumbles.

I chuckle and give him a light shove. "Go. I'll wait."

With a dramatic sigh of exasperation, he adjusts the bag on his shoulder. "Yes, ma'am."

Just as he turns to walk toward the locker rooms, Lucy comes up from the heavy bag room on the far side of the gym. She perks up when she sees me.

"Dani," she says happily. "I was just about to text you. We're doing a self-defense seminar for a bachelorette party next week and we need some women to show the moves on the guys. Want to help Remy and I?"

I perk up at the question. "Are you kidding? That sounds amazing, I'm so in." I look at Aiden. "Are you doing it?"

Aiden lets out a groan, his head dropping to my shoulder. "You get way too excited about the idea of bitch-slapping me. Should I be worried?"

This time, I'm the one that smacks a kiss to his cheek. "You should be worried when I *stop* getting excited about the idea."

"Here, here," Remy calls from the mat.

"What is it about you women being so violent with your own boyfriends?" Tristan asks in a confused tone, looking to Jax for an answer.

Who just raises his hands in surrender. "Don't look at me, I'm the only one around here whose girlfriend *doesn't* want to punch him in the face."

"Lame," Remy and I say at the same time. And then grin at each other in victory.

"Okay, back to the topic at hand," Lucy says, attempting to tamp down on her smile and failing. "You in?"

"I'm in. Just text me the day and time and I'll be here."

"Wonderful," she says, turning back toward the bag room.

Right before she reaches the door, she calls over her shoulder, "And if you like it, maybe we can get you in here to start training."

My resounding *yes* comes at the same time as Aiden's *no*.

"Not a chance anyone is teaching her how to fight," he growls. "I already have to peel her off of drunk assholes at the bar. If we teach her how to fight, *I'm* going to end up in jail one of these days when a couple of said asshole's buddies decide they don't care that a girl is beating up their friend."

I turn to give him a sour look. "Are you saying you wouldn't enjoy taking on some bad guys with me? I'm sure Batman and Robin have loads of fun fighting them."

He narrows his eyes at me. "In this instance am I Batman or Robin?"

I only smile in answer.

"Jerk," he mutters, poking a finger hard enough into my side that I yelp. Then he's bending down to throw his gym bag over his shoulder and turning to head toward the showers. But before he does, he grips me firmly by the nape of the neck and gives me the kind if soul-altering kiss that he usually reserves for when he really loves me.

"Perfect girl," he breathes against my mouth.

I'm too breathless, too overwhelmed by the love I feel for him in return, to respond.

When we get back to my apartment, Aiden opens the door with his key and promptly throws himself on the couch, looking every bit as comfortable as he's become in the past few months.

"Are you still good to have dinner with my dad this weekend?" he asks me.

"Yeah, I already finished edits for the City Hall job," I respond, unpacking my computer from my backpack and placing it in my usual work spot on the kitchen counter. "But don't forget we have Rachel's baby shower *next* weekend."

He lets out a groan. "Why do I have to go to that again? That's a chick thing, aren't men outlawed at those things?"

I let out a heavy sigh. "I have no idea. I just know Tommy begged me to make you go. Plus, if I have to play weird baby-in-the-ice-cube games, then you're suffering with me."

Aiden only blinks at me. "I don't know what that means but now I'm scared." When I only laugh, his eyes narrow.

"Alright fine," he concedes. "But you owe me."

"Yeah, yeah, you'll get a blowjob out of it," I concede with a chuckle.

It's silent for a few moments, the only sounds in the apartment those of my fingers tapping on my keyboard as I power my laptop on and pull up the pictures I secretly snapped of Aiden's training today. It doesn't take me long to get lost in the shots of my man in his element, mesmerized by the images of him sweaty and focused on tearing down his teammates. It isn't until I hear Aiden say my name that I look up from my computer.

"Come here," he murmurs, opening his arms to me.

I abandon my computer without half a thought. Not because Aiden is more important than my photography, but because if I said I wanted to keep working, my boyfriend wouldn't even hesitate to smile and say *okay*.

That reason alone is what makes it so, *so* easy to love him.

I settle on top of his chest where he's lying on the couch. His arms close around me instantly, and I can't help nuzzling my face into his neck and absorbing his essence with a deep inhale.

I'm so comfortable with his closeness that I don't even flinch when he asks his next question.

"Think you'll ever want kids one day?" he asks quietly, his lips pressed to my hair and his hands rubbing comforting circles on my lower back.

I take a moment to think about it. I can't say I've ever seriously considered the question, but life nowadays looks a little different than it used to.

"Maybe one day," I answer eventually. "Although I can't say for sure. I never really thought of myself as a mom. I always just kind of pictured myself as the cool aunt." I lift my head so I can look down at my boyfriend. "Would that bother you?"

A smile stretches across Aiden's face, even as he shrugs his answer. "I could be happy with either. As long as I get you."

I want to roll my eyes at how corny his words are but the smile that appears on my face kind of undercuts the gesture. I know I fail because Aiden chuckles and wraps one arm around my lower back and weaves his other hand into my hair.

"Stop faking it, you and I both know you can't win this fight," he murmurs, then lifts up to press one, two gentle kisses to my lips.

I don't bother answering, I just return a kiss of my own,

increasing the heat of it by slowly sliding my tongue in his mouth. When he groans and tightens his grip around my waist, I know I've successfully distracted him.

I can't help grinding my hips down into his any more than I could stop a kiss like this once we've started. Even months later, the passion between Aiden and I has never waned, never become anything less than the thing that first brought us together. Some days I even consider it the foundation of our relationship, but then he makes a comment that's so *Aiden* that I'm immediately reminded his friendship has become equally, if not more, important. Our physical and emotional connection has become so interwoven that there's no way to ever separate it, no way to even think about if we're more friends or fuck buddies.

We're just… everything.

My hand has just started trailing down Aiden's chest to his waistband when he suddenly flips me on the couch and settles his body on top of mine. And before he even begins to kiss down my neck, across my collarbone, down to bite my nipple through my tank top, I know what he's about to do.

"I've never met a man that enjoys going down on women as much as you do," I say with a breathless laugh. But I don't stop him, because with that obsession also comes a skill level that has made *me* equally obsessed with his tongue.

"And you never will again," he growls, taking my pants in his hands and tugging them down my legs. When he sees that I'm not wearing underwear, his reaction is every bit as feral as I expected it to be when I decided to forego them this morning.

He wraps his arms under and around my thighs, then tugs

once, *hard*, until his face is buried between my legs and his tongue is sliding along my soaked entrance.

"Oh *God*, oh God," I start chanting, sinking my fingers into his hair and arching further into his mouth.

His tongue slips up to my clit, circling once, twice, until he suctions his mouth over it with the perfect pressure. I never have any chance of holding out when he's eager like this.

True to form, I'm two seconds away from detonating when the strokes of his tongue slow and become lazy. By now he knows exactly what it takes to get me off, so the movement is definitely intentional.

I let out a frustrated growl and tug his hair.

"Don't you dare stop," I grouse. "We are *not* adding edging to our sexual arsenal."

Even his chuckle against my skin is a turn-on, the vibration of the sound making a shiver run through me. But just when I think he's going to pick it up again, he replaces his tongue with his thumb, slowly rubbing circles on my clit as his eyes lift up to mine.

"What about marriage?" he asks, pressing a kiss against the inside of my thigh.

My brow furrows and my head lifts up to stare at him. It takes me a moment to formulate a response, but when I finally do, all that comes out is, "What?"

"I asked about kids, now I'm asking about marriage," he says with a grin, dropping another kiss to my skin. "Eventually."

With my impending orgasm still tightening my muscles and lighting my skin on fire, my reactions are beyond delayed and still very much confused.

"If this is your attempt at a proposal, I swear to God I'm going to—"

"Not a proposal," he assures me. "Just asking how you feel about it."

"While you're going down on me?" I practically shout—outraged not by the idea of marrying him, but because the sneaky bastard waited until *now* to ask me. Because he knows I'm at my most honest when I'm lost in the lust he can so easily sweep me up in.

He only shrugs in answer, then moves his thumb down to my entrance so he can slowly slide it inside me.

"You are *such* an asshole," I complain, the words sounding breathless as I drop my head back to the couch. "We only just got past our relationship hang-ups. Marriage shouldn't even be a topic."

And I know what he wants to say. Because I know Aiden better than I know myself these days, and he never goes a single day without letting me know how he feels about me. How infatuated he is with me, how much he appreciates my body and the physical attraction between us—how much he loves getting inside my brain and finding out new things about me.

How much he loves me.

So I know exactly why he's asking about marriage and babies. It's not because those are things he wants right now—or even ever—but because every day he looks for new ways to love me. To make me happy.

"Alright fine, we'll put that conversation on hold," he says after another pause. "What about moving in together?"

And then his tongue goes back to circling my clit.

For a moment, I revel in the feeling of his mouth once again pulling pleasure from my body. Eventually, my eyes close and my orgasm begins to climb.

When I'm *right there*, he pulls away just long enough to growl my name.

And just like that, the command has me blurting out my honest answer.

"Yes, I want that." As I balance on the precipice of huge sensations, the words rush out of me. "I love the idea of starting my day with you every morning, and getting to sleep next to you every night. I want to live with you because I don't ever want to go another day without you."

And at my whispered confession, pulled out of me in a blur of pleasure and happiness, he gives me everything I could want—and more.

I come with a gasp, my legs tightening around his head as he licks me through an explosive release. I've barely come down from it when he straightens up and hurriedly pushes his pants over his hips. He drives inside me with a possessive growl.

Dropping his chest to mine and settling his weight on his forearms beside my head, I close the distance between us by wrapping my legs and arms around him and pressing a greedy kiss to his lips. More and more I like feeling anchored to Aiden, a habit that's a far cry from how much I used to want space.

"Perfect girl," he groans, his thrusts increasing in their intensity. "*My* girl."

"Yes," I gasp. "Always."

We're both instantly on the verge of another release.

Anytime he gets lust-drunk confessions out of me, he always becomes immediately insatiable for me. Just as I do for him.

"If we move in together, I'm it for you," he says, his gaze focused on my face. "I'll never, *ever* hold you back, but you'll be stuck with me by your side for everything that comes after this. I love you too much to ever let you go."

And the only word that I can answer with is a whispered, "Good."

It's enough to catapult us both into oblivion.

He captures my mouth with a searing kiss, groaning into my mouth when he feels my body clench around him. Then he's driving once, twice, before his hips still and I feel him empty inside me.

It's a claiming I never expected to love as much as I do.

He drops his forehead to mine, his labored breaths mingling with mine. Then… a huge grin stretches across his face.

"So when am I moving in? Or are we going to look for a new place?"

I let out a surprised laugh. "God forbid anyone tries to hold you back from what you want. Your single-mindedness is intense."

He shrugs and drops another kiss to my lips. "It took me forever to find you. Sue me for not wanting to wait any longer to spend every day with you."

I shake my head at his antics, but there's a smile on my face. Truth be told, I don't really want to wait any longer, either.

"How about you move in here while we look for a place that's right for the both of us?"

Aiden's face lights up like a kid on Christmas morning. "I

think that sounds like a perfect idea." And without a second's hesitation, he pushes off of me and stands up. Once he's hastily righted his clothes, he extends his hand to me and says, "Let's go."

I look up at him in confusion. "What? Where?"

"My place. We have to get me packed up."

"What?" I yelp. "Right now? I can't even feel my legs yet!"

His smile turns sly. "That never stopped you from bolting out of my bed before. If you can run away from me immediately after sex, then you can run toward a life with me, too."

And although my expression softens with affection at his words, Aiden has no interest in making this an emotional moment. Which he proves by reaching down to grab my arm and tossing me over his shoulder in a fireman's carry.

"Aiden! I'm still naked, you caveman, I'm not ready!"

He lets out an exasperated breath and lets me slide down his body, though he doesn't allow any space between us. With an arm wrapped around my waist and his other hand sinking into my hair, he anchors me with his usual possessive hold.

"Fine, go get ready," he mutters. "But hurry up. I've been wanting to ask you that for weeks."

At that, I melt in his arms. I wrap my arms around his neck and tilt my face up to his with a genuine smile, pausing to study this incredible man and soak in the love that he showers me with every single day. I take a moment to be grateful for this new life that he's opened for me and never once allows me to second-guess.

"I love you," I tell him in a whisper, the words coming easier every time I say them. This time, it feels like a relief to press the words like a brand to his lips. And when he returns the kiss with a whispered *I love you, too,* there isn't a single moment in my life I've loved more.

Until, of course, the kiss escalates and a groan rumbles through Aiden's chest.

"Okay, maybe one more time. Then we'll go."

And I'm still giggling as he throws me back down on the couch.

ACKNOWLEDGMENTS

Writing this book was unlike anything I ever could have predicted. You'd think by a fourth book I would at least have a basic handle on the writing and publication process, but NOPE. The theme of this book was pure chaos. I'm going to completely change up the normal order of my acknowledgements because this book relied on a whole different group of people than usual.

First, and foremost, Kenzie from NiceGirlNaughtyEdits is a literal angel. I shout her praises after every book, but this one had her rising to a whole new level. Not only is she absolutely brilliant with her comments and consistently takes my 3 star manuscripts to 5 star books that I can be proud of, but she also tackled a whole new challenge with me for this book: rewriting the entire ending the weekend before it was released. I knew the last few chapters didn't feel right, but it wasn't until 3 days before upload that I figured out how to fix them. And this gem of a woman, instead of letting me flounder in the chaos of my own making, worked through her weekend with me until it felt like it got the ending it deserved. I just… have no words. Nothing but thank you.

Along those same lines, Papa Castle and my betas Amanda, Nicole, and Sam, gave motivational speeches that David Goggins would be proud of and talked me off the ledge multiple times during the last few weeks before release. Not to mention the invaluable manuscript feedback that I get from the girls for every book. Without any of them, this book would not have been what it is.

To my husband, who experiences the bulk of my mood swings during every publication: I'll never say this to your face, but you're a saint. Thanks for dealing with this insane career that I've picked (and for always volunteering to test out certain scenes with me). I appreciate your sacrifices.

To Krista, my wonderful PA who puts up with my last-minute… well, everything. You, too, are a saint, and I'd be floundering in this industry without you. Thank you for everything that you do for me.

To Dora and Maria, for always offering amazing beta feedback and for helping to shape this story into what it needed to be.

To my family, friends, readers, *everyone* that has supported me throughout this writing journey, all I can say is *THANK YOU!* Without you, a book is just some ink on a dead tree. Thank you for loving this book as much as I do and for helping to share the fun and sexy story of Aiden and Dani. I love you all more than words can describe.

ALSO BY NIKKI CASTLE

More in the **Fight Game** Series:

Book One: 5 Rounds
Book Two: 2 Fights
Book Four: 1 Last Shot

Or if you want more fun, quick spice, check out the **Just Tonight** novella series!

The Stranger in Seat 8B

ABOUT THE AUTHOR

Nikki Castle is a wife and dog mom from Philadelphia who writes spicy love stories about alpha MMA fighters and the women that melt their badass, playboy hearts. She's a full-time romance author during the day and spends her evenings running a Mixed Martial Arts (MMA) gym with her husband, who is also a retired fighter.

Nikki has been writing in one way or another since she was a teenager. She pursued an English and Philosophy degree in college, and finally decided to sit down and fulfill her longtime dream of writing an entire novel when quarantine began in 2020.